Jit'Suku Chronicles
Sons of Amber

Starcrossed

BIANCA D'ARC

This book is a work of fiction. The names, characters, places, and incidents are products of the writer's imagination or have been used fictitiously and are not to be construed as real. Any resemblance to persons, living or dead, actual events, locale or organizations is entirely coincidental.

No part of this book may be used or reproduced in any manner whatsoever without written permission, except in the case of brief quotations embodied in critical articles and reviews.

In a universe decimated by biological warfare, can former enemies unite to create a new peace out of the ashes?

A warrior-priest is the only one who can heal a failing empire...

Newly crowned Emperor of all jit'suku, Tigh has come back from self-imposed exile as a warrior monk on the sacred mountain. He had given up his claim to the throne in favor of his beloved brother, and turned his back on worldly things. Tigh would never know what had driven his brother to the madness of releasing a biological weapon on the humans, but the fact that it turned on its creators and came back to the jit'suku to deal out untold death, mostly among their precious female population, would forever stain Tigh's memories of his twin.

A starship captain with famous ancestry and a killer reputation...

They call her Valkyrie for the way she swoops into battle and usually saves the day. After losing her beloved ship in an ambush that almost cost the Valkyrie and her crew their lives, Captain Gineva Starbridge is cooling her heels at headquarters, waiting for a new assignment, when the Emperor shows up, in person, looking to broker peace.

For every warrior, there is only one woman who is his true mate...

When Tigh sees Ginny across the crowded audience chamber where he has come to make an unorthodox proposal to unite their two ravaged peoples, he can scarcely believe his fortune. Could she be the one woman meant for him? He had come before the human Council, on his knees, to offer his hand in marriage to any human female that would help him in his quest to forge a lasting peace. But, when he sees Ginny, he knows she is the only woman who will do. Can they navigate a rocky road, with enemies on both sides plotting against them, to unite two warring cultures, into one lasting peace?

DEDICATION

To all those who reach for the stars...

Thanks to my editor, Jess, for helping fix some very old writing. I started this book years ago and never quite found a way to finish it until just a few months ago. I guess it was finally the right time. Thanks also to Peggy for her assistance eliminating the last of the typos. Any that remain are my fault, I'm sure. LOL

Special thanks to Dad, the real rocket scientist, inventor, troubleshooter, and innovator, who fostered my love of science, space, and technology from a very young age.

PROLOGUE

Excerpted from the Jit'Suku Warrior Code

The Rules of Warfare

The First Rule: Never make war on your own kind.

The Second Rule: Oldsters and children are to be respected. Unless they raise arms against you, a true warrior shall let them pass unmolested. Likewise, a true warrior shall never attack females, for they are the image of the Mother Goddess and the bringers of life.

The Third Rule: Never take the coward's path, for only the brave will earn a place in the Mother Goddess's hall of honor.

The Rules of Love

The Nij-ta: Love's first kiss will reveal a warrior's true mate and he will have no other ever after.

The reluctant mate should be wooed with care. If she refuses after three requests for marriage, she may be coaxed, but only by pleasurable means. If ever she repudiates her mate, the true warrior will respect her wishes and live the rest of his life alone, watching over her welfare from afar.

A true mate is a gift from the Mother Goddess and never to be disrespected. A true warrior's most sacred responsibility is the protection of his mate, for she is the image of the Mother Goddess and the bringer of life.

Honor above all.

*

Tigh downed his last opponent cleanly. That made thirty-two for the day. Enough.

The high priest called him forward after Tigh had helped his opponent back to his feet with friendly courtesy. Courtesy, even in defeat, was a mark of the Zenai priesthood, just as humility was valued in a victor.

High Priest Jurdan motioned for Tigh to walk with him. It was an honor rarely afforded to even such a highly-ranked novitiate. Tigh fell in step beside him, waiting to hear what the wisest of the elder priests would say.

"You have learned our teachings well, but I fear your time has finally come to leave us." The spry old man held out a communiqué bearing the royal seal, and Tigh felt his heart drop. He'd left behind the home that was rightly his and cut all ties to the empire years ago. Surely, they could have no use for him now, after all this time in self-imposed exile.

Tigh took the crystal pad with a heavy heart, pressing his thumbprint to the elegantly concealed reader. The small holographic screen revealed the face of one of his father's oldest friends and advisors. Torm had been there for Tigh and his brother, Elius, when their parents had died. Torm had been the one to break the sad news and had acted as Steward, dealing with the day-to-day running of the empire until Tigh and his twin came of age.

When Torm had retired, Tigh joined the priesthood, clearing the way for his beloved brother to have what he always wanted—the throne.

"Elius is dead." Torm's strong voice rang out from the hologram. His face was lined with age and what looked like worry.

Torm's stark words didn't surprise Tigh. For three days now, he had suffered strange dreams, omens of bad tidings that could reach him even here, on the isolated mountaintop that was the Zenai retreat.

"Elius was stabbed by his wife, the Empress Marla, in his sleep, moments before she succumbed to the mutated virus that is, even now, raging through our galaxy. Tigh, you're needed. The empire is in ruins. Elius's virus has turned on its makers, and the techs tell me it may destroy us utterly, killing most of our females as we insanely tried to kill the humans' males." In the holo, Torm sighed heavily. "You may not have heard of this where you are, but Elius became obsessed with defeating the humans, once and for all, after our defeat at Alpha Richtar Sept. A scientist named Gruber came to him with a virus he'd designed. I don't have all the particulars yet, but it was somehow targeted to a specific gene on the human Y chromosome. Since only human males have this Y-shaped chromosome, it was thought to only affect the warriors of their galaxy. Gruber claimed that releasing the virus on human worlds would kill all their warriors within three generations, leaving the females unharmed. Elius used this justification to move forward with the release, but Gruber was wrong. Many human females became sick, aborting male children and damaging their reproductive systems. They were changed on a genetic level, and many are now barren. It has fueled their fire to fight against us."

"Dear Goddess, no." Tigh's whispered words went unheeded by the recording that continued to play.

"Many human females now man the ships they use to defend their systems. And they are fierce. They fight with even greater intensity than their warriors did. Many field commanders left the battle when they realized most of the enemy fleet is now staffed with females, but Elius's hand-picked commanders shame themselves and our people by making war on women. Now, that terrible virus has mutated and come back to us. It kills our women, Tigh. The specific gene it targeted in humans was on the Y chromosome carried only by the males, but in our people, it targets something on both X chromosomes carried by all females. Males are spared, they believe, because we only have one X chromosome." Torm's old face grew pained in the hologram. "Tigh, my own daughter is gravely ill as I record this message. You've got to come back to the capital, as I have, to bring some order to the mess your brother left."

Tigh felt heaviness in his heart. His brother was dead, and from what Torm said, his people were in serious trouble. He'd given up his claim to the seat of power in favor of his brother and Elius's future children. He wasn't sure where he stood legally, but he would act as an advisor, if necessary, or in any capacity where he could help set things right.

"Elius's daughters are sick," Torm went on. "They tell me the youngest girl is only hours from death. He had no son," the holo continued. "You will be heir to the throne, once more, if things go as I fear and both princesses succumb to the virus."

Tigh switched off the holo. He couldn't bear to hear any more. The high priest stood silently at his side, watching him with troubled eyes.

"What should I do?"

The old man narrowed his eyes. "The Mother Goddess has seen all that has transpired. You already know your duty, Tigh. We've long suspected your path lay not with the priesthood. It's why we have denied you the final vows and will continue to do so."

Tigh felt defeat in his heart. It was not something a jit'suku warrior could stomach easily.

"Then, I must leave the Zenai and do what I can for the empire."

The priest patted Tigh's slumped shoulders. "You must follow where the Mother Goddess leads. There is much wrong to put right, and it seems you are the instrument to do it."

"If I'd taken the throne, none of this would ever have happened." Regret filled his heart. He'd loved his brother and thought to give Elius the one thing fate had denied him.

Tigh couldn't believe Elius had released a bioweapon on the humans. It was an act abhorrent to their warrior nature. Tigh was amazed any of his people would have gone along with such a plan. Apparently, much had changed since he'd sought refuge on the Zenai mountain, years ago.

"Did you ever think that perhaps, She sent you here so that you could learn the right way to govern the empire? The Mother Goddess has plans far deeper than our small minds can comprehend, Tigh. Trust in Her, and all will come right, according to Her plan."

CHAPTER 1

One Standard Human Year Later

Emperor Tigh came as a supplicant before the humans' Governing Council. Begging was not something a jit'suku warrior normally did, but dire circumstances called for drastic measures. Over the past year since he'd claimed the throne of his failing empire, almost all women of childbearing age and younger among the jit'suku had died.

But the humans had women. And Tigh had learned through his endless study of their peoples' respective histories, some human women could, and had, bred with jit'suku males in the distant past.

The humans had few fertile men. Large numbers of human women had been sick with the virus, yet survived. As a result of the damage done to them on a genetic level, they would never be able to conceive from a human male, but some twist of fate would allow those same women to produce female children with more resilient double X chromosomes with jit'suku males.

The answer to both the human problem and the jit'suku problem was clear, though it would be difficult to carry out. Enemies must become not only friends, but lovers. Tigh knew, in order to show the way to his people, he must select a mate from among the humans—if any human female would have him.

He'd given up hope of finding his true mate and would settle for any woman that would at least be friendly towards him. What he did, he did for his people. He'd failed them once already by allowing Elius to have the throne that should have been Tigh's. He would not fail them, again. He would take to wife the first human woman that would have him and get her with child, proving to both races that they could merge and end their fighting, once and for all.

It was an ambitious plan, and it would be his life's work. Tigh had risked all by entering human space, seeking audience with their Governing Council over his advisors' objections. Only old Torm and a small contingent of Tigh's most loyal warriors accompanied him, steadfast by his side, willing to face any consequences his actions might bring. It would be well within the humans' right to put them all to death without even hearing what he had to say. The use of a bioweapon was cowardly and not something a jit'suku warrior should countenance. Yet, it had been done. Tigh could hardly fathom his twin's reasoning, but he would make up for it, if he could.

And so, he found himself before the Governing Council, ringed by women of power and their aides. Tigh noted a few males, as well—undoubtedly some of the famous Sons of Amber he'd heard about from his tech advisors. The humans had found a way to outsmart the virus, but it would take generations to restore the balance of male and female, and they would be forever changed on a genetic level, since the Sons were genetic creations of Dr. Amber Waithe and her team.

They were not fully human any longer. Their genetic codes had been modified to make them immune to the virus and able to father over ninety percent male children, with successive generations normalizing to about fifty percent within a few generations as the race recovered. It was a brilliant plan, but the jit'suku had no such similar strategy.

Without women, they were stuck. Condemned by their own arrogance.

Tigh moved to the center of the Council chamber, all eyes on him as he was called to speak. He moved deliberately, knowing his actions were being recorded for posterity. Slowly, he sank to one knee, his ancient sword of office at his feet, head bowed in the traditional gesture of surrender, seldom seen from a jit'suku warrior. What he did here, he did for his people. Some would see it as weakness, but the wise among both races would understand the nobility of his actions. Or so he hoped.

One of the few males on the Council rose and moved to stand before Tigh. His death could come now, Tigh thought, and it would be justified. But all he'd learned of humans and their history made him hope they'd want to know why he surrendered first, before exacting retribution. He was counting on human curiosity to let him plead his case.

"I know you had nothing to do with the release of the virus, Tigh, warrior-priest and newly crowned Emperor. Your surrender means little, and I do not accept it."

Tigh rose to face the other warrior, meeting the dark-haired man eye to eye. Tigh respected the steel he sensed in the other man, the unrelenting dominance and the honor in his words. He was also surprised at the man's knowledge of Tigh's past.

"It's true I was not aware of what my brother had done until recently, but I took over his sins when I took his throne."

"A throne that should have been yours to begin with."

Tigh bowed his head in acknowledgment. "Another sin for which my people—and yours—have paid too high a price. I would never have released any kind of bioweapon. I could not. It goes against every teaching of my faith and tenet of our Warrior Code. I still don't understand why Elius did it, but none of that matters now. What matters is how we fix the problems the virus has created and rebuild our societies."

"We've found our answer," Dr. Amber Waithe said from

her seat on the Council. Tigh recognized her from the reconnaissance holos he had of all the Council members. He knew, too, that this genetically manipulated man standing before him was Commandant Michael Amber, leader of the Atlantia fleet, which made up a substantial portion of the humans' fighting forces.

Tigh turned to the scientist, motioning also to Torm who stood forward from the small group of warriors who had been allowed into the chamber with him.

"You have come up with an elegant, but long-term solution, Dr. Waithe, and are to be commended. I can, however, offer a more immediate solution that will bring the added benefit of ending this war between our peoples for all time."

Murmurs rose through the Council chamber, and Tigh took it as a good sign. Councilor Torm passed a collection of data crystals to the famous geneticist through her aides and returned back to his place among the jit'suku warriors.

"Councilor Torm, who lost his own daughter to the virus, has just given you complete documentation from our best med techs and scientists. I'm sure you all know, by now, that the virus my brother allowed to be released has mutated and turned back on us. It has killed our females in massive numbers, as it killed your males. I've made a personal study of our peoples' history, including especially, the time of the Three Hundred Year Peace, when my ancestor, Tren, mated and married a human female. She was the daughter of an Enhanced human warrior, and I believe now, that these early tamperings with your genetic codes included jit'suku DNA. Otherwise, my techs tell me, the virus could not have mutated enough in your populations to turn against us. It is the small amount of undocumented jit'suku DNA in some of your people that bridged the gap from human to jit'suku and brought our own terror back to us."

The Councilors looked surprised and concerned, though Dr. Waithe seemed intrigued most of all. She had the knowledge of genetics to puzzle this through, and she also recognized the value of the information he'd just given her. She flipped open the accompanying dossier and sorted through some of the information he'd had prepared for her.

"You've given me the means to destroy you utterly." Dr. Waithe silenced all in the room with her soft statement.

Tigh bowed his head. "Without our women, we are already dead."

Silence reigned for a long moment.

"What do you propose?" This from the leader of the Council, an older woman named Mathilde Grey who had been a very successful lawyer then Galactic Court judge before being voted to her current leadership position. She was a shrewd woman who made tough decisions. Tigh had studied her record in some detail, looking for clues to the woman's personality. Everything he read indicated a decisive nature tempered by wisdom and compassion. He was counting on that compassion to save them all, and now was their moment of truth. Perhaps the first of many. Or the last of his life.

"A blending of our races." The murmurs in the chamber were back, louder this time. "Jit'suku do not make war among ourselves. It is our First Rule of Warfare. Now that we know for certain there is jit'suku DNA in humanity, our warriors are thrown into chaos. Once my people believe what the scientists are telling them, they will cease all hostility against humans."

"But how do you make them believe?" Leader Grey asked, drawing attention as silence reigned, once again, in the large chamber.

"By joining with humanity in a visible statement, as my ancestor Tren did. By making a human woman my empress."

Murmurs became loud talking as the listeners erupted in various reactions to his words. So far, no one seemed ready to kill him, so Tigh figured he had a good chance of pulling this off.

Tigh took a moment to look around the room, gauging reactions, taking note of people he hadn't really seen before.

There were many, many women here, and only a handful of men scattered throughout the large chamber. They were all big men with similar features. They looked like brothers, and Tigh realized they were—of a sort. They were undoubtedly Sons, made from similar genetic material, though there was surely enough diversity built into their codes to assure successive generations would breed properly.

His eyes returned to Michael, the warrior standing just a few feet from him, and he noted the small female aide now delivering a message to him. Suddenly, Tigh was struck. This woman… She seemed somehow familiar…somehow important. Tigh took an almost involuntary step forward, breathing deeply to sort out her delicious scent from those of the rest of the room. She was close enough that he could scent her curiosity as she watched him stalk nearer. He also felt a warming thrum within his own body, the recognition of a mate that had never left his people, primitive as it was.

This was a woman he could see as his empress. This woman just might be the one who could mate him and make him the happiest of men. And she was human.

Tigh could hardly believe it. She was a vision. A military woman with wavy brown hair and eyes of hazel green. Her uniform made her look neat and trim and altogether proper. It also made him want to see what she looked like out of that very prim uniform.

Michael must have noticed Tigh's fascination, for he placed himself in front of the woman, blocking Tigh's path. He might have challenged the Son of Amber, right there in front of everyone, but the leader's voice called him back to his purpose.

"Dr. Waithe, what do you have to say on this issue? How would this 'blending' impact human genetics?"

All eyes turned to the woman who had laid the groundwork for the fight against the virus.

"I would like more time to study this, but off the top of my head, I can tell you that the infusion of more jit'suku DNA would be a benefit to future generations on a purely genetic level. Now, politically, you'll have to decide for yourselves, but as for continuance as a species, my research tells me that jit DNA, when mixed with our own, creates very advanced beings, with high resistance to disease and improved sensory perception and reflexes. I don't think it's much of a secret, anymore, that this was how my long-passed predecessors created Enhanced spec ops soldiers during the Rim Wars. What the emperor said about us is correct. There is residual jit'suku DNA already laced throughout humanity from those early experiments. It wasn't widely known due to the Genetic Purity Movement at the time, but many of the Enhanced soldiers went on to have children of their own, and those children reaped the same benefits of Enhancement. It got watered down a bit over the successive generations, but the DNA is still there, and it's spread throughout most of the human worlds."

The leader nodded. "So then, it's not really a question of introducing jit DNA into our own gene pool, but merely adding more?"

"Essentially, that is true," Dr. Waithe confirmed.

The leader turned back to him. "What do you propose?"

Tigh tried to hide his excitement. It would not do to act the fool at such a crucial moment. Better to appeal to their generous human hearts.

"We have many motherless boys among our people now, as you have many women who might enjoy the chance to raise a male child. I would guarantee safe passage for any woman who wants to come to our galaxy to visit, at first, or settle, if they wish to stay. Our orphanages are overrun, and our men are, in many cases, unable to cope. Many wish to get away from the reminders of their loss. If you permit, I'm sure a few jit'suku men and their children would relish the chance to come to your galaxy and make a new life among your women, as well. My plan is to make such movement completely voluntary. It is only up to us, as leaders, to remove the obstacles and allow for it." He read skepticism on many faces, particularly those involved with the military. "You can, of course, put limits on how many men you allow through, and where. For my part, I will place no limits on the number of women who may want to come look for a mate or a child among my people. We can use all the help we can get."

"And who would you take as your empress to cement the deal?" Leader Grey challenged him with an odd smile. "I'm too old for you, sadly." Her little joke broke the tension in the chamber and startled laughs from several ladies.

Tigh bowed his head gallantly towards the leader, but everything in him was focused on the alluring scent of the female who stood just behind Michael Amber. Tigh turned back to face the other man, meeting his eyes with a plea in his own that the Son seemed to understand. Michael moved aside, and the brunette beauty was once again revealed, a welcome sight for Tigh's hungry heart. She was radiant, and a little uncomfortable with all eyes now focused on her. Still, she stood her ground, and Tigh noticed, for the first time, she wore the uniform of a high-ranking military officer. He grinned at the thought. She would make one hell of an empress.

"I'll take her, if she'll have me."

Shocked gasps sounded through the room, but he paid them no mind. No, all he wanted now, was to take the beautiful girl in his arms and see if she could actually be the one his heart thought never to find in this lifetime.

He strode toward her, noting with pleasure how she faced him with curiosity and very little fear. When he stood toe to toe with her, he smiled gently to put her at ease.

"Forgive me, but I must know…"

His words were for her ears alone as he pulled her lithe body into his arms and kissed her soundly. Her lips were plump and soft under his, yielding after the first moment of stunned surprise. She swayed against him as his tongue sought and gained entrance to her mouth, and her unique flavor blossomed across his senses as no other had ever before. Her scent flooded him, the feel of her humbled him.

This was his woman.

The Mother Goddess was surely smiling on him from her home in the stars. To put this special woman in his path at this moment was the sign he'd hoped for but hadn't dared expect. For each jit'suku warrior, there was one special woman who was his other half, the mate to his heart. He often knew her on sight, always upon their first kiss. The Emperor Tren had known his own human mate when he first met and kissed her. So too, did Tigh know this small human woman—a warrior woman, no less—was his perfect mate.

A hand on his shoulder pulled him back to his senses. Michael, the Son of Amber, spoke behind him.

"You'd better let her go, or, emperor or not, I'll kick your ass for manhandling one of my officers."

Tigh pulled back, shaking his head to clear his senses, but it didn't quite work. Luckily, the girl in his arms looked just as shaken. Though he hadn't held a female of any species in many years, one never did quite forget the look of an aroused woman. Tigh licked his lips and noted the way her dazed eyes followed the movement of his tongue.

Drawing back farther, he felt eyes on them and knew he was making a scene, but he couldn't help himself. When she swayed, he steadied her, doing more for his cause—had he but realized it—with a simple kiss than he ever would have done with words. The romantic display would be broadcast over and over on every human world in the coming days, setting many lonely female hearts aflutter.

When she could stand on her own, Tigh stepped back and sank to one knee once more, only this time it wasn't in surrender, it was in supplication.

"I would give you my heart, if you will but take it." His eyes held hers, only slightly above his kneeling height. She was a petite little thing, even for a human.

"You don't even know me." Her low voice whispered through him, sealing itself in his soul.

"My heart knows yours. The Mother Goddess put you in my path at this most important of moments. That's all that matters. But I know you humans do things differently." Tigh stood with a sigh. "I will court you," he searched her uniform for her nametag, "Captain Starbridge. I will show you that we are meant to be together. Then you will consent to be my bride."

Tigh couldn't help the smile that lit his face. The woman stared at him as if he were crazed, but he couldn't contain the joy that bubbled inside him. Not only would they forge a lasting peace, but he would do it with his destined mate as his empress. Life simply could not get any better for a man in his position. They had a rough road ahead, for a certainty, but with his woman at his side, he could face anything that came.

Captain Gineva Starbridge was overwhelmed by the kiss. An emperor—her sworn enemy, no less—had just kissed her senseless in front of the Governing Council and half the galaxy's media. This must be the way her spec ops soldier ancestor, John Starbridge, had felt all those centuries ago when the intergalactic superstar, Diva, had agreed to be his wife.

Ginny didn't like the limelight and had never sought it out, though from time to time, she'd been interviewed about her famous ancestors or feted for her military victories. But she'd never—ever—been kissed by an emperor and then proposed marriage in front of all of humanity. This definitely took the cake.

"Well, Captain Starbridge," Leader Grey prompted her. "What do you have to say to the emperor's offer?"

Ginny was stymied. To refuse outright could spell disaster. She didn't want to be solely responsible for killing this peace initiative before it even began.

"I...I don't know what to say, ma'am."

The leader nodded as if in approval of her answer and turned to the rest of the Council. "We will take some time to go over the materials you've brought, Emperor Tigh. In the meantime, you and your party will remain here as guests of the Council."

"Thank you, Leader Grey and Council members. We're

pleased to remain while we work out the details of what I hope will be a lasting peace for all our people."

Oh, the man had a silver tongue, Ginny thought, watching him woo the ladies of the Council. A talented tongue too, she allowed, now that she'd been knocked nearly off her feet by his ardor. Under any other circumstances, Ginny would welcome a man like him with open arms, but her past and her future were colliding in the person of this very stubborn emperor, and she didn't know where to turn or what to do.

Leader Grey dismissed the Council, drawing the special session to an end with a resounding ring of her gavel. Instantly, noise erupted from the gathered councilors and their aides, but Ginny stood rooted to the spot as the emperor turned back to her.

"Would you give me just one thing before we part?" His voice was a seductive purr that sizzled up her legs. "Give me your name, sweetheart."

She considered him, thinking her name was little enough to give. It wasn't like he was asking for a kidney, after all.

"Gineva Magdalena Starbridge, but my friends call me Ginny."

An odd sort of recognition played over his handsome features. "Gineva is a beautiful name for a beautiful woman. But I've read about another Magdalena Starbridge in my ancestor's journals. Maggie, they called her, although many knew her as Diva. Is she your ancestor?"

Surprised by his knowledge, Ginny nodded. "She was a spy in the Rim Wars, though that didn't come out until well after she and her husband John were lost in the Pyramid."

"She was also second-generation Enhanced, though I don't know if your family was aware of it. I've heard the subject was taboo among humans for many years. My ancestor, Tren, knew her and thought, at one time, to marry her, but she turned out not to be the woman for him."

"She married John Starbridge after orchestrating his escape from the Emperor Tren."

Tigh's smile nearly melted her bones. "Tren recorded later

that he'd let them escape. He was so disappointed that she wasn't his mate, he fell into depression for a time, but she'd promised to send other second-gen Enhanced women so that he might find his true mate. He did eventually find the woman he sought to be his empress, just as I have found you."

"Now, wait just a minute—"

Tigh backed off, his manner appeasing. "Forgive me, but can't you see it's meant to be? You carry jit'suku DNA within you. I recognized you the moment I saw you. You are my mate, and you will come to realize that what I say is true in time. I'll try to be patient, but I warn you, I never mastered the art of patience. It was one of my main failings as a novitiate."

"You were supposed to be some kind of priest, weren't you?" She couldn't help her curiosity, though she probably should have gotten away from this disturbing man as quickly as she could.

Tigh nodded. "After giving the throne to my brother, Elius, I secluded myself on Zenai mountain and didn't know about anything that occurred until after my brother died and I was called back to the palace. I would have stopped all of this if I could. What he did is inexcusable, and all jit'suku bear the shame of his actions. It is a dishonor we will carry all our days."

"I'd like to hear more about your ways." A deep male voice broke in from behind them, and Ginny belatedly realized her commanding officer, Commandant Michael Amber, stood behind them, listening in. They both turned their attention to him. "Perhaps you and your men will join me and my staff for dinner tonight?"

The emperor looked to her, then back at Michael. "If Captain Starbridge will be part of that company, I will most happily accept your invitation. As for my men, I know they are interested in meeting humans in friendship rather than across a field of battle. Each member of my group is a volunteer, chosen from among hundreds, especially for this mission."

Michael seemed to look over the small group of warriors with an assessing eye. "All who come in peace are welcome at my table, Emperor Tigh, and Captain Starbridge will be there. She's part of my staff, right now, between ships, as it were."

Neatly maneuvered into spending more time with this strange, upsetting man, Ginny had no choice but to comply.

CHAPTER 2

"Is the future empress taking calls?" Ginny heard her mother's teasing voice coming from the com panel located in the main room of her cabin. She'd just finished her duty shift and dreaded what came next. Apparently, the first in the long line of humiliating events to come was a call from her mother.

Janet Kerlew-Starbridge was normally the best of mothers, but when it came to her daughter's personal life—or lack thereof—she was like a dog with a bone. It didn't help that Ginny was embarrassed beyond belief to discuss certain things with her mom. Ginny took after her father. He was more sedate and reticent while her mother was outgoing and emotional. She saw the universe differently and had a vastly opposing opinion of how Ginny should run her personal life.

For one thing, after Ginny's brief engagement ended, her mother had counseled her to get on with her life, but she just couldn't move on so quickly. The argument had been a sore point between mother and daughter until the plague made them forget their petty quarrel. For another, Ginny's mother didn't understand her daughter's desire to join the military. A trained nurse, Janet Starbridge couldn't comprehend Ginny's need for revenge or her desire to defend and protect the rest of humanity against the continued jit threat. Yet, they loved each other deeply and spoke often, even though Janet Starbridge lived on-planet, and when Ginny wasn't onboard her ship, she had a compartment in the Bachelor Officers Quarters, BOQ for short, on-station.

Ginny sighed and threw her uniform jacket toward the couch, hitting the button on the small private com unit that would answer her mother's planetside call. She had to get this over with sooner or later.

"I'm here, Mom. And I'm not the future empress. Not yet, anyway," she grumbled.

"Could have fooled me. That man laid a kiss on you the likes of which I have never seen." Janet Starbridge made a fanning motion in front of her still-young face on the viewer with long, elegant fingers. She looked a lot like her daughter but wore pale pastel colors and floaty fabrics while Ginny actually preferred the starch and starkness of her dark uniform. "Does he kiss as good as he looks?"

Ginny huffed as she tugged off her shoes and propped her aching feet on the table that fronted the couch. "I won't dignify that with an answer."

"That good, huh?" Janet chuckled. "So, what are you going to do? Are you tempted to say yes and become the empress of all you survey?"

Ginny squeezed her eyes tightly shut. "I just don't know."

"Oh, sweetheart." Her mother's voice dipped to comforting tones. "You could be an instrument of peace. But can you forgive them—forgive him—for what those people have done to us? I don't envy you this choice."

"I'm supposed to be having dinner with him tonight. With the commandant and all his staff too, but I can just bet they're going to seat me right next to the emperor."

Her mother shrugged her elegant shoulders. "What can it hurt to get to know the man? It's not every day one dines with an emperor, after all."

Ginny kept her mother's words in mind when, as predicted, she was seated directly next to Emperor Tigh at

Michael Amber's formal dining table. The rest of his command staff was present, including his wife, Colonel Leah Blackfoot-Amber, though Ginny sorely missed her own bridge crew. The command staff was a friendly bunch, but because Ginny was often out in the field with her ship, she didn't know many of them very well. And she definitely didn't have the close relationship with any of them that she had with her loyal crew. The core of her ship's crew was waiting, with her, for their new assignment. They were on-station as well, but not high-ranking enough to be included in this exclusive company. Darn the luck.

Tigh had no such problem. He'd brought quite a few of his men with him to the dinner, including the kindly-looking older gentleman who'd been at his side in the Council chambers earlier. Councilor Torm was his name, she remembered as she smiled slightly in greeting, taking the seat the emperor held out for her, right next to his own.

"You look lovely, Captain," Tigh murmured near her ear as he assisted her.

She looked up, and his handsome face was entirely too near. Quickly, she looked away, trying to hide the blush that wanted so desperately to rise in her pale cheeks. "Thank you, Your Highness, but dress uniforms are very much alike, I'm afraid."

Tigh sat close at her side. "Perhaps, but the way you fill yours out is entirely unique...and gorgeous."

Again, that flush of embarrassment wanted to rise, but she tamped it down. She made no response, guessing he would probably argue his point, just for the sake of small talk, and she had no patience for that. She wanted nothing more than to get this dinner over with and escape back to her compartment. She wasn't cut out for state dinners and all the trappings and politics they entailed.

Emperor Tigh, surprisingly enough, seemed to share her attitude, though he hid it better. Small movements of his hands indicated his discomfort, though you'd have to be sitting practically in his lap to notice. He was a very controlled

21

man, but his eyes gave him away. He didn't have the ruthlessness she'd encountered in many of the jit ship captains she'd faced in battle, though she knew he was a trained warrior. Still, he didn't seem as aggressive as the other jits she'd fought. Then again, a state dinner was quite a different setting than a battlefield. Still, she watched him, curious about the man who seemed so different from others of his race.

"Emperor Tigh." Michael spoke once everyone was seated. "You already know Captain Starbridge. Allow me to introduce my wife, Leah." Michael went around the table, introducing the rest of his command staff. They were all women and all very high-ranking military commanders. When he was finished with the formal introductions, Tigh sat forward and did the same, adding a bit of personal information about each of his men.

"Councilor Torm was advisor to my father," Tigh said of the old man who sat at his right hand while Ginny was on his left. "He retired to his family when my brother took the throne but recalled me from the Zenai when Elius died." The old man nodded, looking serene as only an accomplished statesman could under such close scrutiny. Tigh turned to the next man, sitting down the long table among the human women.

"Captain Halith Zen of the flagship Jendai Zoluu. He was recently promoted to captain and is a longtime friend. His mother was a trusted councilor to my parents on social matters, and we practically grew up together. When I left for the Zenai, he joined the fleet, serving in home sector, protecting Solaris Prime.

"Executive Officer Jimnai Burk is also an old friend. We studied together in the Zenai monastery on Solaris Prime for several years before I left for exile on the mountain. He is a third-level novitiate but has also been a member of the home fleet for many years.

"Hansa is Armsmaster on this mission, though he has served as Captain of the Imperial Guard and Armsmaster for the Fleet. He objected to Elius' actions and was imprisoned for over a decade on Volhul for his views."

The women regarded the giant man with varying degrees of alarm and pity. Even in the Milky Way, the infamous prison of Volhul was well known. It was spoken of in fearsome tones, used as a threat to keep wayward soldiers in line. Few who went there were ever seen again.

"Xeer is one of the guard corps on this mission and is the new master of the Palace Guard. We also trained together for a time in the Zenai monastery on Solaris Prime, but Xeer's true skills lie with weapons and technology. He is a galaxy-class sharpshooter."

Michael nodded approvingly. "As is Captain Holmes." He nodded to the older woman seated about halfway down the long table. "She shoots competitively several times a year. It's always a pleasure to see her bring home the trophy. Perhaps we can arrange a match between her and Mr. Xeer while you're here."

Xeer nodded, holding one hand over his heart in respect. "It would be an honor." The smile he sent the female captain was both daring and friendly. This Xeer seemed like a bit of a tease, and he was handsome enough to sweep most women off their feet. The ladies would have to watch that one. He was a rascal, if Ginny was any judge.

Tigh introduced a few more of his men, and then, dinner was served. It consisted of a few courses but was thankfully shorter than Ginny had feared. Tigh was pleasant company, if a bit overly solicitous. He talked with everyone, but somehow, his attention never seemed to stray far from her. His pale blue gaze followed her at all times, not in a creepy way, but it was definitely disconcerting.

Ginny felt like she was under a microscope. Not only was the emperor watching her every move, but so was everyone else. Her small hope that her fellow officers wouldn't make a big deal out of Tigh's impulsive proposal quickly dissolved. Before the first course had even been removed, she'd been asked the question she'd been dreading.

"What are you going to do, Captain Starbridge?" Leah Blackwell-Amber asked from just a few seats away. "Are you considering accepting the emperor's proposal?" A hush fell over the table, even though Leah had spoken in moderate tones. It seemed everyone wanted to know the answer.

Including Ginny.

She had no clue what she should do. The question had preyed on her mind for hours now, and she was no closer to a resolution. Tigh, himself, was a temptation. Just on a purely physical level, he was a handsome man with the startling combination of thick black hair and palest blue eyes. He could have been a vid star in the old days, if he hadn't already inherited an empire.

Men were few and far between these days, and the idea of having one to herself was definitely intriguing, though it wasn't something she'd ever expected would come her way. Especially not such a handsome and obviously fit specimen. She was attracted to him, despite her better judgment, but she couldn't be ruled by hormones. She had to think through this decision and do what was best for all concerned, not just for her raging hormones.

"I'm not certain what I'll do, yet," she hedged. "I mean, I'm considering it, but I haven't made up my mind."

"But you could end this war, once and for all." One of the older human officers sounded almost scornful of her hesitancy.

Ginny had to tread carefully. "I realize that, of course. And I, too, want peace. But there are other factors to be considered."

"Like what?" the abrasive officer wanted to know.

Tigh held up one hand, signaling for silence. "Please, let us not talk of this at table. Ginny will make up her mind in good time. I'd prefer she not be pressured." He smiled to soften his words, and the older officer seemed to relent, sitting back in her chair while one of Tigh's hands covered Ginny's on the table. It was an obvious show of support that was oddly comforting, though Ginny felt a little foolish holding hands like a schoolgirl at what was essentially a state dinner.

"Thank you, Your Highness." Ginny pulled her hand out from under Tigh's, tucking it firmly into her lap.

The rest of the dinner went well after that, though Ginny remained uncomfortably aware that she and the jit emperor were the center of much speculation and curiosity. She hated the limelight but had learned to live with it while in port. On her ship, she could be as anonymous as the next captain, but every time she docked lately, there was a contingent of newsbots ready to follow her every move.

It was a hazard of the job. After some initial embarrassment at being caught in a few odd-looking situations while on-station, she'd learned to curb her movements so she would never again be embarrassed in the media. Being a ship's captain had garnered her a certain amount of publicity, and her war record was openly discussed in the media. She saw no sense in giving the galactic news corps anything salacious to speculate about her personal life.

But then, Tigh had happened. He'd turned her life into intergalactic news fodder, and no matter what her answer to his proposal, she knew she would have to live with the fallout for years to come. If she said yes, the newsbots would never be gone from her life. If she said no, speculation would run rife, as would condemnation from many people. If she refused his offer of marriage, would she prolong the war? She didn't know, but even she could foresee that she'd take a lot of blame in certain quarters were she to refuse.

She couldn't let that influence her decision, of course, but it was something she'd have to deal with if and when the time came. For now, she had a lot to think about, and Tigh wasn't making it any easier.

He was the soul of courtesy at dinner. He also entertained her with witty and insightful conversation. His wasn't a practiced charm. He was more earthy. More real than she had expected. His appeal was on a more basic level. An instinct more than a considered thought.

Oh, the man was dangerous, indeed.

As the meal ended and the small party broke up, it was strongly suggested by the commandant himself that Ginny allow the emperor to escort her back to her compartment. Since she was already in officer country, as they called it, the walk to her cabin was a relatively short one. She had been in the middle of denying Tigh's request to walk her there when Michael Amber had intervened, convincing her to accept.

Of course, Tigh couldn't be allowed to wander around the station on his own, so a trail of guards—both human and jit'suku—followed along behind them as they walked slowly toward Ginny's berth. Tigh seemed to want to linger while Ginny wished he'd move a little faster. She wanted out of her dress uniform. She wanted the comfort of her own quarters. And, most importantly, she wanted away from the disturbing emperor who seemed convinced, somehow, that she was the right woman for him. The right woman to be empress, for Pete's sake! Ginny still couldn't wrap her head around that dizzying idea.

"What is your schedule like tomorrow?" Tigh asked conversationally. She wasn't fooled. He was looking for more opportunities to harass her. She mentally chastised herself. To be fair, he was an interesting companion, and if not for the marriage offer that lay between them like the proverbial eight-hundred-pound jungle beast, she would have welcomed his attention.

"I'm on first shift," she replied. "Then, I have training scheduled with my bridge crew. Even though we don't have a ship of our own at present, we try to keep our skills sharp."

"Then, you're expecting a new command soon?"

She couldn't find anything to object to in his tone. He'd stuck to less volatile topics all during dinner and seemed to be following the same path now that they were alone—except for the guards, of course. She breathed a sigh of relief.

"Any day now, they say. I flatter myself to think they want us back patrolling the rim as soon as possible."

"From the little I've seen, it is not flattery to think that you are valued highly by your people. Your commandant seems inordinately interested in your welfare." Tigh made a face that was hard to interpret. It seemed part jealousy, part respect, with a touch of concern.

"Commandant Amber is an accomplished leader and a good strategist. I credit his deployments with our success in this war. He knows where to put each of us to play to our strengths. Of course, his wife plays a large role in that work, as well. Leah was his XO for several years before they got together. Now that they're married, it seems like the partnership of commandant and executive officer has blended into a wonderful marriage of equals." She heard the wistful note in her own voice and quickly turned away, glad they were nearing her hatch.

Tigh's hand on her arm stilled her. As she turned to face him, still several yards from her door, she noted the entourage of guards draw to a stop, just out of earshot. Then, all she saw was Tigh's beautiful blue eyes, watching her with concern.

"That is what I want too, Ginny. A partnership. A life mate who will support me as I support her. Don't you think we could have that together?"

His earnestness touched her heart and tempted her to candor. "Why me, Tigh?" Her words were the barest whisper.

He took her hands in his and raised them to his chest, resting them over his heart as he stepped closer, into her personal space. She was mesmerized by the look in his eyes, the seriousness with which he took her question.

"Warriors often know their true mate on sight and always from their first kiss. Among my people, we call it the nij-ta. The mate test. When I first saw you in the Council chamber, I was stunned. I have never, never felt the way I felt when I first saw your beautiful face or breathed in your delicate scent. No other woman has ever made me want her from first glance, and after kissing you, I know no other ever will. You were made for me, Ginny. As I was made for you."

"You know all that from a single kiss?" She wasn't really

buying it, though it was awfully romantic. It sounded crazy, but she'd felt the magic of their first kiss. She'd felt a tingle she couldn't ever remember experiencing before.

"For jit'suku warriors, the nij-ta is all it takes. For my own part, I believe the Mother Goddess put you in my path, at this time, as a sign. Many warriors search their whole lives and never find their true mates. When I went into exile with the Zenai, I thought I would dedicate my life to the Goddess and never marry. With Elius on the throne, I could not have children. They would have thrown doubt over Elius and his heirs by their mere existence. I was fine with all of that. For all his faults, I loved Elius."

"You gave up your throne for him," Ginny observed. "You must have loved him a great deal."

"We were twins. He was the other half of me for many years. Some might say now, he was the bad half, but I don't like to believe that. He wanted the throne while I did not. I thought to give it to him, to give my brother the one thing in the universe denied him by an accident of birth."

"Did you ever stop to think that your Goddess allowed you to be born first for a reason? Perhaps Elius was never meant to rule."

Tigh's expression actually hurt her. It held all the pain, the torment and doubt that he held at bay when in public. For the first time, she saw him as a man who had lost as much, if not more, than they all had. He had suffered the loss of his twin and the disillusionment of learning his brother had been a monster. His sister-in-law and nieces were gone, as were many others she didn't know. His life's work on the Zenai mountain was in ruins. He couldn't go back and do what he wanted. He had to pick up where his brother left off and try to salvage the situation the best way he could.

This proud warrior had surrendered.

That, in itself, should have told her the character of the man who now faced her with such grief in his eyes. He had suffered too. Both their galaxies were shattered, and it was up to them to pick up the pieces.

"Oh, Tigh." Ginny moved the final distance between them, pulling one of her hands from beneath his to cup his cheek. "I'm so sorry." Her whisper hung between them as they gazed into each other's eyes, sharing their pain for a long moment. Finally, Ginny turned her head and laid it over his heart, hugging him, offering comfort.

Tigh's arms went around her and drew her close. He bent his head, and she felt his lips nuzzle into her neck, but not in a loverly way. Their embrace was about compassion, not desire. Not at that moment. Though, she could feel that the warmth of his arms could easily ignite a fire in her blood that would be hard to quench. It had been so long since she'd just been held by a man.

She felt him kiss her hair, his big hands stroking her back with soothing motions. She didn't ever want to leave the safety of his arms, and the thought surprised her. She hadn't felt this way since she was a young girl in the first throes of love. But she didn't know Tigh well enough to love him. Did she?

"Your heart is as gentle as your spirit is strong, sweet Ginny." His words rumbled past her ear, igniting a little shiver that she was loath to let develop any further. She pulled back, putting a little space between them as she looked into his eyes.

"You really think I'm the woman for you? That isn't just a line?"

He seemed puzzled. "Not a line, as you put it. I have found my mate in you, Ginny, as the Mother Goddess willed."

"I wish I had your faith. It's not so easy for humans, you know. We don't have the kind of instant recognition you seem to believe in."

"I have faith enough for both of us. I promise you now, if you agree to be my bride, we will have a beautiful life together. There is no unfaithfulness among true mates. We will be partners and helpmates, and if you cannot love me now, I hope, in time, you will come to love me as I already love you."

She was shocked. "You love me? You barely know me."

"You are my true mate, ordained from the Mother Goddess. I couldn't do anything other than love you, but you are right. I do not know you, and the voyage of discovery is proving to be as enchanting as my first sight of you, Gineva Starbridge. I can only hope you will enjoy getting to know me, as well."

She gave him a shy smile, sensing his need for reassurance. He'd just gone out on a huge limb. She'd give him a little something for his efforts, if only in the way of comforting words.

"I can honestly say I've never met a more fascinating man than you, Tigh." She'd slipped into using his first name in her mind and nearly cringed at her familiar use of it, but he seemed encouraged.

"And I can say I will never meet a more fascinating woman, Ginny. Together, we could reshape the universe, if you will agree to be my partner."

"Partner? Or trophy wife?"

He puzzled out her meaning then scowled. "I meant every word I said. We will be partners, Ginny. While it is true I came here with the intent of marrying any human female that would have me, once I saw you, all thoughts of that plan went by the wayside."

"Well, you're honest about that, at least."

"I am honest about everything, Ginny, as you will come to learn. As a novitiate of the Zenai priesthood, I cannot lie."

Ginny thought about that for a moment. He seemed in earnest.

"If that's true, you're a freak among politicians."

"But I am not a politician. I intend to be a ruler. Playing politics is what hurt my brother the most, I believe. Though I will never know what his exact thought processes were, in reviewing the records of his decisions, I saw a pattern of knee-jerk reactions to political pressures. I will not repeat his mistakes. As a first step, I have dismissed most of his councilors and emptied the court. I intended that my wife and I will start from scratch when we return to Solaris Prime."

"I think that's a wise choice."

"You see?" He beamed at her, a teasing light in his stunning eyes. "We already agree on something. I think we will find there are many other points of harmony between us, if we but look for them."

Ginny chuckled as she moved completely out of his embrace and turned to her hatch, which was a few yards away. He followed, of course. She turned at the portal and looked up into his eyes.

"I had a good time tonight. Thank you for being the perfect escort and the perfect gentleman." She leaned up and gave him a kiss on the cheek.

Tigh surprised her by drawing her close with his hands around her waist. She didn't resist. The guards were down the hall if she needed help, and she knew a few moves to defend herself should he suddenly turn aggressive. She didn't think he'd attack her. He was just too controlled, too honorable for that kind of thing.

But he would kiss her.

Tigh moved in and sealed his lips to hers, firing that strange tingling sensation throughout her limbs. No other man had ever made her feel this way, but it had been a very long time. Maybe that was why she responded to him so powerfully.

Whatever it was, she reveled in his firm touch, his tender exploration of her mouth with his tongue, his caressing hands on her back and buttocks. He lifted her into his hardness as his ardor increased, and she was with him. There was no way she could lie to herself. Her body wanted Tigh. Almost obsessively. But her mind was in control, even if her body wanted her to strip naked in the hallway and let him have his way with her in front of God and everybody.

He pulled back before she could embarrass herself, and it was Tigh who saved them both from a lot of gossip. Oh, the guards would no doubt talk about the hot kiss they'd witnessed, but a goodnight kiss was a far cry from what she really wanted, now that Tigh had excited every last nerve in her body.

He let her go by slow degrees. She was chagrinned to find her legs unsteady once more. Only Tigh had ever been able to make her weak-kneed with just a kiss. That alone made her wonder just what he might be able to do if she let him make love to her. She might not survive.

"Goodnight, sweet Gineva."

"Goodnight, Tigh." She was still in a daze as she entered her compartment.

CHAPTER 3

Stepping outside her quarters the next day, Ginny accepted sharp salutes from the two sentries standing on either side of her portal. Sometime in the night, someone must have given the order for guards to be placed by her door. She wasn't altogether comfortable with that but had no doubt Tigh's rash actions in the Council chamber had something to do with the stepped-up security.

Ginny was completely shocked, however, when she stepped out into the public hallway and was immediately surrounded by newsbots and even a few live reporters. Never in her career, even after some of her major victories in battle, had she been so hounded by the media. Luckily for her, the sentries made themselves useful as she ran the gamut from the hallway to her office in the secure military wing on the other side of Atlantia Station.

"You have a tough decision to make." Commandant Michael Amber entered her office unannounced about midway through the morning. Ginny looked up at him in surprise, rushing to stand, but he waved her formality aside. He motioned for her to remain seated as he pulled up a chair in front of her desk.

"Sir?"

"I can't order you to accept or decline the emperor's

proposal, Captain, but I wanted to let you know that, either way, I will hold no prejudice against you. If you refuse him, your place is assured here, regardless of what the news media tries to say about you. And, you should know, they're already talking."

Ginny felt her stomach sink. She'd purposely avoided watching the news out of fear that she'd be the center of speculation.

"I was afraid of that."

"I can understand your reluctance to feed the media frenzy, Captain. Which is why I advise you to make your decision quickly. The longer this drags out, the worse the media will become. We've already had three attempted breaches of security by stealth model newsbots. One was found hiding in a corner of the Officer's Mess just half a standard ago."

Ginny was appalled. "I'm sorry, sir. I had no idea—"

He waved her apology aside. "I know you couldn't have expected such a rabid reaction to this situation, and the situation itself is not of your making. Just keep in mind that more than an impulsive emperor is awaiting your answer." Michael stood and headed for the door. "If you need time off to think or consult with your family and friends, just say the word. The sooner his proposal is answered, the sooner we can get back to normal around here."

"Yes, sir. I'll do my best."

Michael gave her one of his rare smiles. "You always do, Captain. That's just one of the reasons I'll regret losing you if you agree to the emperor's plan. But, for the sake of peace, it might just be worth it. Think carefully before you decide, but do it quickly."

He left her office, leaving Ginny in even more turmoil than before. She'd expected it would be bad, but she hadn't realized just how bad. She needed to make her decision and let the emperor know. He deserved to know her answer first, before anyone else.

That thought in mind, she pulled out a rarely used pen and

paper. Some things had to be done according to tradition. She didn't know if she'd be able to face Tigh in person, and a digital transmission was out of the question, due to the possibility of media infiltration. She'd have to write him a good old-fashioned letter.

It took most of the rest of the day, but in writing the letter, Ginny had a chance to organize her thoughts. By the time she finished, she knew her answer. Folding and sealing the envelope, she directed a sub officer to deliver it by hand.

Tigh would have it within minutes, and there was nothing left to do but make her way back to her quarters. Ginny ducked the newsbots in the open areas of the station and sealed herself in for the night.

*

The jit'suku emperor stormed Ginny's private compartment in the BOQ, bypassing her security measures as if they didn't exist. Anger shown in every line of his long, hard body.

"How dare you?" Ginny was stunned and angered by his abrupt intrusion into her domain.

He shook the paper of her letter in front of her nose. "What is this?"

Suddenly, she was on the defensive. She knew it had been cowardly to send him a letter rather then tell him in person, but she'd been afraid of his reaction—and her own reaction to his stirring presence. The truth was, she couldn't trust herself to turn him down if she had to look into his eyes.

"It should be quite obvious."

"You refuse my offer?" His voice modulated as he dropped down on the couch next to her, but with some space between them. "Don't you want peace?"

"I want peace more than anyone, but you should have asked a different woman. Not me."

"But why?" The gentle pleading in his voice started tears behind her eyes, but she refused to let them fall.

"I have my reasons."

Anger flared again, in his haunting eyes. "Fine. I'll not have you come like some virgin sacrifice, cringing all the way to my bed."

"I'm not a virgin." Defiance laced her tone.

But her words didn't have the desired chilling effect on him. Rather, his volatile temper erupted into sarcasm laced with amusement. "Good, then. We at least have that in common."

"I thought you were celibate."

"I have been. But, before I declined the throne in favor of my brother and sought sanctuary with the priests, things were different." The spark in his eye told her just what things he meant. His anger dissipated, and his face softened somewhat, making her uncomfortable with his continued scrutiny. "Who was he?"

She sighed and sank back on the couch, thinking for a long moment. She didn't want to share any of her painful past with this disturbing man, but he deserved a better answer to his proposal of marriage. Perhaps if she told him the truth, he'd leave her be.

So deciding, she rose to get the holo off her bedside table and brought it back to him. She sat at his side, closer than before, so he could see the small image as she switched on the viewer. It played for a while before she spoke.

"His name was Paul."

Emperor Tigh watched the man's image with mixed emotions. The holo showed a young, pale human, with blond hair and dark eyes, handsome in a boyish way as he twirled a much younger version of Ginny in his arms.

"We were engaged to be married, but he died of the virus when it first hit our world." Her voice was painfully wistful as she stared down at the young man's image, and Tigh knew the boy would never age in her heart. How could he compete with a memory such as this?

How could he not at least try? Ginny was the woman he

needed by his side. He needed her compassion, her strength and her courage if they were to make this peace plan work. He would have liked to also have her love, but he wasn't sure if that could ever be. Still, his senses told him, this was his woman. He'd rather have her—even without her love—than any other woman in the universe. He needed her. It was that simple.

"You loved him very much."

"I did." Finally, her watery eyes rose to meet his. "Tigh, you have to know. There are other reasons a younger woman would be better suited. For one thing, I'm nearing the end of my fertile years. Even if I could somehow conceive, I couldn't have very many children." Her voice broke as she looked away again. "But the biggest problem is that I'm barren. I was infected with the virus and nearly died. It's left me scarred on the inside, the doctors tell me. I've tried to get pregnant a number of times, but with no success."

Anger flared in his veins. His woman had tried to mate with another! Tigh knew the primitive fury was unjustified, but he could barely stop himself from hunting down and killing each and every man who had dared touch his mate. They'd probably be Sons of Amber, he knew, since few other human males were left, and most were sterile.

"Who?" He couldn't stop himself from asking. "Who did you want to father your child?" If it was a man he knew, Tigh wasn't sure he could stop himself from trying to kill him the next time they met, but he needed to know.

"Ezekiel Amber," she said sadly. Her tone didn't sound lover-like, and it caused Tigh to stop and rethink. "Always Ezekiel."

"But he's mated, I heard."

Ginny nodded, acceptingly. "Lucky man. Yes, he's married, but he still makes deposits to the sperm banks. When I decided to try to have a baby, I looked through the holos to find the Son who looked most like Paul. I thought, if I could have a little boy that might have Paul's blond hair, I could pretend it was his child. I could pretend he'd given me that at least. I was going to name him Seth, in honor of Paul's father. It's what we'd discussed before he… Before he died."

Tigh's anger defused in favor of heartbreaking sympathy for this poor girl. She'd lost so much. He could hardly blame her for wanting to ease her loneliness with a child.

"Love is the noblest reason of all to marry," he said softly, taking the holo from her hands and switching it off, "but there are others."

"To end the war, you mean?" She didn't protest when he put the holo on the table in front of them.

"And for children."

A tear leaked out of one eye to flow down her cheek. He caught it with his thumb and rested his palm against her soft skin. His fingers tunneled into her rich brown hair. She was the most beautiful creature in the universe.

"But I can't have children."

"Not with a human male, perhaps, but the scientists tell me jit'suku men and human women who've been damaged by the virus should be able to create female babies. I believe it has to do with the redundancy of your X chromosomes, though I am no genetics expert."

"So you said when you came to the Council. It's one of the reasons they're considering this proposal. Many women who were sick with the virus might want the opportunity to try living with one of your men, if it meant having babies and establishing peace, even after all that's gone on between our peoples. But as emperor, you'll need a son to carry on your direct lineage."

He moved closer, pulling her into his arms. "All I need, is you, Ginny. Any children we have will be a blessing, but whether male or female doesn't matter to me in the slightest."

"By your laws, a girl can't rule the jit'suku."

Tigh shrugged, pulling her closer. He saw the heat flare in her lovely eyes and smelled her arousal. She wasn't indifferent to him. No, not at all.

"I never wanted to rule. If we have no boys, another will rise to be emperor. It matters not to me. The Goddess will decide our fate and that of our people."

He kissed her then, silencing her words. He couldn't help himself. She was in his arms, soft, feminine and so in need of the comfort he could offer, it nearly broke his heart. Why did she not see she needed him almost as badly as he needed her?

His tongue dueled with hers as if made to do so. Her flavor fired his senses, her scent invaded his very being, taking him over and making him harder than he'd ever been before. This was his woman. Of that there was no doubt.

Praying she'd come around to his way of thinking, he lifted his head, hoping to see agreement in her eyes. Or, if not agreement, then perhaps a softening toward him. He would take any little advantage at this point, but he would not leave this planet without his mate. That much was clear.

"Please, my heart, say you will marry me."

The racing thoughts behind her beautiful eyes gave him hope. At least she wasn't turning him down outright this time.

"On one condition."

It took a moment for her words to sink in. She was agreeing, but what would be her condition? She could have anything, and she probably knew it. Now, he would learn her true measure. Would she want riches or grand concessions? Tigh almost dreaded hearing her demand. She could ask for the universe, and he would find a way to give it to her.

"What is it?"

"I won't marry you unless we're sure I can conceive. I want to be pregnant before we marry. I won't saddle you, or your people, with a barren queen."

Relief surged through him. His heart hadn't led him astray. This woman was truly the one for him and his people. She would be a wise and caring empress and would serve their people well.

"Empress you shall be, my sweet Gineva. And fulfilling your request will be my pleasure."

"Good." She moved back from him and stood briskly, heading for the com. "Then, I'll schedule an appointment for tomorrow at the insemination lab."

Tigh was right behind her, snaring her waist and pulling her back against his hard chest, her back to his front. His hardness nestled into the soft flesh of her ass as if it'd found a home.

"You'll do no such thing."

"But we need to know exactly when I'm ovulating." She sounded exasperated, but she wasn't fighting against his hold. No, she seemed to snuggle her warm, feminine self against him without even being aware of it. He liked that. A lot. "I know it's in the next day or so. We're right around the time, but with the damage done to me by the virus, we need to time this exactly right. The clinic will be able to inseminate me with the highest probability for success. And they may be able to tell us if there's anything we can do so you can have a male heir."

"No." He nipped the lobe of her ear as she wrapped her arms over his, around her waist. He felt the shiver run down her spine as he licked into the whorls of her delicate ear. She was so responsive to him, so perfect for him. How could she not know they were meant to be together? "You should know the jit'suku sense of smell is more highly developed than that of humans." He inhaled her luscious scent, rubbing his nose along the sensitive cords of her neck. "You are nearing ripeness now, Ginny."

"Oh, God. You can smell that?"

He chuckled at her outrage. "Mmm-hmm, and it smells divine." He licked her neck, making her shiver. "Tastes divine too."

"Tigh…"

He liked the sound of his name on her lips, especially in that soft, breathy whisper that went straight to his groin.

"Know this, my sweet Gineva—any children we have will be conceived in the time-honored way. Girls or boys, matters not to me. Whether one or an army, matters not. Science is what got us into this mess, and science will have no part in what happens between us from this day forward. We will have our babies—or not—according to the will of the Mother Goddess."

She turned in his arms to face him. "Just so we're clear. I won't marry you if I can't get pregnant, Tigh. You'll need children to prove to your people that this peace is real and viable."

"I trust in the Goddess. You were meant for me, Ginny." He shrugged. "That fact is undeniable. All else will happen as She wills."

Her head tilted as she gazed up at him. "You've said that before. You believe in a Goddess, not a male deity? I find that odd for such a male-dominated race. And why would a priest in a Goddess culture practice celibacy?"

Tigh pulled her in so that her soft thighs rested along his, the hard ridge of his erection nudging her slight tummy. She was so womanly, so beautiful, he never wanted to let her go. He knew she was stalling for time, but she also needed to learn about his culture, and this bit of curiosity was a good sign.

"When a Zenain priest takes his final vows, he is essentially marrying the Goddess. He pledges his life to her and all his strength. He vows to be faithful to her for the rest of his days. Luckily, I hadn't yet taken my final vows." He winked at her, and she blushed so prettily, he had to lean in and kiss her heated cheek, but she'd asked a question, and he wanted to answer so that she'd feel free to ask more in the future. He would never stifle her curiosity. He loved her quick mind and knew she'd need to learn a lot to assimilate into the life of the jit'suku empress.

"Our deity is female because there is no higher power in the universe than that of creation. It is you women who harbor that power within you. We men play our part too, but ultimately without the female, all life is lost." He thought sadly of the tragedy that had called him from his mountain retreat. "We learned that the hard way when my brother's asinine plan to destroy you destroyed us, instead. Men have flocked to the temples since, repenting and praying for guidance. I believe the Mother Goddess sent us to you—the people we'd tried for so long to destroy—to help us see the error of our ways and to restore balance among all Her children. For I've come to learn that you humans are Her children, as well. In my search of your histories, I've found many instances of Goddess worship, predating even your advancement to the stars."

"The God of my childhood is male, Tigh." Her voice was soft, tinged with a bit of apprehension.

"Don't worry, my heart. I've looked into the teachings of your native religion since meeting you. There are female deities in your culture too, enough to calm the fears of my people and allow you to retain your own beliefs, albeit in private. In public, it may be a different matter, but I will handle the religious obligations of emperor, if you wish. There are very few, actually, so it shouldn't be a hardship for you at all. We believe, as you do, in religious freedom, though the majority of our people worship the Mother Goddess in various forms."

"I see you've thought this all out very thoroughly."

He nodded. "It is my nature to plan for all contingencies." Tigh pressed his hardness against her hips, unable to stop himself. Her proximity was firing his senses almost beyond control.

Tigh felt her shiver and sensed anxiety in her ripening body. She was afraid of him, and he didn't like it at all.

"You, of all people, have no reason to fear me, sweet Gineva. I would never harm you." He kissed her hair softly, backing off just a tiny bit though he couldn't bring himself to let her go now that he had her finally in his arms, where she belonged.

"I didn't think you would," she admitted in a small voice. "It's just that...I haven't been with a man since Paul." She fairly choked on her embarrassment, and he could feel the heat in her flaming cheeks as she pressed her face against his chest, hiding her eyes. "He was the only man I ever made love to. It's been a long time, and you're...very different, and a bit intimidating."

Pulling her close, Tigh rocked her in his arms, seeking to comfort. "I'm dominant. It's the way most jit'suku men are designed, especially the warrior class. I can't help that, but I can promise that I will never, ever cause you harm in any way. Not intentionally. I may bumble and hurt your feelings because I don't understand your culture, but I expect you to tell me when that happens, and I will listen. We need to talk freely between ourselves to make this work. I know that. But, when it comes to making love, you'll follow my lead, and I can guarantee you'll enjoy every moment. Trust me in this, at least, sweetheart. I'll bring you pleasure and never let you doubt you made the right choice by joining with me."

He shuffled her back toward her large bed as he spoke, tumbling down with her onto the soft mattress as he bent his head. Taking her lips firmly under his, he sought entrance with an unrelenting stab of his tongue and was granted access with an eagerness he hadn't quite expected. She seemed to like it when he gave her no choice. He'd have to file that information away for later consideration. Could this strong woman harbor a secret submissive side?

Tigh nearly laughed at the thought. If it were true, she was the best possible mate for him—a lioness in public with a keen mind and a compassionate heart to rule their people at his side, and a bedmate willing to let his dominant side reign over their pleasure. The Goddess surely knew what She was doing when She created this beautiful woman to be his mate.

Through tragedy for both their peoples, they would triumph, and the first part of the plan was getting his mate pregnant. He had to prove to her, and to his people, that this union of jit'suku and human would save both races and finally bring peace. Everybody would win after the devastating losses of the past tragic years. Jit'suku males would be free to colonize in the human galaxy, as human females would be welcome in return. Eventually, there would no longer be two separate races. The genetics would blur, and all thoughts of war would be ended as the volatile jit'suku temperament was steadied by more stable human influences, and both races would prosper—as one. It was the only way.

Not that it would be an easy road.

But the first step would be a pleasure. Quite literally.

Tigh loomed over Ginny on the wide bed, kissing her deeply as his hands roamed over her body. He tried to be gentle but still managed to tear some of her garments in his haste to be rid of them. She, in turn, used her dainty fingers to unclasp his robes of state, baring him with much more ease and grace than he was managing.

With a grumble of annoyance, he eased up, releasing her from his kiss as he struggled with the fastening of her lounge pants. The string had knotted and would not come undone. He was ready to find a knife and cut the darn things off when he heard her giggle for the first time.

The ultra-feminine sound nearly stopped his heart. Such a light-hearted sound would enchant any hardened warrior, but coming from his destined mate, the tinkle of her laughter sent bubbles of happiness through his soul. His breath caught as he met her sparkling eyes. She was laughing at his eager fumbling, and he didn't mind one bit. He would act the clown to see that innocent, carefree expression on her face. For just a moment, he glimpsed the girl she'd been before the virus, and knew the boy she'd loved then had been the luckiest man in the universe to have this magical creature all to himself.

Tigh wanted her love, almost desperately, but he counseled himself against being greedy. She would love him—or not—in the fullness of time. He'd read enough to know that humans didn't always recognize their true mates. Often, they lived their entire lives without ever realizing the other half of their soul was out there, just waiting to be found, and most never found them at all. It was a sad state of affairs. But Tigh knew, without a shadow of a doubt, Ginny had been made for him. Hopefully, she would realize the reverse was also true at some point in their lifetime together. He would wait for that day, and pray for it. On the day she gave him her love freely, he would be complete.

"Help me?" Tigh smiled at her as their eyes met and held. She was so open to him in that moment, he felt his heart cracking, widening to admit her into it. He knew she would remain there always, deep within his soul.

With a shy but eager nod, Ginny moved her dainty fingers to work on the knot he'd made. Meanwhile, he threw off the rest of his heavy robes and tossed them to the floor. The robes of state were necessary while he roamed among the humans, but damned uncomfortable. Luckily, they'd been designed to be easily removed should the need for combat arise. Tigh was left in his supple leather leggings that had been specially designed to allow a full range of motion and the bands across his chest that held a few primitive, bladed weapons that were his specialty.

A Zenain priest novitiate never traveled without his weapons, if he could help it. True, the humans had confiscated all of the more advanced weaponry he and his men had brought, or made them leave it locked up on their impounded ship, but they seemed to think nothing of the primitive blades and fighting sticks he habitually carried.

He could have done without them, of course—a Zenain priest is taught to use his entire body as a weapon—but practicality demanded that weapons be carried when possible. Against a laser pistol, a throwing knife could be surprisingly efficient. Close range combat would bring his hand-to-hand skills into play, but Tigh knew he could never strike a woman except under the direst of circumstances. However, if one was shooting at him, a well-placed, disabling throw of one of his blades wouldn't offend his warrior sensibilities.

As the robes dropped away, he settled back at her side on the large bed. She was concentrating so hard on the knot he'd made in her drawstring, she seemed almost surprised when he moved one hand up from the strip of bare skin at her waist to work on the little buttons of her shirt. She smiled nervously up at him as the knot came free, and they ceased to move for a timeless moment, just staring at each other like lovestruck children.

"I'm going to prove to you that we belong together, Ginny. How can you doubt it?"

She tilted her head, and the moment was broken. The fire in him rose, though, as her eyes dropped to his chest and widened. The lick of her lips told him she liked what she saw.

CHAPTER 4

Tigh was more than muscular beneath his robes. He was downright beautiful. As finely honed as any man she had ever seen—though of course, she'd seen few outside of holos. Still, he had the perfectly honed chest of an athlete, which she hadn't expected. Those fancy robes had hidden his warrior nature, and a band of bladed weapons worn familiarly over his heart.

"In my head, I knew you were of the warrior caste, but I never imagined..." Her fingers trailed over the warm leather, her eyes helplessly following the contours of his amazing chest.

"I trained with the Zenai priests for over fifteen years." His deep voice purred through her, rumbling in her core. "It is a warrior priesthood. Every day, I trained my body for defense of self and others. It's something I still do."

"I can tell." Her eyes devoured his muscular form as he sat up and unstrapped the band of bladed weapons, baring his magnificent chest completely. Every movement sent his corded muscles rippling, setting off similar shockwaves in her midsection as she watched his male perfection. He was amazingly potent.

"I'm glad my form pleases you. I already know I'm going to love your body as much as I admire your soul." He held

47

her gaze as he loosened the drawstring and pushed her pants down and off. His eyes never wavered from hers as his hands followed the path, stroking down her thighs and calves, caressing and enflaming her with his touch alone. "When I saw you in the Council chambers, I knew you were perfect. My warrior mate. I could ask for no better match in all the universe."

"Then, you don't mind women of rank? I thought you jit'suku warriors all wanted perfect little feminine dolls to obey your every command." She tried to make light of her words, but inwardly, she'd worried about what he'd want from her. She was used to being in command of her own ship. It would be hard to subjugate her will to a powerful man, and she'd wondered how any sort of relationship between them could work.

"In lovemaking, I will want to be in charge. It's my nature. But in life…in life, I want a partner. An equal. Someone to share my burdens as I share hers. I don't want a weak woman." He leaned in to kiss her lips, once, softly. "I don't think you're weak, Ginny. Not for a minute." His whispered words made her catch her breath. "I like that you'll challenge me, as I will challenge you. We will have a partnership in the truest sense of the word."

Ginny gasped as one of his big hands slid between her legs. His hand was calloused, warm, and infinitely possessive. He was laying claim to her, quietly, and with few words, but he was definitely mastering her body. She could feel the wetness gathering in her core, responding to his slightest touch. Oh, this man was dangerous.

But she was loving every minute of it.

To have such a powerful, masculine being focused so totally on her was a new and exciting experience. It had been too many years since her first forays into lovemaking with Paul. They'd been inexperienced and very young. She saw now that Paul was a mere boy when compared to this exciting, intoxicating man who now dared to claim her. She'd loved Paul, and she always would, but Tigh was teaching her things about her body she had never dreamed. And they hadn't even really started yet.

"When we join, you will understand the rightness of our being together." His hand moved, one finger daringly dipping into her folds, circling lightly as she gasped. "Your body already knows me. It wants me."

"Tigh…"

She couldn't give voice to the shocking things she wanted to say. She wanted him too, but how could she feel so deeply, so quickly? She'd only just met the man, but already, she felt somehow a part of him. It felt as if a piece of her would be missing if, for some reason, he left. She would be incomplete. The very idea of it frightened her, but it also made her want to investigate where these foreign feelings were coming from. It was tantalizing. There was more there, waiting to be discovered, and she wanted to explore it all…with him.

"Yes, my love." His strokes grew bolder now, more demanding, and her body rewarded his moves with more slick wetness. His eyes held hers as his grin deepened. "Will you come for me, sweet Gineva? Will you come on my hand and let me know the depth of your passion?"

If he didn't stop touching her soon, she was afraid she damn well would. And then die of embarrassment. It had been so long since a man had touched her and never like this. Never with this knowing, this intense longing in his eyes.

"Tigh, I don't want—"

He shocked her silent by insinuating one long, thick finger into her core, all the while his thumb continued to rotate around her clit. "This isn't about what you want, Gin. In this arena, it's all about what I want. And what I want most, right now, is to discover your passion. I want you to come for me. I want you to show me what you like so that I can learn to pleasure you." He kissed her lips then placed little biting kisses down her jaw and throat until his face nuzzled in the barely hidden mounds of her cleavage. Just two small buttons held her top together, and as she watched in fascination, he ripped them off with his teeth, spitting them across the room with barely leashed impatience before returning his mouth to her chest and nudging the fabric away, once and for all.

His hot mouth traced paths over her breasts, zeroing in on her nipples as his finger began to stroke in and out, in a maddening rhythm. His eyes looked up as he bit down gently, but with a hint of his dominance, on one aroused nipple, and she bucked in the brightest orgasm she'd ever had.

His fingers possessed her throughout, his eyes followed her every movement, learning and, it seemed, relishing her response. She came and came against his stroking hand as he watched, a satisfied, almost smug smile on his face that she couldn't find fault with. Not when she was feeling so sinfully delicious, all because of him. The man had magic hands. Not to mention that sexy mouth of his. Or those washboard abs.

Ginny sighed as she mentally cataloged all his magnificent features. She was only halfway through her list when he removed his wonderful hands from her body. But he didn't go far. Tigh lifted her arms and dragged the remnants of her shirt upward. She thought he was undressing her, but he left the sleeves to tangle around her hands, using the rest of the fabric to secure her to one of the bed posts. He'd tied her up.

She hadn't thought she could feel anything remotely arousing after that massive orgasm, but she was wrong. His act of dominance—tying her up, for heaven's sake!—turned her on like a switch. She felt herself cream and knew she was leaving a wet spot on the sheet, but she didn't care. Her body was primed and wanted that hard cock she could see making a deep ridge in his leggings.

If she'd been free to move, she would have tackled him, but as it was, she had to wait for him to make the next move. She didn't have to wait long.

Tigh stood next to the bed, and her head swiveled to watch him. He was so close. He made short work of the lacings on his leggings, but it seemed to take him an inordinate amount of time to work them down over his amazingly muscular buttocks.

He was stripping for her.

The thought sent shivers down her spine and shocked her eyes up to his. He was smiling as he winked at her, and she knew her suspicions were correct. This bold man was taking his time, teasing her, tantalizing her, in a way she'd never known a man could do outside of holos and vids. Paul had been all business when it had come to making love. He'd stripped quick and met her under the blankets, almost shy about his body, but Tigh... Tigh was something else altogether.

Tigh was a man, sure of himself and his appeal to women. He licked his lips as he watched her body move. She found it impossible to hold still, and his sinuous movements as he undressed made her squirm.

"Do you like what you see?"

He'd worked his leathers low on his abdomen, but his cock was still hidden.

"I haven't seen anything yet." She chuckled, daring him, wondering only belatedly if she was pushing too far. But he just grinned and pushed down his leggings in one smooth move that bared him completely. Her mouth went dry.

He was magnificent.

Thick and long, and oh, so aroused. Taking in the whole picture of him, she realized he was male perfection. Perfectly balanced muscle and grace, his body was long, lean, muscular and in beautiful proportion. His cock was proportional too. It was the largest one she'd ever seen, even counting vids and holos. She wondered absently if all jit'suku males were built on such a grand scale. If so, the human women they entertained would undoubtedly be a happy bunch of girls.

Leaving his leggings behind on the floor, he stepped toward her until he was at her side, his hard cock directly in front of her mouth. She looked up into his eyes, reading the command there. She knew what he wanted. Dare she?

Sucking cock wasn't something she had a lot of experience with. She'd only done it a few times with Paul and hadn't thought herself particularly skillful, though he seemed to like it. But Paul hadn't been built like this man. And somehow, she hadn't ever felt the same unbridled desire to taste him as she was feeling for Tigh. It felt disloyal, so she shut the thoughts of Paul from her mind.

But Tigh was waiting, and hoping, if she was reading his expression right. He'd said he was dominant, but it was good to see he wouldn't force her. She needed that. She needed the reassurance to know that he wouldn't push her beyond what she could handle. Oh, he'd definitely stretch her comfort zone—and a few other places—but she could see the respect in his eyes for her safety and wellbeing. It meant a lot to her and gave her the courage to try to please him in return.

Boldly, she stroked out with her tongue, licking around the head of him, liking the groan of pleasure from deep in his throat. Feeling her way as her confidence increased, she took more of him into her mouth. Tigh stepped forward slightly, to make it easier for her, and her mouth was suddenly full of cock.

Blissfully full of cock. The way she wanted her pussy to be as soon as she was done here. Ginny almost giggled at the thought. He was already corrupting her, and they hadn't even had sex yet.

"I like the way you suck me, Gin." His voice caressed her senses. "I'm going to fuck your mouth now, little one. Just relax."

His muscles strained as he moved forward and back, just a bit, moving lightly in and out of her mouth. She could tell he was trying to be as gentle as possible, wary of hurting her. It would be easy to be overwhelmed in this position, and again, his care with her wellbeing impressed her.

She could taste the saltiness of his desire, and she sucked harder, hollowing her cheeks as he moved in and out. He groaned and pulled out. Ginny was surprised by her disappointment. She'd never swallowed before, but she wanted to drink Tigh down and know his taste. The idea should have been shocking, but somehow, it just seemed right. She was becoming very possessive of this man she'd only known for a day or two. The idea should have frightened her, but she couldn't summon the fear that she'd always had of jit'suku warriors.

Since coming to know Tigh, her old fears were proven false. The jit'suku were just men. All right, she amended, they were incredibly tall, amazingly fit, skilled warriors, but men all the same. They seemed to want the same things all men wanted—a willing bedpartner, a warm meal, a safe home, and in Tigh's case, at least, an equal partner to share his life, if his earlier words were to be believed.

But she did believe him.

"Come back, Tigh. Come in my mouth." She found herself fairly pleading for his come. Not something she'd ever done before. But this man was special, she was discovering, in so many ways.

He bent to kiss her sweetly. "No, honey. I want to be inside you when I come. I want us to find pleasure together. But I promise you can have all you want, another day. Today is for making babies."

Reminded of the point of this exercise, Ginny blushed. She was so embarrassed. She'd forgotten this wasn't about making love—it was about cementing a deal to make peace.

"I'm sorry." Her voice was small, her face turned away from him.

Tigh sat on the side of the bed, looking down at her with concern. He saw her shame and puzzled over it. How could she go from intense, sexy heat, one moment, to painfully shy mortification, the next?

"What's this?" he asked softly. "You have nothing to be sorry for, Ginny. You are the most beautiful woman I have ever seen and much too good for the likes of me. I want you, sweetheart. All of you."

Her sad eyes lit the tiniest bit as she looked up at him. "I feel like an idiot. Untie me?" She tugged on her hands, and he knew it was wisest to comply, this once. Something had changed here, and he needed to understand what it was. If his cock would just let him think straight enough to do so.

After he released her arms, she sat next to him on the side of the bed. She refused to meet his eyes. "I said I was sorry because I forgot our goal here for a moment. Let's just have sex and see if I can get pregnant. That's what's important. I'm sorry I distracted you."

"Distracted me?" Tigh could barely contain his astonishment, or his glee that his woman had responded so fully to him she'd forgotten all her reservations, including her very reason for agreeing to bed him. "Sweet Gineva, you are the sexiest woman I have ever known." He tackled her gently and swept them both down onto the bed. He rose over her, insinuating one leg between hers, ready as he'd ever been to make them one. "When we're married, you can distract me all you want, but first, I have to get you to agree to be my wife. That's the most important thing. Not babies or even our people. What matters most to me, in this moment and in life, is you. Having you, my destined mate, at my side through whatever comes. Having you in my bed every night, in my home every day, wherever that may be. Being in you as often as possible, in every way. Those are the things that matter to me most as a man. This is about Tigh and Ginny. Not about anyone or anything else. Just you and me."

He could see tears start behind her eyes, but they weren't signs of distress. No, her smiling face told him his words had touched her, and he was glad. He wasn't an eloquent man, but he was glad he'd found the right words to reassure his little human mate. He was sure he'd make even more mistakes as they made their way in life together, but he would make up for each and every one—if she would only agree to be his wife.

He levered himself over her, placing his knees between hers on the bed, widening her legs as he made a place for himself. Gently, he lowered his body until he rested on his forearms, just above her. His hardness nudged along the sweet line that was flowering open, dewy and waiting for him. His chest brushed her magnificent breasts, the hard nipples puckering up into his flesh as he reached down to kiss her.

"You are all I will ever want in life, Ginny. You are my most basic need." He held her eyes as he pushed gently forward with his hips, joining them little by little. "This," he pushed deeper, slowly, giving her time to adjust to his size, "is what we both need." He pushed inward, her wetness allowing him to glide, though the fit was tight. Still, her body was made for him, elastic and willing to bend around his size, expanding to take him in and hold him tight.

He pushed all the way home and just stayed there for a moment, savoring the feeling.

Tigh's possession was like nothing she'd ever experienced before. His cock was so long and thick, it filled her completely, almost painfully, but the edge of pleasure soon removed any pain there might've been. He lay thick and hard within her, filling her, for long moments as his eyes held hers in a magical communion. It felt as if his soul touched hers in that moment, though she was probably being fanciful.

Still, as they locked together, something in her heart clicked with his, joining them in more than just body. She could just feel it. Though, she didn't pretend to understand it at all.

Then, he started to move.

Gentle, at first, he moved within her, letting her get accustomed to the feel of him. He was so big, his muscles so powerful, she felt a little overwhelmed by his size, but in a good way. He melted her bones with the powerful, steady motion of his body over hers, in hers. She liked the way he moved, accelerating his rhythm and moving with him after the first few strokes.

"That's it, sweetheart," he encouraged her as he picked up the pace. "A little more now. You can take it."

"Oh, God, Tigh!" She moaned as he moved faster and harder within her, lighting little fires throughout her being. He felt so good. Nothing had ever felt quite like this before.

"It's gonna be quick, this time, Ginny. It's got to be." He was panting above her, and she could see the lines of strain on his face. "Come with me, baby. Come with me now!"

Tigh moved even more powerfully within her, driving her passion higher until she burst in a shower of sparks. Ginny cried out as she hit a peak and tumbled over, higher than she'd ever been before. Tigh was with her every step of the climb, shouting his own release as he came inside her, filling her with warmth, bathing her in his essence.

Whether they made a baby or not, she would never trade this experience for anything in the universe. Being made love to by a jit'suku warrior such as this was something she wouldn't have missed for the world. Though of course, if things worked out as he hoped, she would be in his bed for the rest of their lives.

Offering a quick prayer, she hoped for a baby. She hoped for a reason to marry this man and keep him in her life and in her bed for a good long time to come. Just that easily, he'd won her over.

But it was more than the sex. It was the respect he'd shown her before, during and now after, as he withdrew and lay at her side, breathing hard. He seemed to actually care for her, aside from the need to gain her compliance with his plan for political purposes. He seemed to truly want her in his life, and that was a miracle to her in itself.

CHAPTER 5

Tigh woke her with a soft kiss. When he pulled back enough so that she could see his face, he was grinning from ear to ear. The satisfied expression in his eyes touched something deep down inside her feminine core. She purred inwardly, knowing that she'd put that smug expression on his face, and she knew something very like it must also be gracing her features.

"Today is the happiest of days." His joy was almost infectious. She found herself smiling along with him as she sat up in the large bed.

"Why? What's today?"

"Today..." Tigh swooped down close to nuzzle her neck, breathing deeply. He sat back, as if savoring the scent of her. "Today is the day you'll agree to be my mate."

"Are you saying—?" Her mind spun with the possibilities. "You can tell that too?"

"Yes, my love. You are most definitely pregnant, I'm happy to report. You smell divine." His husky voice touched a chord deep inside her as he moved back down, breathing her in and kissing her neck, her jaw, her cheek and then finally, her lips.

He kissed his way up her cheeks to her eyes, and only then did she realize she was crying. Tears of joy flowed down her face as she contemplated the realization of a long-held dream.

"Thank you, Tigh!" She threw her arms around him, nearly launching herself into his arms. She rained kisses down his cheeks, her hopes flaring as the reality of his words settled in. She was pregnant—if his nose could be trusted. "I have to get tested. Just to be sure." She pulled back to meet his shining eyes. It was clear he had all the proof he needed, but she believed in being thorough.

"And then, you'll marry me?"

Slowly, she nodded. "Yes, Tigh. I'll be glad to marry the father of my baby. Our baby. Oh, God! I'm so happy!" The tears continued to flow down her cheeks as he held her, rocking her and kissing her, sharing her joy.

Later that morning, with an armed guard protecting them from the ever-present gaggle of newsbots and reporters, Tigh and Ginny went to the compound's clinic for the quick test that would prove him right...or not. Ginny held her breath when the med tech pricked her finger for a blood sample, then scanned her tummy with a hand-held device. Five minutes later, they had their answer. Gineva Magdelana Starbridge was most definitely pregnant.

Possibly with twins.

It was still too early to tell for certain, but there was a high probability that she was carrying twins. The very idea of it blew her mind. After all this time, and all the effort she'd put into trying to get pregnant, it seemed almost anticlimactic to have achieved her dream of nurturing not just one but, most likely, two tiny innocent lives within her body.

Ginny walked on air as they left the clinic, and the reporters seemed to sense that something was up. Sure enough, not an hour later, news of her pregnancy—filled with rumor and supposition—was being broadcast on every newsfeed.

Tigh hadn't left her side. In fact, he'd practically moved into her quarters. He'd taken over one corner of her suite and set up a portable comp station where he sat, monitoring the news while attending to affairs of state.

"We've got to do something about this." Tigh's voice cut into the lovely daydream she'd been having about the twin girls she was going to have in just nine short months.

"About what?"

"Have you seen the news?" Tigh sat on the couch next to her and switched on the vid. Flipping through the feeds, Ginny saw the media had her alternately pregnant, unable to get pregnant, diagnosed with some dreaded disease or being fitted for implants at the emperor's request. There were ever more outrageous explanations being created out of thin air for their visit to the compound clinic. Some made her laugh out loud, and some sparked her anger.

"What can we do?"

Tigh sighed as he switched off the vid. "We need to hold a press conference."

"A press conference? Tigh, maybe now is a good time to tell you that I'm really not very comfortable speaking to the media."

He put his arm around her shoulders. "Don't worry. I'll do most of the talking, if that's your wish. I don't like it either, but it's clear it needs to be done before they go any farther into the realms of fantasy trying to explain a simple clinic visit."

This time, it was Ginny who sighed. "I guess you're right."

Tigh pulled her in close for a quick hug, kissing the top of her head. Releasing her, he got to his feet and touched his wristcomp to signal for one of his aides. Within a few moments, the wheels were set in motion for a press conference later that very day.

It wasn't something she was looking forward to.

The press conference itself was both better and worse than Ginny had expected. Better, in that the questions were mostly inquisitive rather than hostile, and worse, in that they were incredibly invasive.

One of the younger female reporters got hung up on the

particulars of how conception had taken place. She was probably too young to comprehend the fact that babies didn't used to be conceived in a lab as a matter of course.

"But how?" she asked, rather insistently. "We've been following all your movements. No one reported seeing you visit the insemination lab."

Tigh pulled Ginny back against his chest, folding his hands over her tummy in a very familiar fashion, stating his implicit right to touch her silently, but firmly. The older women understood the subtle signs of genuine male affection and protectiveness, but the younger girls—most of whom seemed to be reporters—didn't seem to get it.

"These babies were planted the old-fashioned way, and we enjoyed every minute of it." Tigh patted her stomach with a roguish grin and a wink she could see reflected off the monitors while Ginny blushed to the roots of her hair.

She could hardly believe Tigh had just told the galactic media they'd been having sex. It wasn't something she was comfortable discussing by any stretch of the imagination. Sex was something private, not something to talk about with complete strangers, much less publicize. And that naughty little wink? She'd have a thing or two to say to him once they were alone.

"Did you say babies? Plural?" Thankfully, another reporter moved the questioning forward.

"It's too early to know for certain," Ginny said quickly, glad for the change of topic, "but the clinician stated there was an eighty-five percent probability of twins based on the test results and family history."

"You're a twin, aren't you, Emperor Tigh?"

"Yes," he said, loosening his arms but not letting her go. "I had a twin brother." Ginny knew talking of his lost brother was a touchy subject. It was Elius who had loosed the virus and tried to destroy every last human in the galaxy. Humanity had no love for Elius, but he was still Tigh's brother—his twin—and Ginny felt an odd pang of sympathy for the man who had lost not only his brother, but his faith in that brother.

"And do you have twins in your family, Captain?"

"Yes, as a matter of fact, my mother is a twin. And there are twins on the Starbridge side of the family going all the way back to Diva and John Starbridge's sons Jack and Zach Starbridge."

"So, you're pretty confident you carry twins, then?" one of the reporters asked from out of the crowd.

Ginny nodded. "Fairly confident, and very hopeful. I've wanted to get pregnant for a long time. This is a dream come true for me."

They'd talked about whether or not Ginny should reveal her failed attempts to get pregnant. Tigh wanted her to speak on the subject in order to give hope to other women in the same predicament and, of course, to further his cause in the court of public opinion. But Tigh left it up to her whether she would delve into her painful past experiences with failed insemination attempts or not.

At that moment, Ginny decided to be brutally honest with the galactic media. She knew there were hundreds of thousands, if not millions, of women out there who'd been through similar experiences. Those women deserved to know the truth. They deserved her honesty and the faint flickering hope she could provide that somehow, they too, might also have a chance at their own impossible dream. It was the very least she could do for the women—and for the cause of peace.

The more she thought about it, the more Ginny realized Tigh's plan for merging the two races was the only sensible solution. Humanity might be able to rebuild, and even the jit'suku might eventually find some way to rebuild their society, but together, each would stand stronger and recover more quickly than they would on their own. Together, they would evolve into something better—a people who had hopefully learned from their predecessors' mistakes, never to be repeated.

*

Tigh moved in to Ginny's suite the next day. It was, of course, much smaller than the rooms he'd been given, but it suited them both. For one thing, Ginny refused to move into his rooms, citing her need to remain in the Bachelor Officer Quarters—albeit the comparatively luxurious compartments set aside for those with high rank like herself—so as to be available should the commandant need her. She and her bridge crew were assigned to his staff while they waited for their next ship assignment.

"What happened to your last ship?" Tigh had asked with genuine curiosity. He didn't have access to his intelligence gathering specialists, so his information on Ginny was limited to what his men knew or could find out.

"The good ship Sarasota." Ginny raised her glass in a brief salute. "She survived that last battle, but just barely. We took some good hits off your captains, but in the end, we were able to defeat them."

"How many?" Tigh felt anxiety rise in his blood at the thought of this special woman being in such danger from his people.

A pained look crossed her face. "Two of your cruisers faced us. The Bel'al and the Gin'kil. They left me no choice but to destroy them both."

Tigh remembered the details from the briefings he'd received since coming down off the Zenai peak. The loss of the Bel'al and Gin'kil had been grievous indeed, and details of that battle were still sketchy on the jit'suku side. He was appalled to think Ginny had faced two such fierce ships and come out the victor, though it had to have been a close thing since her ship had to be scrapped soon afterward.

"How many of your ships were there?"

She took a quick drink. "Just us. The Sarasota was on picket, protecting one of the lesser jumpsites when your ships came through."

"You got them as they jumped then?" It would be dicey,

but he could understand how two fierce jit'suku ships might fall to one human vessel, given the element of surprise, but she shook her head.

"I wish we'd been that fast, but our orientation was bad for their angles of entry. We had to maneuver around, and by the time we were in good position for engagement, your ships were online and targeting us." She refilled her glass with cold water and downed a portion quickly. "That was one hellacious battle. It went on for several hours as the three of us blocked and parried all over that sector. I thought for sure, they were just keeping us busy while a larger invasion force came through, but apparently, those two ships were acting on their own."

Tigh nodded. "From what I've been told, the captains of the Bel'al and Gin'kil were conducting deep recon and thought one small human ship would be an easy victory. At least, that's the last message they sent to their command before jumping. After that, we have little information on what happened until your side notified us of their destruction through diplomatic channels."

"I'm sorry, Tigh." She turned away from him. "This is going to be so hard. Your people will never forgive me or my people for the lives we've taken and vice versa. I don't know why I thought this could work." She stood and paced agitatedly toward the window.

Tigh came up behind her and placed his hands on her shoulders. "Can you forgive me for abdicating in favor of my brother?"

Ginny turned to face him, startled by the unexpected question.

"You couldn't have known what he would do with the power, Tigh. What Elius did wasn't your fault."

His eyes shut, and he pulled her closer. She went into his arms without protest, feeling the tension in his hard body.

"I'm glad to hear you think so, for I cannot help but ponder how different things would have been had I chosen to fulfill my duty as firstborn." He held her, seeming to draw comfort from the gentle embrace. Ginny had to admit, it felt really good to be held in his arms, even when they weren't having sex. Just being close to his powerful male body was a forgotten pleasure.

"It's no use wondering what might have been and blaming yourself for the actions of another."

He drew back slightly to kiss her forehead. "Thank you, Ginny." He drew back farther still and looked down into her eyes. "There's been much blood shed on both sides of this war. If you can forgive me for what I did—or at least, failed to do—then we have a beginning."

"But your men will know I'm the captain that took out over a dozen of your ships. I don't think they'll forgive that easily at all."

"A dozen?" Tigh seemed shocked.

"At least, over the years I've been in command." She nodded, proud of her record, but not of the lives she'd had to end in order to defend her home galaxy. "The Sarasota was a great old ship, and my crew are among the best in the fleet. We were a small ship, but we were mighty."

"The jit'suku respect a warrior's prowess—even an enemy's. It will be hard to think of a woman as a warrior, but they will know of your accomplishments once they know which ship you captained, and you will have immediate respect, if not acceptance. There is some formal reparation we can make to the families of those whose lives were lost to you that should further that respect." His eyes sparkled as the wheels of his mind spun. "We can build on the respect, Ginny. In time, I think my people will accept you. You come to Solaris not as a vanquished enemy, nor as your people's sacrifice for peace. You'll come as a respected adversary turned truce-talker. And our true bond will give my people hope for the future, as will your pregnancy. Since the loss of our women, my people are almost totally without hope. I think they will accept you, and other human women, with open arms and minds, hoping you will forgive our aggression and save us from ourselves."

"Oh, Tigh. I hope you're right." Over the comp, a discreet bell chimed, signaling that she was wanted in the commandant's office. "I've got to go." She tugged away from him gently.

"Will you be back for dinner?"

She paused, surprised by the intimacy they'd fallen into so easily. "Do you want to eat here in my quarters?"

"I thought it might be nice. Unless you're tossing me out?" His blue eyes beseeched her, and she felt her heart melt—along with several other regions of her body.

"No, you can stay here, Tigh, though why you'd want to share this tiny suite when you had a posh diplomatic apartment at your disposal, I can't imagine."

"I want to be anywhere you are, Ginny. Whether posh or not, matters not to me. All that matters is that you are there. Then, it is my home."

She smiled at him, pulling his head down for a tender kiss. "You say the sweetest things, sometimes."

*

Ginny and Tigh ate dinner together in her suite later that night as she thought through her plans for the trip.

"Tigh, can I bring some women with me to Solaris?"

"Of course." He leaned in to kiss her cheek affectionately. "You can bring whoever you like. The more the merrier, as you humans say."

"Good. Then, I'd like to ask my bridge crew if they'll come. Those women are like family to me, and I'd like to have them around, if they're willing to give up their careers—at least for the time being. It's a lot to ask of them, but I think a few will want to come with us. But, Tigh," she placed one cautionary hand on his forearm, seeking his full attention, "they are very active women. They're not used to sitting around doing nothing. They've been trained to run a battleship, and they're among the best in the fleet. Do you think we can find something to occupy their time on the journey, and some kind of productive jobs, if they want them, when we reach Solaris?"

"You're a good captain to think of you crew's comfort." Tigh sat back in his chair and sighed. "I will be frank with you. Jit'suku women, except in extraordinary circumstances, do not serve in our military. The gender roles in our society are—were—very clearly defined. Women tended to the home, raised the children, managed the finances. Men of the warrior classes protect and defend, manning the military and training. Men of the various worker classes help provision the warriors in whatever way their skills are suited. It worked for us for millennia, but now that our women are mostly gone, we are in chaos." Tigh scratched his chin, thinking through the possibilities. "Perhaps your women will help forge change in our traditions, but it will not be an easy road."

Ginny chuckled. "It wasn't for our ancestors either." Tigh looked surprised so she explained a bit of human history, starting with the suffragettes up to her time, hitting the highlights. Tigh seemed duly impressed, and a little alarmed, so she decided to calm some of his fears. "To be honest, many of us would never have pursued careers in the military if all our men hadn't been killed. I know I'd planned to be a teacher before the war turned ugly, but when women started filling the empty posts in the fleet, I signed up. I know a few of my bridge crew were the same. They might welcome a chance to do less martial tasks, but none of my ladies are loafers. They'll want meaningful work, not just busy-work."

Tigh nodded gravely. "We will endeavor to find something suitable for them. I think I and my crew should make every effort to learn about these women on the journey so we can help them assimilate into jit'suku society. I hand-picked the crew for this voyage, and most of these men have strong diplomatic skills. They can help."

Ginny snorted with amusement. "I can't say the same of my ladies. Most of them say what they think and damn the consequences. Only respect for rank kept them in line. Now that we'll be acting as civilians, we could very easily have a few intergalactic incidents on our hands before we even leave port."

"I'll warn my men." Tigh laughed. "But I think they'll be so glad to see women coming back with us, they'll forgive just about anything." His brows drew down as his face sobered. "We've all been worried about the fate of our race. Human women are the only hope we can see for the continuation of the jit'suku as a people."

She sensed the concern in him and felt it echo through her thoughts as well. "But you won't be fully jit'suku anymore if your plan succeeds. Your people will have human DNA too."

"That's probably for the best." He placed his napkin aside and rose to face the window. "From what I've been told by our techs, the human DNA will temper us, make us more rational in the long run. That is something the jit'suku have needed for generations. I can only imagine it was the stresses of fighting an unwinnable war that caused my brother to make such an irrational, untenable decision to release the virus. That so many of his people had to feel the same to carry out those immoral orders says much for the irrationality of my race on the whole."

Ginny came up behind him, placing a comforting hand on his shoulder. "Then, why do you seem so perfectly reasonable, Tigh?"

She meant it as a little joke, perhaps as a compliment, but when he turned, she saw the fierce expression on his face. She drew back a little, alarmed at the sudden change, and he let her go.

"I can be just as irrational as the next jit'suku warrior, Ginny. You give me too much credit." He sighed, and his expression changed, became weary somehow. "I've spent the past years meditating and honing my skills on the Zenai mountain. That training allows me to see a bit more clearly, perhaps, than others of the warrior class."

"You were going to be a priest, but your brother's death changed your plans. I'm sorry for you but glad the empire is in your hands now, Tigh. Your brother would have kept fighting until all of us were dead."

"As many still wanted to do, sadly." He turned away again, but she caught the look of utter defeat on his face as he turned. "Until the women started dying." His tone was so bleak, she felt tears gather behind her eyes. "But the high priest wouldn't allow me to take my final vows. He knew all along that the priesthood was not my path. But my training is something I will never forget. It guides me and grounds me."

"I respect that, Tigh." She moved to stand next to him at the window. "You're a good man and a wise emperor."

They remained silent for a long time, staring out at the human city below, thinking deep thoughts. Their silence was companionable, their moods meshing as they grew increasingly comfortable in each other's presence. At length, Ginny sighed and turned toward Tigh, breaking the solemn spell.

"Tomorrow, I'm going to meet with my bridge crew and ask if they want to come with us. I think, tomorrow night, we should have dinner with them, with your men too, so they can all meet each other and get an idea what we'll be in for. I think, if my ladies have a chance to meet your men, they'll be better able to decide whether they really want to come with us or not."

Tigh looped an arm around her shoulders and drew her to his chest. "A sound plan, sweetheart. My men will be on their best behavior. I'll tell them to wear their dress uniforms."

"Oh, no, Tigh." She drew back and smiled up at him. "I want this to be a casual affair. Not formal. I want them to interact as naturally as possible. They need to see you and your men in your everyday mode so they can get an idea of what you're really like."

Tigh laughed, and she was warmed by the sound. "I can't promise they won't act like asses, trying to impress your ladies, but I'll pass the word."

"Good. I'll make all the other arrangements through fleet command. Michael owes me a few favors."

"Favors?" Tigh sounded jealous, and she liked the possessive squeeze of his arm around her waist. "And just what kind of favors would a Son of Amber owe to my bride?"

She shrugged. "Oh, nothing much. I just saved his life. Twice."

Tigh laughed aloud. "The leader of the Atlantia fleet owes you not one, but two life debts? These are tales I'd love to hear."

"Maybe when we know each other better. After all, a woman likes to keep some secrets." Ginny smiled at him, and he just shook his head.

"I see I'm going to have to keep my wits about me in this partnership of ours," Tigh said, his expression open and amused. "But that's a good thing. Neither of us would do well with a passive partner, I think."

"You could be right about that," Ginny replied, nodding as she acknowledged the absolute truth of his words.

CHAPTER 6

Sometime later, Ginny stopped in the hall just outside the briefing room. She spared a smile for her master-at-arms, Chief Henriette Sonata, who stood ready to announce her into the room. Tigh had escorted her this far, but Ginny wanted a chance to talk to her bridge crew first, before he met them.

"Just give me half a standard, okay?"

Tigh leaned down to plant a firm kiss on her lips. Ginny was very conscious of their audience, but she'd grown a bit more used to Tigh's dominant ways over the past days. He wouldn't let her out of his sight without some token of his care—a kiss or hug or something even more demonstrative. He smiled down at her as he let her go. She could feel the reluctance in his lingering fingers as he slowly let go of her hand. They'd been together almost constantly since that fateful night when they'd first made love. It was a bit overwhelming, but when she was with him, everything just felt so right, she didn't question it too closely.

"Half a standard, Ginny. That's all I can take."

His low voice rumbled through her veins. Only Chief Sonata's amused grin kept Ginny from running back into his arms as Tigh walked away on quiet feet. She nodded to her crew member, and Chief Sonata opened the door, calling for attention from the assembled crew.

Ginny straightened her uniform jacket as she walked into the room, receiving the salutes that were her due as a ship's captain. Though they were informal when working, her crew was highly disciplined and respectful of the traditions that went with wearing the fleet uniform. Ginny stepped to the front of the room and put them at ease, immediately feeling the curiosity and excitement coming from the assembled women.

"Sit down, everyone," Ginny said on a sigh. "I've got a lot to tell you."

"Then it's true? You and the jit emperor?" Tiggy O'Roarke, the finest coms specialist Ginny had ever worked with, asked.

Chief Sonata ambled in from securing the door and smiled widely. "I can confirm it." All eyes turned to the grinning woman. "He walked her down here. And may I say, ma'am," the other woman winked at Ginny, "hubba, hubba. That is one fine lookin' man."

Laughs met the chief's outrageous statement, and Ginny was glad Henriette, called Henny by her friends, had broken the ice. Ginny laughed with them as they all sat around the conference table.

"Thanks for that assessment, Chief. He is rather handsome, I think, but you'll all get to see for yourselves in a half standard hour. I've asked him to come meet you."

"Holy crap!" Tiggy started fussing with her curly hair. "We're meeting royalty? And me, having a bad hair day."

"Tig, you're always having a bad hair day," one of the others teased. "Get over it."

"Don't worry. Tigh's a really great guy. Not stuck up at all, even if he is the emperor now, since his brother's death."

"Is it true he knew nothing about what Elius did?" Cat, her medical officer, asked with concerned eyes.

Ginny nodded gravely. "Tigh was training to become a priest. He was cut off from jit society for years and had no knowledge of what his brother did until he was called back from the Zenai mountain."

"Zenai?" Henny asked, her pale blue eyes narrowing. "I've heard about them. They're supposed to be like the ancient monks from Earth who created the fighting forms. Zenain priests are supposed to be some of the toughest warriors the jits have to offer—and that's saying something. But it's said they won't fight for anything other than in defense of others. Their path is the path of the protector. Honorable folk, they are."

Ginny knew Henny had a deep interest in all forms of martial arts and was herself a ninth degree black belt in the ancient art of jujitsu. She led the exercise classes all of the crew enjoyed, training with them in the ancient ways. She was also a galaxy class competitive fighter and had been from a very young age. Henny had a small mountain of medals, ribbons and trophies in her locker from all the competitions she won against men and women alike before the virus.

When the virus started killing off the males, Henriette, like Ginny herself, had answered the call and joined the fleet. Ginny had known Henny most of her life. They'd grown up together and joined the military together but hadn't served on the same ship until Ginny's second assignment. They'd worked together to save their small ship after a particularly nasty engagement with the enemy, during which the captain and most of the bridge crew were killed.

That had been Ginny's first taste of command, when she brought that ship limping back to port. Subsequently, when Ginny had been given her first real command, she'd been able to hand-pick her bridge crew. There was no question in her mind when it came time to pick a master-at-arms. Henny was the only woman she wanted in that key position of defense and strategy.

"I believe Tigh has been very honest and forthright with me. I'm beginning to trust him."

"You're carrying his baby," the doctor said quietly, "aren't you?"

Ginny nodded, unable to hide the smile or the tears

gathering in her eyes. Getting pregnant was something most women wanted, but few were lucky enough to experience in this post-virus world.

"I am pregnant," Ginny confirmed, "and I'm going to Solaris with Tigh and his crew when they leave here. I wanted to offer you all the same chance." She stood and started to pace—a nervous habit she'd picked up while captaining the Sarasota. "The jits have few women and are completely devastated by the loss. I really think that my going there, my being pregnant, will give them hope for the future and give us all a chance for peace."

"We heard the emperor's speech before the Council. They've been broadcasting it over and over on all the news streams. Do you really think it'll work?" Tiggy asked.

Ginny nodded. "I do. Think of it. A chance to bring a lasting peace after centuries of warfare. A chance to change both our races for the better and leave two thriving galaxies to our children."

"Not to mention all those hot, horny men tripping all over themselves to get into our panties." Henny's earthy humor caught Ginny off guard and made her laugh out loud, as did all the women. Leave it to Henny to break the tension and bring them back to the nitty-gritty.

"There is that. And ladies, if Tigh is anything to judge by," Ginny blushed hotly, "I think you'll enjoy every minute of it. So what do you say? Think about it? I'd like to have some female company on Solaris, and Tigh's promised we could find useful, satisfying work for anyone who doesn't want to sit around all day eating bon bons. There are a multitude of tasks for which the male jit'suku are not prepared. They're muddling through, but I think they'll be glad to see women of a compatible species, even if they were at war with humanity for centuries."

"I'll go, Captain. There's nothing holding me here, and you'll need someone to watch your back." Henny was the first to answer, and it warmed Ginny's heart.

"Thank you for that, Chief. Look, I don't need your

answers right now. I want you to think about this carefully before you decide. I want you to meet some of the jit'suku men and study up on what we might encounter once we reach Solaris."

A discreet knock sounded on the door before it opened. Tigh walked in, his handsome face smiling for her alone, it seemed, though he looked around at the assembled women. A few tried to stand, but he motioned them to sit with a gentle smile.

"I didn't mean to interrupt." Tigh stood next to Ginny, unable to keep from touching her. He put one arm at her waist, but it wasn't enough. He wanted to draw her back into his embrace, but he knew that would be too much, too soon, for her crew and perhaps for her, as well.

"Your timing is impeccable, actually. I was just going to tell them what we had cooked up for tonight." Ginny leaned back against the small credenza against the wall and smiled up at him. "Why don't you do the honors?"

Her smile warmed him from the inside out. By the Goddess, this woman was special. Each time he saw her, he wanted her more.

"Gladly." He turned toward the gathered women, taking just a moment to clear his mind. Ginny so easily stole his wits, he'd have to be careful. "I'm Tigh," he introduced himself simply. It would be better, he decided, to be informal with these women. If the relationship between them and Ginny was anything like the relationship he'd had with his own crew, informality would be the order of the day to winning them over.

"Oh!" Ginny stood and came forward. "Let me do the introductions first." She fussed a bit as she blushed, and Tigh was enchanted. "Sorry. Um, this is my executive officer, Lieutenant Sally Darlington." She indicated a brown-haired woman who sat in the first seat on the right. Ginny then continued around the table. "Doctor Cat Heller." A dark-haired woman with startling green eyes nodded at him.

"Ensign Krysta Verity, navigator, Ensign Tiggy O'Roarke on comms, Chief Engineer Justina Soto, Chief Henny Sonata, master-at-arms, and Chief Penny Amato, payload master."

"Ladies." Tigh nodded at them, receiving smiles of varying friendliness in return. "I've looked forward to meeting you all. By now, you know what dire straits my people are in. Ginny has consented to be my wife." He reached for her hand and held it close to his heart. "We plan to return to Solaris within the week, and I think Ginny would like some female company on the trip, as well as on Solaris. There are few women left among my people and little hope. Ginny represents hope. Hope for my people and for the future. Hope that we can salvage something out of the ruin that we drove ourselves into." He had to fight against the sadness that always threatened to envelop him when he thought of what Elius had done to their people.

Ginny squeezed his hand, and his gaze met hers. She was so very special, so very perfect. She didn't yet realize how much she'd come to mean to him in such a short time, but she would. He'd spend the rest of his life proving his love to her.

"To that end," he continued, knowing the women watched him carefully, "I'd like to invite you all to dinner tonight. My crew will be there, also. It will be a chance for you to meet and mingle, to discuss anything and everything in a casual atmosphere. I want you to learn about us, so you can make an informed decision on whether to stay here or come with us to Solaris."

Ginny stepped up to the table. "This is strictly casual. No uniforms. No fancy dresses. No state dinner theatrics. I've ordered a buffet in the BOQ conference room and reserved it for us for the night."

"Roger that, Valkyrie," the one called Tiggy said with a cheery grin.

Tigh's ears perked up, and for a moment, he thought he must be hearing things. "What did you just call her?"

Tiggy looked up at him in surprise. "That's her call sign.

75

Valkyrie." Then the small woman blushed. "It's from an ancient Earth myth. The Valkyries were some kind of handmaidens to ancient gods. They were warrior women who would swoop down out of the sky to reward the valiant and carry them off to heaven or some such. Our captain earned the name for the way she always seems to swoop in, out of nowhere, to save the day."

Tigh's heart nearly stopped in awe. "Your human legend is very similar to a closely held prophecy of the Zenai. We call such women Velkir, and all Zenain priests await the day when the Mother Goddess sends them to our aid."

Tiggy laughed innocently. "Well, your wait is over. The Valkyrie and her crew are bound for Solaris."

Tigh looked stunned as Ginny stepped forward. "Now wait a minute, you haven't given this enough thought. I don't want any snap answers, and I won't hold you to any decisions you make now, without meeting the men first."

"Come on, Captain, you know we would follow you anywhere," the master-at-arms said cavalierly. "Did you really expect we would let you go off on your own?"

"Oh, Henny." Tears gathered in Ginny's eyes. "You guys are the greatest. But my decision stands. Meet the men first, then think over your decisions very carefully. You can change your mind right up until the moment we depart."

"No need to think any further, Captain. I'm going with you." Henny laid her palms flat on the table in a decisive move.

"All right, Chief. I'll take that under advisement." The mischievous light in Ginny's eyes spoke volumes of her affection for these women, and her master-at-arms, in particular. Ginny turned her smiling face toward him, then back to her crew. "We have a long duty shift ahead of us then dinner. I suggest we get to work."

Tigh had a lot to think about. He had to consult the nearest database of ancient Earth legends and talk to a few of his men who also had Zenai training. This revelation of his future wife's call sign could mean much more to him and his people than he previously thought. But he couldn't say anything yet. He had to puzzle out the congruencies and possibilities before raising hopes among his crew and his people.

"I'll leave you ladies to your duties then," he spoke perfunctorily as he made to leave. He had a lot on his mind, but he couldn't leave his woman without a parting kiss. She walked him to the doorway, and he pulled her into his arms. "I will see you tonight, if not sooner."

"Tigh, I have work to do."

"I know," he said in a voice only she could hear, "but I can't stay away from you for long. It's a need I have to be in your presence."

She ducked her head slightly. "I know how you feel. It's the same for me. I don't understand it, and I'm not sure I entirely like it."

He kissed her cheek tenderly. "It is what it is. Such is the way between true mates. In time, perhaps, we'll grow accustomed to it, but for now, I need to be near you." He kissed her lips then, with just a hint of the passion he always felt now, just beneath the surface, when she was near. The other women in the room made their presence known with a few low whistles and hoots. Ginny pulled away, blushing beautifully. Tigh smiled as he leaned around her to wink at the assembled ladies. That they were comfortable enough to tease their captain said a lot for her style of leadership.

"I'll see you ladies this evening." With a parting wave for the crew and a last caress to Ginny's soft cheek, he left. He had much to do before this evening.

Tigh found his most trusted adviser, Councilor Torm, in the library that had been made available to them.

"Tigh, my boy, it's good to see you. Though all of us are envious that you have found your mate so easily among the humans." Torm eyed him suspiciously. "She is your true mate, right?"

Tigh nodded. "Without doubt. She is the only one for me.

I would not lie about such an important thing as that. In fact, you know as a Zenai novitiate, I cannot lie."

"A rare thing in an emperor." Torm sat heavily at the table he'd been using as Tigh joined him. "So, why have you left her side? Newly mated, it is very difficult to be parted."

"I'm experiencing that firsthand." Tigh rolled his eyes as he called up a new display on the library table. "But she has work to do, future empress or not. Plus, I've just learned something that I need to research a bit more before we go home. Torm," he sought the older man's counsel, "do you know what the humans call my intended mate?"

Torm's eyes narrowed. "Velkir-y."

"You knew?" Tigh was shocked at the knowledge in the older man's gaze.

"You didn't?" Torm countered. "Ah, but then, you were stuck away on that mountain and never heard about the humans' victories against some of our most talented captains. You never heard about the ace the humans called Velkir-y. At first, when intelligence reported her call sign, many thought it blasphemy. We thought the humans were taunting us deliberately. It caused many ship captains to go after her, targeting her and her ship, the Sarasota, specifically." Torm sighed heavily. "Which, in turn, caused many of our ships to be lost."

"She was that good?" Tigh felt his spine tingle in awe and a bit of fear at the idea of what his little mate had done in the war and how much danger she had been in.

Torm nodded. "She is that good. Her crew is the best the humans have to offer."

Both men were silent as Tigh thought over the ramifications of the human ace captain being his true mate, and the best female crew being the first women to come to Solaris. If he didn't know better, he'd think the ancient Zenain prophecy was coming to pass. But it had been many thousands of years since the Zenain priesthood had been formed to protect and preserve the teachings of the Zenai in preparation for a time when the ancient prophecy would be fulfilled. Tigh doubted that a prophecy of millennia could come to fruition during his time, but somehow... Somehow, all indicators seemed to point to that awful truth.

"They were not taunting us." Tigh's voice was low as he called up the human legends from the database. He turned the viewer to Torm, switching on the three-dimensional display. "They call her Valkyrie, after one of their own cultural myths."

Torm read furiously through the material, as Tigh did. The parallels between the legendary warrior maidens of ancient Earth and the prophesied women of the Zenai were uncanny.

"The high priest must see this."

"I agree." Tigh called up all the data he could on Valkyries and saved it to a disposable chip until he could get it fed into the memory banks of his ship. If the prophecy really was coming to pass now, during his reign, this was only the beginning. Changes would be coming—some good, some ill—but change was certain. If this was the time prophesied all those thousands of years ago.

"Tigh, we must prepare ourselves, if what we suspect is true." Torm gripped Tigh's arm urgently.

"Yes, old friend. But tonight, we dine with the Velkir-y and her crew. It is the first step in getting to know them. The first step of many on what promises to be a long and winding path."

"Goddess only knows where it will lead us."

Ginny was kept busy all day, preparing reports and readying those who would replace her on Commandant Michael's staff, now that she was definitely leaving with Tigh. She also spent time in meetings with Michael and several of the high councilors. They gave her advice on a multitude of subjects, each with their own individual perspectives. Most wanted her to gather intelligence on the true state of the jit'suku people, their defense capabilities, and the status of their fleet.

While there hadn't been any attacks over the past several

standard months, few were willing to accept that the war was truly over. There hadn't been one final decisive battle to end it. For many, the lack of such a confrontation was troubling.

But Ginny was more than willing to give Tigh the benefit of the doubt, at least for the time being. She was coming to trust him in ways she never would have believed just a standard week before. Whether her judgment was impaired by the intensely physical relationship they shared, she couldn't judge. She knew her objectivity was off when it came to Tigh. She accepted that as a consequence of their new relationship, though she tried desperately to keep her eyes open for any suspicious behavior.

After all, it wasn't all that long ago since they had been bitter enemies. Enough jit'suku captains had tried to kill her that she was wary of any and all overtures from Tigh's people. Yet, somehow, she couldn't apply the same standards to him. It was as if her heart just wouldn't let her see him as an enemy, even though her mind knew he now ruled over all the jit'suku forces.

Dinnertime came all too soon. Ginny rushed back to her quarters to freshen up and change into civilian clothes, but Tigh was there before her. He caught her off guard, pulling her into his arms as she entered the suite.

"I missed you," he growled against her cheek before swooping in for a long, hard kiss.

Ginny couldn't disagree with that sentiment. She welcomed his kiss enthusiastically, returning his ardor kiss for sweet kiss, lick for exciting lick, touch for arousing touch. Before she knew it, they were prone on the floor, just inside the door, and Tigh had half her clothes off. His own clothing followed close behind, flung across the room in wild abandon, the only concern on both of their minds how to get skin on skin as quickly and completely as possible.

They came together fast and hard. Ginny was breathless with desire as Tigh joined their bodies together. There was no waiting. No finesse. Just a stark fury of need. She felt it just as strongly as he apparently did because it took only a few powerful thrusts before she was keening on the edge of total insanity.

She cried out as she came, and a moment later, he joined her, groaning as her name fell from his lips. She might've blacked out for a moment, because the next thing she knew, Tigh was lifting her in his strong arms, carrying her toward the bed. He placed her on it, but she sat up, recalling her schedule prior to this unplanned—and very pleasurable—interlude.

"What time is it?" She looked at her chronometer, cursing at the numbers she read there. "Damn. We're going to be late."

As it turned out, Ginny and Tigh walked in only a few minutes late to the dinner she'd set up earlier. She was on the receiving end of a few pointed looks from her crew, but if the men gave Tigh any guff, it was well hidden. Or, perhaps, his guys were too well disciplined to let their thoughts show.

All of Tigh's men were warriors born while Ginny's crew were women who had chosen to do other things with their lives before the virus. They'd turned to soldiering as a second choice, in a crisis, and it was probably easier for them to remember how to be civilians than it was for the jits.

The meal was set up buffet-style so everyone could mingle. It was working as Ginny had planned, for the most part, except for Henny.

"You're not mingling, Chief Sonata." Ginny stopped by Henny's post against the wall on her circuit of the room. She'd noticed Henny holding back, watching all from her position against the wall. One of the jits had, in fact, done the same on the other side of the room.

"Sorry, ma'am. Just getting the lay of the land."

Ginny snorted. "Likely story. Get some food, Hen. That's an order."

"I'll move when he does," Henny's eyes were locked on her counterpart across the room. The man was watching her, too, and Ginny sensed a grudging sort of respect pulsing between the two.

"I'll ask Tigh to get your friend over there moving. Does that satisfy you? I'd hate to see this devolve into a pissing contest, because you know, he'd win. It's just a matter of equipment."

Henny laughed out loud as Ginny intended. When she began walking, Henny fell in step beside her. They stopped by the buffet, and Ginny supervised while Henny filled a plate. Tall and muscular, Henny was a woman who ate. She didn't pick at her food like smaller, less physically active women.

The dinner, while not an unqualified success, certainly went a long way toward making the women more comfortable in the presence of the jit'suku men. There were even a few budding friendships, if Ginny didn't miss her guess. Maybe even a romance or two that could be in the works.

Ginny wouldn't have thought it possible, but then again, she'd never really seen most of her crew in social situations with men before. They'd mostly come together as a group after the virus had decimated human males. The few males that were left were spread out over vast distances, so a gathering like this was unheard of, even in military circles.

Parties with near-equal numbers of males and females had been the norm when they'd all been growing up, but since the virus, there were always way more women than men and few occasions to celebrate much of anything. As a result, while the dinner was a good first step, it was also more than a bit awkward.

However, one positive thing did come out of it. Every one of her crew decided to go with her to the jit'suku galaxy. Now that they'd had a chance to meet the men in person, nobody had changed their minds. In fact, some were even more convinced than ever that they would like to come along.

CHAPTER 7

Michael Amber asked to speak to Ginny privately the afternoon before she was to depart with the jit'suku emperor. Ginny knew there would be a debrief of some kind, but Michael's words and actions were a bit more than she'd expected.

"It would be naïve to think your journey with these men will be a smooth one," Michael faced her across the large desk in his office. "I'm sending along some security measures should you run into trouble. Your security chief is being briefed as we speak, and she'll fill you in on the particulars of the equipment. Right about now…" he leaned back in his chair and dropped the paper he'd been holding onto his desk, "…I'm supposed to be giving you a pep talk about how your people thank you for your sacrifice, etc, etc, etc. Let's take that as said, Ginny, and let me talk to you person to person here." He leaned forward once more, his gaze intense. "You don't have to go if you don't want to. Despite what's been said and promised, if you decide right before the ramp goes up on that ship that you don't want to go, all you have to do is signal me, and I'll get you out of there. That's a promise you can count on. I don't give a damn about politics. I'll get you out, if you want out."

"I don't know what to say, Commandant." She searched

for a response. "Thank you for the offer, but as of right now, I'm committed to seeing this through. I'll remember though, if I get cold feet."

Michael burst out laughing. "The day the Valkyrie gets cold feet will never come."

"You have more confidence in me in than I do, Commandant."

"Please, call me Michael. You're going to outrank me to a considerable degree in a few days' time, Empress."

That was something she still hadn't quite come to terms with. The reminder of what she was moving toward made her wince.

"Destiny is a funny thing, Ginny. I was born to my fate and had a lot of time to accept it, but you're just starting down a road that will take your life in a completely unexpected direction." His insight was startling. "You can either fight it or accept it. My advice is to go with the flow. I never expected to marry either, but when the right person comes along, you're better off to accept what could be rather than stubbornly cling to what was."

Ginny boarded the jit'suku ship the next day. Tigh had brought her aboard a few times during the past days, to show her where things were and familiarize her with the layout. She'd moved her kit into his stateroom, putting the rest of her belongings that she wanted with her in her new home—it was really odd to think that she was moving to an entirely new galaxy to live—in the hold of the ship. The rest of her crew had done the same as they'd all made preparations to leave the only galaxy they'd ever known.

Each evening, she'd met up with her crew for an informal debrief on the day's events. She wanted her crew to learn all they could about their new ship, just as a safety precaution. The ship wasn't the new command they'd all been expecting, but they were a crew, and they were going to be on the jit ship for a while, so it was only smart to learn what they could while they were there.

One thing Ginny hadn't quite expected was that her family would demand to go along. Not only her mother, but her aunt and young cousin were sending items to the ship, to be placed in the cargo hold. And, on the day of departure, they presented themselves for embarkation and would take no answer other than "Welcome aboard".

Ginny had to give them all credit. As the voyage began, they seemed to be settling in well. Her crew was a bit restless as the first week of travel time came to a close. They'd had an escort to the galactic rim and had crossed over into jumpspace with little fanfare. The travel time in the jit'suku galaxy would be a bit longer because Solaris Prime was a bit farther from this jump point, but the ship was functioning perfectly, and there was very little for the women to do.

When Henny suggested getting together in the gym for a little martial arts practice, Ginny was only too happy to agree. They set a time, and her crew met up at the gym as planned, much to the surprise of the jit'suku men who were off-shift and using a few of the exercise machines at the time.

Henny led the class, and the jit'suku warriors watched in fascination as the women went through the drills. Ginny was glad of a little exercise, though she was mindful of her condition and didn't push as hard as she usually would. She was more amused by the men's reactions to their display and had to keep from laughing a few times at the expressions on some of their faces.

Forgetting them, she focused on her movements, stretching her body and relishing the physical activity after too many days spent idle. She didn't notice a whispered conversation between a young jit'suku and an older officer. Nor did she notice when the younger man was dispatched, on the double, from the gym area.

*

The young medical corpsman, Pier Sal'Omval rushed onto the bridge, sinking to one knee before Tigh as he sat in the command chair. Tigh sighed in weary annoyance. He'd told the youth, time and again, such a show of respect was unnecessary, but the young medic had his own ideas of what respect was due his emperor and a novitiate of the Zenain Order. Tigh realized early on the youngster was probably more impressed with Tigh's Zenai training than his position as emperor. It never failed to amuse him when the youth watched his short workouts in the gym area with obvious fascination.

"What is it, Pier?"

"Jin'tal, I was sent to tell you…" A pained look crossed the young man's face. "Sire, the women are using the gym for some kind of fighting practice."

Tigh nodded. "I gave them permission to use the gym during off shifts."

"Yes, sire, but they are fighting." The young corpsman sounded suitably appalled that human females should be engaged in such exercise. "And your intended is among them."

Tigh stood abruptly. "Ginny is fighting?"

"She is with them, though I did not see her engaging in combat. Still, Med Officer Jek'al thought you'd want to know and sent me straight to you."

Tigh was already striding out the door as quickly as his long legs would carry him. "You're damn right I'd want to know. Ginny should not be risking her health in such a way when she is pregnant."

The corpsman hopped to keep up, his shorter legs a disadvantage when walking next to Tigh's superior height. Wisely, the boy kept silent, merely following as Tigh's temper flashed. He was angry at the thought of what might happen to his reckless human mate, but it was fear for her safety—and that of the babies—that truly ruled his racing heart.

When Tigh reached the gym, he found the human women arranged in an orderly row, practicing blocks, strikes and kicks in formation, being led by the blonde master-at-arms, Henny Sonata. Tigh stopped abruptly in the door, taking in the scene. It looked like every off-duty male was poised around the perimeter of the large space, watching the women with varying degrees of amazement and awe. The women, by contrast, appeared to pay them no mind as they swept through graceful choreographed movements that were startlingly similar to the drills he'd learned in his first years with the Zenai.

They followed Henny, movement for movement, though it was clear she was the most skilled of them all. Still, many of the women had high levels of skill, the ability dropping off slightly as they went down the line.

Tigh saw Ginny moving fluidly on one end of the line. She was skilled, it was plain to see, but he doubted if the women's pretty movements could translate to effective combat with a man of his size. Tigh strode forward as the women faced away from him, his one thought to get Ginny clear of the danger of being kicked or struck by a misplaced move on the part of her fellow practitioners.

He came up behind her, grasping her around the waist without warning.

The next thing he knew, Ginny was responding as if he was an attacker, moving with quicker moves than he would have credited, slipping out from his hold and moving to incapacitate him, as well. Of course, at this point, his own training kicked in, and he avoided her blow, which could have done some serious damage, but she was overbalanced and falling in a way that might injure her.

Sweeping out and down, Tigh used all his skill to quell her retaliatory moves while bringing her gently under his control. She moved so fluidly another man would be hard pressed to keep them both upright and in one piece, but Tigh was one of the most highly-ranked students of the Zenai warrior priesthood.

"It's me, Ginny," he whispered as she came to rest in his arms. He could feel her muscles quivering under his hands as she realized who held her and what they'd almost done. The whole episode had taken just seconds. "Are you all right?"

She swatted his chest. "Don't sneak up on me like that!" Ginny backed away, and he let her go, duly chastened.

"You're right. I didn't think before moving to protect you and, as a result, put you in even more danger."

Ginny tilted her head, her momentary anger seemingly stymied by his heartfelt apology. She studied his face, her own eyes questioning while the women stood motionless behind them, watching with wide eyes. Tigh knew every warrior in the room was watching the byplay, as well, but all that mattered to him was Ginny. She was all that was important in his existence. Her safety and the safety of their babies was paramount—for so many reasons.

"I was in no danger."

Tigh's anger, fed by fear for her safety, battled within him. He strove for calm but knew his eyes flared.

"Fighting practice is best left to those who are not pregnant."

"We weren't fighting." Her jaw set stubbornly, but then she seemed to think better of it and relented. "I wasn't going to participate in kumite, just in the kata practice. I thought that was safe enough."

"What is kahtah and koomitay?" He spoke the words phonetically, unfamiliar with the terms for which his translator had no data.

Henny strode forward, her assessing gaze traveling up and down Tigh as she asserted her authority over the exercise class. "Nice moves, Your Majesty." She grinned lopsidedly as he gave her his attention. "Kumite is the fighting practice. Sparring is another word for it. Kata is what you saw us doing when you came in. Defensive and offensive moves choreographed in ancient patterns. No contact is involved. I wouldn't want to risk an accident with the captain's health and wellbeing, I can assure you. There is little risk of injury in kata practice at this level."

Tigh turned toward the woman who was leading the class, clearly an expert in her field, but risk was risk, and Tigh was unreasonable where Ginny was concerned. He knew it, but he couldn't do a damn thing about it.

"I respect your reasoning, Armsmaster, but it is difficult for me to see Ginny at any risk at all."

Ginny surprised him by stepping forward, her hand resting on his forearm gently as her eyes searched his. "I wouldn't risk the babies for anything, Tigh. I want them as much, if not more than you do." Her soft gaze tightened just a bit. "But I refuse to sit on my ass this entire voyage, getting soft and fat. I need exercise. Even my doctor agrees."

"What if I like you soft and fat?" Tigh moved closer, his words for her alone, though he suspected Henny might've heard, though she made no indication.

Ginny snorted with laughter, her anger fully diffused, and Tigh knew his rash actions had been forgiven. Relief poured through him. He so wanted this relationship to work. It had to work, for their people's good, but mostly just because he was fast realizing he would be hard pressed to live without Ginny in his life if she ever took it in her head to live apart from him.

"I promise I won't be in any danger, Tigh. The worst that could happen is a pulled muscle, and I'm very careful to warm up and cool down properly so that doesn't happen." She moved back. "Let me just finish the kata section of the class, then I promise I'll sit it out when they switch to kumite."

Tigh didn't want to let her do it, but he knew this female was used to making all her own decisions for both herself and her crew. It would be hard for her to defer to his judgment, though he knew she was reasonable. Still, she knew more about the human fighting form than he did, and he had to believe she also knew her own body's limits. He would be a fool to forbid her a simple no-contact workout, if that's truly what it was.

Tigh nodded and stepped back. "You won't mind if I stay and watch?" He tried to sound casual. "I'm interested to know more about your human fighting forms."

Ginny seemed to take that statement at face value and

even smiled as she rolled her expressive eyes towards the throng of onlookers all around the gym. "Why not? The more the merrier, I always say."

Ginny resumed her place in the line of women, and Henny moved back to the lead position. She called out some words he had no translation for, and the class was off again, starting with a choreographed pattern of blocks, then a series of punches and kicks, and some acrobatic moves that took them to all four corners of the room before finally settling back in the position they'd started from.

Tigh was entranced. His woman moved like a dream. The fighting moves were somewhat familiar, though the style was quite different than any of the Zenai fighting forms. Still, Tigh could appreciate the way such moves complemented the women's smaller build and shorter reach. They used their agility and quickness in ways that would counter even larger and skilled opponents. The form was a thing of beauty. As was the woman he watched throughout.

Ginny was graceful and accomplished. While not in the same league as Henny, who led the class, Ginny was by no means a novice at self-defense. Tigh didn't know how he felt about that. Jit'suku women traditionally didn't fight in any form at all. Oh, there were some settlements where the women still had to fight alongside the men, but those were mostly hostile, backwards environments. Civilized jit'suku worlds allowed women to live the lives they were best suited to, cultivating the young, teaching, nurturing, and assisting in the running of governments.

Councils traditionally held representatives from all the facets of jit'suku society—the three W's—warriors, workers, and women. Women held important positions in all levels of society and had responsible jobs. The only avenue they seemed not the least bit interested in was making war, and that was just fine. That's what the warrior class was for.

At the conclusion of the kata portion of the class, Ginny bowed and left the line of women. Tigh warmed when she moved to his side, as if she belonged there. And he realized, she truly did. She was his woman. His future life partner. His. Just his.

As he would be hers. If she would but accept him into her heart.

"What are they doing now?" he whispered close to her ear, encouraging her to tell him more about their ways.

Ginny watched the class pair off after some instruction and begin sparring practice. Tigh watched their movements with a practiced gaze. He had often engaged in just such practice. In fact, it had been a daily event in his life until he had left the Zenai mountain. He was somewhat amazed that the humans would have such similar teaching and fighting methods.

"Henny usually teaches a few moves then allows open sparring. I think she's adjusting her methods somewhat today because of the audience. We're not accustomed to having such a large group of watchers." Ginny's voice was pitched low so that only he could hear her comments. "Okay," she said as Henny called for the group's attention. "Watch this. She's going to demonstrate a new move, using Tiggy as a practice dummy, then allow the rest of the class to work on the same move in pairs."

"We use much the same methods to teach young priest candidates when they first arrive on the mountain." Tigh thought fondly back on his initial years as a novitiate.

Ginny looked up at him, her eyes questioning. "I can't imagine you as a priest, Tigh."

He sighed. "For many years, I thought that was my path in life, but the Mother Goddess had different plans for me."

Ginny placed her little hand in his discreetly as she stood at his side. The small gesture warmed his heart.

"I'm glad."

Little bubbles of happiness rose in him suddenly, like nothing he had ever experienced before. It was joy, he thought with bemusement. Clear, forthright, unequivocal joy. He'd never expected to feel such a pure emotion.

"Me too," was all he could manage between the need to

mask the effervescent emotion running through his veins while on public display, and his desire to keep what little he could of their private lives, private.

"Oh, look at that leg sweep. That's a cool move." Ginny's attention was on the class as it progressed, but Tigh noted happily that her hand remained in his. She was starting to get used to him, he thought with some satisfaction.

"Cool, as you say," he squeezed her hand, "but potentially dangerous for a woman in your condition."

Ginny sighed heavily. "Oh, all right. I concede your point. Getting thrown around when newly pregnant is probably not a good idea."

Tigh refrained from chastising her with a good deal of effort, but he was trying to give her some leeway. After all, she had come to him from a totally different culture, where gender roles were insanely disparate. He had to give her time—and give himself time—to come to terms and meet, hopefully, somewhere in the middle.

"What do they call this sort of fighting practice?" Tigh strove to change the subject.

"Henny can tell you much more about it, but this is an ancient form of martial arts. Back on Earth, many centuries ago, martial arts developed among many cultures. Much of what we have still today, is the same—or as similar as we can manage—as what those ancient monks developed all those centuries ago. Tradition is very important among the teachers and practitioners of almost all martial arts. Henny learned from her father. He was one of the grand champions of his day, and he owned and operated one of the finest martial arts schools anywhere in the galaxy. Students would come to him from all over."

"Did you know him?" Tigh sensed deep feelings just under the surface of her words.

Ginny nodded once. "I was fortunate enough to study with him as a child. Sensei Mick was one of the finest men I have ever known. He was like a second father to me, and Henny was like a sister. She still is."

"I had no idea you knew each other as children."

"We grew up together. Our parents were friends. It was their fondest hope that I would fall in love with and marry one of Henny's brothers. She had six brothers, you know. Of course, they're all gone now. When Sensei Mick succumbed to the virus, then his sons died in short order, his wife killed herself in her grief. Only Henny is left from the entire Sonata clan. She's the only one left to pass on the knowledge her father's line kept sacred for generations."

Tigh was touched by the woman's loss. "If I have anything to say about it, her knowledge will be passed on. Her clan will not have died in vain. Together, Ginny, we can be the means for all those who have lost so much to begin to rebuild."

He could see tears gathering in her lovely eyes as she gazed up at him. Tears that he would never allow in his own eyes, though he felt them in his heart. She would cry for both of them, though he knew she would fight to keep a strong front for her crew. He squeezed her hand, offering what comfort he could.

"It's a noble goal, Tigh. It's the reason I initially agreed to your plan."

"Initially?"

A secretive smile bloomed over her lovely face. "I've since found other reasons."

Tigh liked the mischievous sparkle in her eyes. "Such as?"

"Oh, I think you know."

"The babies, perhaps?" His smiled broadened as he winked. "Or how we made them?"

The enchanting flush on her cheeks was his answer.

CHAPTER 8

Henny called for kumite, and the group set to work. She supervised as the women paired off and tried the new moves she'd set before them. The eyes of the men watching all around unnerved her, but she couldn't let it show. Still, she noted the various looks of admiration, lust, distrust and disdain aimed at them from all sides.

The admiration and lust were easily dealt with, trust could be earned, but the disdain ate at her craw. Henny knew some sort of statement would need to be made. She'd seen it before with warriors in her father's dojo. Whether male or female, when one fighter was underestimated, the best remedy was to prove otherwise.

Henny looked around the room and made note of the most antagonistic looks. Sizing up the few men who really seemed to be sneering at her and her women, she knew she could take them. She'd made a study of the jit'suku fighting methods for years alongside her father. They probably didn't have any moves she couldn't counter. At least not the run-of-the-mill fighters. The emperor now, he was a different story. Henny knew he'd been an elite fighter, even among the jits. He was a novitiate of the fighting priesthood, and she guessed he could probably teach her a thing or two, judging from the amazing juggling act he'd just displayed with her captain.

But she'd never challenge the emperor. At least not unless it was truly necessary.

Henny worked her way around the room toward a pair of warriors who were grumbling among themselves. She moved nonchalantly, positioning herself so they would not realize she had sought them out on purpose. Instead, she made a show of coaching the pair of women nearest the two men she'd targeted.

"They dance well," she heard one of the men say to the other, just loud enough for her to hear, "but they're just girls. They couldn't fight their way out of a sack."

Henny suppressed her grin of satisfaction with effort. Turning on her heel, she walked right up to the big male, her hands on her hips as she craned her neck to look up at him. She was tall for a woman, but all of these men were taller. It wasn't something she was used to, but she could definitely use it to her advantage when fighting them.

"What did you just say?" She challenged him loud enough that the men near him shuffled their feet and listened with unabashed curiosity. Little by little, the rest of the room grew silent as the others became aware of the confrontation in the making. Just as she planned.

The warrior pushed himself up from his negligent leaning against the wall. He tried to intimidate her with his size, but it wouldn't work. Henny had never been intimidated by male muscle. She'd had six brothers and a bear of a father who had taught her well how to use her slightly smaller size to her advantage.

"I said," he paused to look around at those who listened intently all around, "that your moves are pretty, but I'd hardly call it a fighting form."

Henny stared up at him. "I think you just challenged me."

The warrior was smarter than he looked, holding up his hands and backing down. "I don't fight females."

"You will fight this female. You've insulted my house and my ancestors." Henny spat at his feet, knowing the insult could not go unanswered by any jit warrior. She'd studied her enemy well and knew their weaknesses. The entire room grew uneasy, some of the men shuffling and grumbling to themselves.

Bless her heart, the captain was at her side in a flash, the emperor not far behind.

"Sire, she challenges me!"

Henny was surprised by the big lunk of a warrior appealing to his emperor before she could even get a word out. Henny stood back, watching the byplay.

Emperor Tigh's expression was grave but full of respect when he turned to her.

"The women call you sensei, which my intended informs me means teacher. Among the jit'suku warrior class, teachers are held to higher standards than regular warriors, be they male or female. And yes, we have—had—a small number of female instructors, so there is precedent for what you have done here. Was it your intent to challenge this warrior to combat?"

Henny bowed her head in what she knew was the proper jit'suku form of respect. The warriors grumbled. "I have studied your ways, Emperor Tigh. I knew what I was doing when I challenged this warrior. Your crew needs convincing of our skills, and this warrior in particular needs a good swift kick in the—"

"Henny," Captain Gin cut her off, and Henny had to suppress a grin, "do you really think this is wise? Or even necessary?"

"With all due respect, Captain, it is very necessary if we are to establish our place among these men."

Ginny nodded, her eyes speaking volumes. "Don't lose then, Chief." Ginny backed off, her support clear.

Tigh faced the young warrior. "Male or female, when a challenge is issued by a teacher, it must be answered."

Henny knew that the answer could go either way, but if the man refused to fight her, he'd lose serious amounts of face with his buddies. Such challenges were almost never refused, and the troublemaker she'd selected didn't disappoint. His hands moved to the fastenings of his weapons, and he stripped off the belts that held his energy rifle and other arms. This fight would be hand to hand.

Henny grinned with feral intensity as she turned back to her women. This was going to be good.

"Does your Armsmaster know what she's doing, truly?" Tigh asked Ginny as they moved to the side to watch. A space had cleared in the center of the gym area, and the two opponents now faced each other, preparing to battle.

Ginny grinned, her eyes intent on the combatants. "Oh, yeah. Henny's one of the most gifted and highly trained martial artists in our galaxy. Your man doesn't stand a chance."

"Amazing." Tigh stood back, making certain they were well out of range of the confrontation.

"Wait 'til you see her in action. The sensei will be teaching all your men a lesson today."

"Not to underestimate her?"

Ginny sent him a sidelong glance. "Not to underestimate human females, in general, and my crew, in particular."

The fight started after the traditional exchange of respectful bows. Almost immediately, it became quite clear that the jit'suku warrior was outclassed. He seemed slow and bulky in comparison to the lithely athletic woman, who dodged and wove around him. Occasionally, she would get in strikes of her own, but she never once came even close to receiving any of the blows the giant warrior sent in her direction.

After a few minutes, Henny clearly decided to end the battle. She moved in closer to the large man, setting him up beautifully for the leg sweep she had taught the class earlier. In a windmill of flailing arms, the male warrior went down hard, landing on his ass in an ungraceful heap.

A few of his comrades laughed as Henny positioned herself above him for what would be an incapacitating or killing blow. But the final strike would never be delivered. This battle was done. With surprisingly good grace, the big warrior conceded the victory. There was no loss of face in a battle fairly fought.

Henny graciously offered the young man a hand up, and he accepted after just a moment's deliberation. The crowd of watchers seemed still undecided, however. The battle had been too short, and with an opponent who was too young to really test the woman's capability.

But she seemed to realize that. With a scoffing gesture, she motioned to the crowd. "Anyone else? I need more of a workout than that."

Teasing grumbles sounded from the men. A few feet shuffled, and Tigh looked over the room, sending a silent signal to one of his most trusted men. Xeer was a seasoned warrior, who would give the talented woman a good fight. Tigh knew Xeer was skilled enough not to hurt her inadvertently, but he probably wasn't good enough to best her. Xeer was strictly a weapons man who drilled in hand-to-hand combat only because it was necessary.

Nodding imperceptibly to Tigh, Xeer stepped forward. The other men cheered on their comrade, and the new battle was begun in short order.

As expected, Xeer lasted a bit longer than the previous fighter, but Henny easily outclassed him. Tigh was surprised at how handily she vanquished him. With another discreet nod, a third opponent moved forward to face the small human woman. Pantell was just as easily dispensed with, much to Tigh's intrigue. The fourth and fifth were also quickly dispatched.

Finally, Tigh gave up trying to orchestrate her opponents, and his own armsmaster stepped forward. Tigh had every confidence in Hansa. He was the most skilled warrior onboard, after Tigh himself. Hansa had trained with the Zenai as a young boy and nearly perfected his skills in the years since. Though he had not been allowed to learn all the secrets of the priesthood, his knowledge was much greater than most. Tigh figured this match would be a little more even, but this time, the male would win.

But Henny used her size to her advantage. Her graceful movements were faster than the eye could follow, and her strikes were solid. Both combatants were pulling their blows, not allowing the full force of their punches and kicks to impact on their opponent. The goal in this combat was to score points, or prove superior skill, without damaging the opposing warrior. Both were equally skilled in being able to execute their moves without inadvertently harming the other. At the speed they were both moving, such finesse took vast skill indeed.

All within the gym area watched with fascination as the match went on and on. For every strike Hansa scored, the female scored as well. They were well and truly matched.

After long minutes of battle, and increasingly more difficult strike patterns, Henny finally made a mistake. Jumping high to deliver a spinning roundhouse kick, just as Hansa aimed a blow to her solar plexus, they tangled, and she would have fallen hard. But Hansa apparently saw what would happen and chose to break her fall with his own defeat. Putting himself gallantly in the path of her landing, he forfeited the match in favor of saving her from potential harm. There was honor in his actions that all who watched fully appreciated, including the human women, Tigh was glad to see.

Henny bowed low to Hansa, respect clear in her every move.

"You are a skilled warrior with a kind heart, Armsmaster." The sparkle in her eye made Tigh think perhaps there was more feeling there than the gruff woman was willing to display in public.

"And never have I met a woman as skilled in the art of war as you, Master-at-Arms." Hansa's voice was low and respectful, making Tigh proud of the man he'd hand-picked to be his armsmaster on this trip. It had been a good choice.

Tigh sensed undercurrents flowing between the two and

decided to give them some opportunity to speak privately. With a meaningful glance, Tigh indicated the show was over, and it was time to vacate the gym area. His men hopped to, trooping out of the gym quickly, leaving the women behind to gather their belongings in peace. A few stragglers appeared to want to talk with particular females, and Tigh didn't begrudge them the opportunity to talk with the women who were also on their way out the door.

Within minutes, the gym was nearly empty, yet Hansa and Henny remained at the center of the matted floor, speaking quietly. Tigh took it as a good sign.

"Do you think they'll be all right?" Ginny's voice reached him as he turned back to her. Her attention was on the two armsmasters talking intently several yards away.

"Oh, I think they'll be just fine. If I'm not much mistaken, we may have just witnessed the beginnings of a lasting friendship."

"You think so?"

Tigh tucked her shoulders under one of his arms as he steered her toward the doorway. "I know so. Hansa respects anyone who can match him move for move. Your Henny had him hustling. I know that for a fact, for he is my own sparring partner."

"Wow." Ginny's eyes widened as they moved out into the hall. She threw a look back at them over her shoulder, but Tigh guided her down the companionway, leaving the two to some well-earned privacy.

*

Henny's doorchime sounded. She wasn't surprised. She expected Hansa at her hatch right at shift change. He was a little late, but she wouldn't quibble. The alien warrior was like no man she'd ever known before, and if she wasn't much mistaken, he was staking a claim over her for the rest of his crew. It was an annoyingly primitive thing these ultra-masculine jit'suku warriors did when they met a woman they liked, but in this case, Henny didn't mind a bit.

She kind of liked the feeling of being under this amazing man's protection, as it were, though they both knew she could darn well protect herself. It was a cultural thing—a figurative protection that made her feel cherished in a way she'd never been by any human male.

Hansa and she had become close over the journey. They taught each other things about their respective fighting styles and built a respect based on common ideals. Hansa was a warrior's warrior, trained in the jit'suku way, but not unwilling to see the value of Henny's own traditions. She liked that. And she respected his skill as well. There were few beings of any race who could impress her in the fighting ring, but Hansa was definitely one.

He impressed her in other ways too. He was courting her, giving her little gifts and spending every free moment with her. He kissed like a dream too.

Henny had never felt such passion with any other man. Or—dare she admit it—such love. He hadn't come right out and said it yet, but she felt sure he was heading in that direction. Her heart beat faster when he was near, as it was doing now, as she headed for the door to meet him.

With a bright smile on her face, she hit the hatch release, and there he was, the man of her dreams.

"Henny, my love..."

Her heart thrilled to hear him call her his love. It was the first time, and it meant a lot. But her joy turned to dismay as his eyes rolled back in his head, and he leaned heavily on the doorframe. Something was seriously wrong.

"What is it?" She reached out to steady him, and he collapsed in her arms.

"Poison...Warn..."

He keeled over, and she used his momentum to pull him completely inside her room, slapping the panel to shut the door behind them. If there were enemies about, she didn't want to leave him vulnerable.

She tried to shake him awake and quickly checked him

over. He was alive but completely unconscious, and his vitals were dangerously low by human standards. She didn't know what that meant for jits, but she was damn sure going to find out. She couldn't lose him now.

She'd only just managed to find him. In this big universe full of life, she'd found a man she could truly respect and perhaps, even love. It was a miracle…and yet, that miracle could so easily be taken away from her. Henny firmed her resolve and suppressed her emotions. She had to get to the bottom of this.

Hansa had warned her about poison. That meant—unless he was utterly delirious, which she doubted highly—something sinister was afoot on the ship. Henny sat back on her heels, thinking fast. She knew what she had to do.

She activated the tiny, hidden emergency com that connected all the women onboard.

"Alert. Situation alpha blue. Repeat: alpha blue." That was the code for hostile takeover of the ship. Henny didn't believe in going off half-cocked. If Hansa was down, there was a good bet that the rest of the command staff was already unconscious. "Command code, zed niner niner." Henny issued the order that would detach seemingly harmless adornments from the women's luggage. The passive recorders would now go active, following each woman around as she responded to the crisis. The human military and government had equipped them with all kinds of clandestine hardware for just such a contingency. This mission was too important. If something went wrong, both governments would need to know who was at fault and how events transpired. "Secure all stations," she ordered further, laying Hansa more comfortably on the floor of her room then arming herself before heading cautiously out the door. "All hands report in."

Henny closed her cabin door, leaving Hansa within, safe for now. She worried inwardly about his condition, but there was nothing she could do medically until they'd secured the ship. She went down the hall, peering around corners carefully before proceeding, her weapon drawn when the first of her crew started reporting in.

"Alpha en route." That was the captain.

"Beta en route." Henny ticked off the executive officer on her mental list.

"Gamma en route." The nav officer was efficient, as usual.

"Delta. Three downed jits in my hall. En route." That was the doctor, unable to not take note of casualties.

"Epsilon, almost there. Lots of downed jits in the hall." Tiggy's voice was solid, though Henny knew she wasn't the best at hand-to-hand combat. Still, the com officer was good to go in any situation, and if she reached the bridge first and encountered resistance, she'd put up a decent fight.

Of course, Henny wouldn't let her fight alone. As the rest of the women checked in, Henny doubled her speed. She was close to the bridge, and it would be better to have as many women as possible storm it at the same time, in case they met serious resistance there.

She moved around another corner and saw Tiggy sticking to the shadows along one wall. She was good at stealth, at least, even if she'd never be an expert martial artist. Tiggy had better skills with firearms, and that counted for a lot in this kind of battle.

"Epsilon, on your six," Henny warned the other woman of her presence, keeping the channel open. In this kind of emergency situation, all the women would need to hear what transpired with their fellows. Henny moved up to join Tiggy, and the relief on the other woman's face was evident.

"I can't hear anything from inside the bridge. Door's shut tight and locked on voice command."

"I can help there." Captain Starbridge moved up from another hall to join them. Two of the other women were already with her. "Tigh gave me access."

Henny thought about their odds. Five women were gathered now, in the hall outside the bridge. It would have to be enough. She nodded to her captain. "On your order, ma'am."

Ginny looked around at her crew, noting the small recorder drones that followed them all. The little devices were recording all that transpired and were programmed to transmit their signal immediately upon the death of the woman they were programmed to follow. They were failsafes so that the human government would have some idea of what had happened on the diplomatic ship. Ginny was glad of them now. Depending on what they found on the bridge, this mission could very well be over for all of them.

She caught Henny's eye just before touching the pad on the wall that would unlock and override any security measures put in place against the regular jit'suku crew. Only Tigh had such direct access to the ship's computer, and he'd given her the same the moment they boarded as a gesture of good faith. No one else knew, for they'd done it privately, and Ginny was glad for Tigh's foresight now.

She couldn't think too much about him at the moment, though, or she'd lose sight of her goal in a mass of fear and nerves. He might be dead or dying. He might never again smile at her the way he had, and that would be a true tragedy. All of these men on this crew had been so good to her and her women. None of them deserved a sneak attack like this. It was up to Ginny and her crew to fix this. She had to put aside her worry and get the job done.

Ginny palmed the access port, keeping her weapon up and ready. Her crew was arrayed around her, spread three across the wide door. They'd storm in as quickly as possible and face whatever came, together, as they always had.

The door slid open, and the women tumbled in, but there was only one man standing, and Henny easily took him out with a stun shot to the head. He crumpled to the floor, joining the other jit'suku all around him. All of them were unconscious. Including Tigh.

Stars! She let herself feel the fear for him that lived in her heart for one breathless minute before she got her act together. She had work to do to get them all to safety, and there were others better suited to seeing if the damage that had been done would be fatal. Ginny had to trust in her people to look after Tigh and the others while she did what she could to defeat the enemy that was undoubtedly coming for them all.

Ginny made for the command chair and her lover, who was out cold. She couldn't allow herself to be distracted, but her heart gave another pang, seeing him so helpless and pale.

"Doc, where are you?" Ginny called over the still-open com.

"Right here, Captain," Doctor Heller said from the open hatch. "Sorry I'm late."

The rest of her core crew joined them rapidly, and Ginny closed the bridge access, sealing them in. "Doc, can you check internal sensors for any other conscious jits? I'm assuming none of you found any of these boys awake on your trip here, right?"

Negatives answered her question as the medical officer did a quick scan of the ship. "The only normal life signs are from the bridge. All female, except for him." She looked over at the traitor they'd found at the com console when they entered. It was the jit'suku doctor.

"Hansa was able to say the word 'poison' to me before he fell." Henny's expression was tightened with suppressed worry as she moved over to the weapons console and made herself at home.

Ginny looked from Tigh to Cat and back, ruthlessly suppressing the worry that gnawed at her for Tigh and his men. "Can you find out what's been done to them? We can run the ship, but we need these men awake, Doc."

"Leave it to me, Captain." Cat was a capable doctor. Ginny knew, if anyone could figure a way to revive the warriors, she would.

"Captain," Tiggy spoke from the com station. "The jit doctor was signaling three vessels that are now on an intercept course." And there they were. Right on time. The enemy Ginny just knew had to be coming.

Ginny looked over at Krysta, her navigator. "Time to intercept?"

Krysta's expression was grim. "At present speed, a little under a standard hour, Captain."

"All right, ladies," Ginny looked around at the bridge, calmed by seeing her crew once more at the ready, "we have work to do. There are three probable hostile ships out there, and we need to use the element of surprise to our advantage. Henny," she turned to her master-at-arms at the gunnery station, "can you make heads or tails of the weapons systems?"

"Not a problem, Cap'n." Henny was already settling into the much larger chair, easing the adjustable controls to her smaller body size. "I'll be ready when you are."

"Good. Nav, I want you to keep an eye on their formation. Plot me some intercept solutions. I'll look them over in a quarter standard, and we'll plan our action. We're bringing the fight to them. It's the only way to salvage this."

Ginny went over to consult with Henny on just what kind of armament this ship had. She was unfamiliar with this particular ship configuration and needed to know what they could bring to bear on a superior enemy force. All the while, she said a little silent prayer that Cat would be able to find an antidote and restore the men while Ginny and her friends dealt with the bad boys in the big ships. She knew the others had grown fond of Tigh's guys, too, but they were doing their jobs, setting aside their worry and working together to save them all. She couldn't be prouder of her ladies, even if part of her still worried down deep where it wouldn't interfere with the task at hand.

CHAPTER 9

Within a half standard, they were as ready as they could be. A course had been chosen, with contingencies should the enemy ships break their current formation, and Henny was ready with the weapons. Ginny took the precaution of starting some of the recording drones broadcasting back to Earth on a secure channel, in case they were blown up. Chances were the tough little drones would survive even hard vacuum, but it might be better not to take the risk. Peace was too important.

"I've got it!" Cat's voice rose above Ginny's thoughts and the normal hum of the bridge. Cat's expression spoke of triumph and anger.

"Doc?"

"That bastard did poison them." She looked over to where they'd secured the jit doctor against one bulkhead. He was still unconscious. "But I've located an antidote. It will take a while to revive them all, but they should be fine in a few hours, without any lasting injury. Without it, though, they'd have been dead inside of six standards." Again, her cold glare turned on the jit doctor.

"How soon can you administer the antidote?"

"I'll have to go down to the medical lab then patch into the ship's environmental system. That's how he spread it around in the first place, but he didn't count on the fact that this particular poison is ineffective on humans. Or, perhaps, he discounted the possibility that we could pose a threat. We're 'only women', after all." The doctor sneered those words, and all the women on the bridge either bristled or laughed.

"Or maybe he wanted us as hostages." Ginny considered the unconscious man. "Why didn't he succumb? I guess he had some of the antidote in his system already? Or some other kind of counteragent?"

"Yes, ma'am. Had to be. The jit'suku sense of smell is highly sensitive. This is one of the few airborne compounds that can pass by them undetected. And, as you see, it's very fast acting and potent."

"Get down to the lab, Cat. I want these men restored as quickly as possible."

"It'll take a few hours. And they'll be groggy for a day or two."

Ginny nodded. "We can handle the ship for them. Maybe this'll give them some idea of just who they're dealing with."

"If running their ship doesn't, the battle we're about to engage surely will." Henny's grim humor sounded from the weapons console.

"Better switch on their ship recorders if they're not on already." Ginny directed her comment towards the com station.

Tiggy nodded. "They were all on. I think the emperor must've activated them just before he passed out."

Ginny stood beside Tigh, unwilling to displace him, just yet, even though she'd need the command chair in the battle to come. She touched his hand. "He's a good man."

"Captain, I can bring him to the medical lab with me and monitor his recovery." Cat had come up beside her with an emergency gurney from the bridge med kit. It floated beside them on anit-grav cushioning that protected the patient and made them nearly weightless to move. If they could lever him onto it, Cat could move him easily.

Ginny sighed. "I suppose we can't just leave him where he is. He is the emperor, after all. Someone should make certain he comes out of this unharmed." She was torn. She wanted to be that someone but knew she had a battle to fight.

Cat put one hand on her arm, comforting her. "I'll watch over him, Gin. You've got work to do here. Get rid of the enemy ships. I'll take good care of your man while he recovers."

Ginny spared a moment to place her hand over Cat's. "Thanks, Doc. He means more to me than I can say."

With a nod to the other women who'd gathered around to help, they lifted Tigh's inert form onto the gurney and secured him in place.

"Justina and Penny, go with her. On your way, pick up my family from their suite and escort them all to the medical lab and seal them in. I know my mother and aunt can be of some help to the doctor. Then, see what you can do in engineering. We may need someone down there if the enemy ships get in any lucky shots."

"Aye, aye, Captain." The chief engineer and payload master saluted as they formed an honor guard—a heavily armed and alert honor guard—around the emperor's stretcher. With Doc Heller guiding the sled, Ginny walked with them to the door, stopping only to place a soft kiss on Tigh's stubbly cheek before opening the hatch and watching them slide through. She secured the door after they'd turned the corner, the women's recorder droids hovering around the small group, and headed back to her duties with a heavy heart.

There was a battle yet to be fought, and Ginny Starbridge had never looked forward to battles.

But she always won them.

"Krysta, what have we got?" Ginny stood near the nav station, putting off the moment when she would fill Tigh's empty command chair.

"They're on course, as expected. No deviations."

"Good. Can you plot a microburst that will bring us right

up the middle of the two far side ships, with a clear shot at the afterburners of the lead?"

"You don't ask for much, ma'am."

"Only what I know you're capable of, Ensign." Though a younger officer, Krysta was one of the best. If anyone could plot the impossibly tight maneuver at this close range, it was her. "When you have the solution, ping it over to me. I'll pilot it myself."

"Aye, aye, ma'am."

Krysta was a shy creature, but she was in her element plotting the impossible courses Ginny often demanded. Krysta had always been an ace up Ginny's sleeve as she captained the Sarasota through improbable scenarios. A more talented navigator Ginny had never met. She'd need all of Krysta's skill now, if they were to survive the upcoming battle in an unfamiliar ship.

The three enemy ships were close now. With the burst, they'd soon be in the thick of things. Ginny offered up a silent prayer for their survival. More than just their lives were riding on this skirmish. The fate of two entire galaxies hung in the balance.

Ginny couldn't put it off any longer. With a resigned sigh, she sat in Tigh's big chair. She didn't have time to dwell on the mixed feelings being in command of this top-of-the-line ship stirred in her heart for, a moment later, the console pinged, and she had to review Krysta's solution.

"Helm control on my mark," Ginny intoned. She wanted to get a feel for this ship before she piloted it in combat, but there was precious little time.

She gave the signal, and the controls dropped from above, startling her. On a human built ship, they'd have either popped up from below or swung in from the side. Adjusting her seat and posture, Ginny took the reins. It wasn't something she did often, but she'd started her career as a pilot and had always had a penchant for flying anything new or different. In this instance—flying an unfamiliar ship under battle conditions—Ginny knew she was the most able of her crew to give it a go.

The stick was hair trigger, she soon learned. The slightest motion of her fingers or arm spun the ship quickly. It responded faster than anything she'd ever flown, but then, the jits were master shipbuilders, and this was the emperor's own flagship. It had to be the best of the best.

"Whoa, girl." Ginny used all her concentration to learn the feel of this ship in the few minutes allotted. She couldn't do too much maneuvering because the enemy ships, no doubt, still assumed they were still on autopilot. And there was one more thing she had to be certain of before she took out three jit'suku ships. "Tiggy, have you got evidence secured? Are we certain those three bogies are really bad guys?"

Tiggy spun in her seat, her eyes hard as diamonds. "Oh, there's no doubt about it, ma'am."

Ginny recognized that tone. The com officer was royally pissed off, so whatever she'd found in the com logs had to be damning, indeed. But Ginny needed to hear it for herself before she took irrevocable action.

"Play it, Ensign."

"Aye, aye, ma'am." Tiggy spun her chair back around and brought up the records, playing the audio on the bridge speakers so everyone—including the recording drones—could hear. A series of tones played out first. It was some kind of recognition code used routinely in secure communications.

"Doctor?" A strange male voice sounded throughout the bridge.

"Doctor Gruber. It's good to hear your voice again. Everyone's out. It's safe for visual confirmation."

The com screen showed a holographic image from the lead ship of the three now closing on them. A man dressed in beribboned finery stood in front of the console while the com officer put the message through. As if the fop was too important to push his own buttons, Ginny thought. The man looked like a fool.

"Good work, my friend. Captains Sirkin, Redolan and

Merther assure me we are in position to intercept you. We will proceed as planned, staging the scene so our people will believe the human whores at fault for killing our weakling emperor and his collaborators. Groveling before the humans. It's disgusting."

The man couldn't seem to keep his opinions to himself, though he should know better than to voice anything so incriminating on a com channel. Even the most secure com could be hacked. But, in this case, the idiot's rantings were all the proof Ginny needed to justify her actions.

"They are even worse up close than you can believe, Goran," the doctor said. "These females are barbarians."

"Barbarians, eh?" Henny smirked. "He must be talking about me."

"Don't flatter yourself, Hen. That man hates us all," Tiggy observed.

"I've seen enough, Ensign," Ginny said, bringing them back to order. "Log the evidence and put it under seal. We'll need it when we reach Solaris Prime." If we reach Solaris Prime, she thought carefully to herself.

"Coming up on microburst window, Captain." Krysta watched her screen, as did Ginny.

"Henny, I want you to come out shooting when we burst through the middle of their formation. I'll line you up for a simultaneous port and starboard shot. Can you handle the jit controls?"

"No sweat, ma'am." Henny was as calm and professional as always, though her eyes glittered with battle fire. "Get me close, and I'll fry their asses."

"Disable if possible," Ginny instructed. "Kill only if necessary."

"Aye, aye, Captain."

"All right then." Ginny looked around at her crew—her friends. "We get one shot at this. Let's make it count. Krys, count us down."

As they'd done many times before, the women of the Sarasota acted in unison to save all their lives. Krysta gave

Ginny the signal, and she hit the afterburners for a hop into the midst of the three-ship formation. The moment they were clear, Henny hit the guns. Port and starboard broadsides took out half the weapons arrays of two of the ships and knocked gaping holes in their hulls. They were out of the fight for at least as long as it took to stabilize their hulls, which would most likely take hours.

Henny could easily pick them off now, and if they'd still been at war, Ginny would have given the order, but as things stood, she didn't want to take any more lives. There would be justice for these men, but it would be Tigh—God willing—who meted it out. All Ginny had to do was disable them long enough to get her own ship to safety, but there was still one fully functioning warship now powering up for a counter-strike.

"We're clear. Henny, track weapons. I'll try to give you a vector to the third ship's engines." The two disabled ships weren't going anywhere fast, but they still had a few weapons. Ginny would have to keep clear of what they had left while engaging that third bogie.

But this one was craftier than the other two. Or maybe, it was just because this captain had a few minutes to prepare. Ginny had lost the element of surprise, but she'd also evened the odds—as long as she stayed away from the functional flanks of the ships they'd already disabled. It took some tricky flying, but this ship handled like a dream. The more she flew it, the easier it became, and she started to enjoy the feeling of almost being one with the ship as she maneuvered after the leftover ambusher.

She chased him away from the other two, trying to get him out into the open so she wouldn't have to worry as much about those semi-functional ships. He was crafty though. The other captain refused to blink when she played chicken with him. Ginny was forced up and over, taking strafing fire to her belly as she sailed past.

But then, Henny pulled one out of her magic hat and sent a torpedo up the tailpipe of the enemy ship as they passed.

"How in hell did you manage that trajectory, Hen?" Ginny was so surprised, she voiced the thought even as she dove past and out of range of the enemy beam weapons. She had to get into his blind spot to avoid projectiles.

"Captain," Henny was grinning, "this ship has a few unexpected abilities. Rotational and extendable weapons pods, for one thing." She flicked a few switches. "Sorry I didn't figure this out before. I'll have that third bogie down in just…" They all watched a flight of torpedoes speed out from their ship at an impossible angle toward the retreating enemy. "…about…" The torpedoes were going to make it, though the other captain did his best to turn. His ship was too slow. "…now."

Screens lit with the explosion as multiple targets on the enemy ship went up in flames quickly extinguished by the vacuum of space.

"I think that's done him, Captain." Henny checked her screens, as did the others.

"Confirmed, Captain," Krysta said with satisfaction. "All three bogies are dead in the water."

"Com?" Ginny asked as she kept back from the battlefield. She had a few choices for what to do now. She pondered what the wisest course of action would be, but much depended on what the enemy captains did next.

"Signal tones only, Captain," Tiggy replied, "but on a sub-channel. They're looking for their man."

Ginny thought through her options, deciding on a course of action.

"Signal them back."

"Ma'am?" Tiggy turned to look at her.

"You heard me, Tig. Put us on wide lens. I want them to see exactly who just kicked their ass."

"Aye, aye, Captain." Understanding dawned on all their faces as Tiggy turned back with a grin and implemented the order. "You're on, Captain."

"Captains Sirkin, Redolan and Merther, this is Captain Starbridge."

"Get off the com, woman." One of the captains' faces appeared on her screen as he answered. Smoke billowed behind him, so she guessed he was on the second ship. That one had sustained severe damage near the bridge.

"I'm sorry I cannot accommodate your request, because right now, I'm the only one available. You do realize you've committed treason against your emperor. He's not going to be very happy with any of you."

"I will take my chances with him before I deal with a bridge manned by females." A second jit face popped up on her screen, next to the first.

Ginny didn't rise to the insult. "Have no doubt, you will deal with Tigh when he recovers from the poison your collaborator tried to kill him with. For now, I just wanted you to realize you—all three of you—were defeated by a ship captained and crewed by supposedly inferior humans. Female humans, at that. Take a good look, men. And remember, we could have killed you. Instead, the Valkyrie and her crew spared you today. I hope you'll remember that when you face justice before my husband-to-be."

"You're the one, then." A third face joined the other two. "The captain of the Sarasota. The one who blasphemes our beliefs."

"Tiggy, send our friends the data files Tigh gathered from our archives about the Valkyrie." Ginny maneuvered away from the scene of battle. "Gentlemen, a little reading for you while you await justice. My call sign was never intended to be any kind of insult to you or your religion. The legend of the Valkyrie is an ancient tale from Earth. Until Tigh showed up, we had no idea my call sign was what had your men gunning for me. I won't apologize, but I thought you should know."

Two of the three captains looked skeptical. The other dour puss seemed intent on mistrusting every word she spoke.

"I'd love to stay and chat, but I have a schedule to keep. If you're not here when Tigh wakes up, may your Goddess have mercy on your soul. We know who you are, and all evidence has been duly logged. End transmission."

Tiggy hit the control, and the screen blanked.

Ginny maneuvered the big ship into open space and turned control back to Krysta, who put them back on course.

"I'm almost sorry to give back the helm. This baby flies like a dream." Ginny stood from the command chair and stretched her legs. "Tig, any news from Doc?"

"She's been busy, Captain. She put your family to work, and they've searched all decks, picked up a lot of the men who fell at their posts and took the injured ones to sickbay. Antidote has been distributed through the air system, and a few of the younger ones are beginning to come around."

"All right." Ginny wanted to see Tigh. It was an imperative in her blood. She had to see him now. "We're not completely out of the woods here. We have one traitor in custody, but there may still be more. We can't let down our guard. Krysta, you have the helm. Henny, I want you to intensify scans. Tig, keep an eye on com both inside and outgoing from this ship. I don't want any more secret signals."

"Aye, aye, Captain." Tiggy set her controls.

Henny shot her captain a questioning look as she headed for the hatch. "I'm going to seal you in here. I don't want anyone else gaining bridge access until Tigh's awake."

"What about you, Captain?" Henny asked. "You should have an escort. Like you said, we may not have all the conspirators."

"It's a chance I'll have to take, Chief. I'm going down to Medical to check on the emperor."

Ginny sealed her crew in the bridge and headed for medbay at double time. A few groggy jits slumped against the walls, but few were moving at any speed. When she hit the medical area, her mother met her at the door. The patients were lined up in the hall.

"How is everyone?" Ginny asked after her mother let her in.

"A few broken bones, some contusions from folks falling

on things, but nothing serious. Most of them are starting to come around. Doctor Heller has the emperor and Councilor Torm in the far corner." She pointed behind her as she secured the door, and Ginny set off in that direction, finding Tigh easily enough.

She stood next to his bed, taking his big hand in hers. "Tigh," she whispered. "My love, wake up." She leaned down and kissed his cheek, whispering encouragement in his ear. She stroked his hair with one hand, waiting long minutes by his side, until he began to stir.

"Ginny?"

"I'm here, Tigh. It's all right."

"Where am I?"

"Medbay. You were gassed. All the men were."

Tigh's eyes narrowed as he struggled to focus. "Are you all right?"

"Doc said this particular poison doesn't affect humans. My crew is fine. We took over the bridge and captured one traitor."

"The doctor." His eyes clouded with memory of betrayal.

"Yes, Tigh. I'm sorry. He signaled three ships. We had to fight our way out."

"Who?" His eyes closed wearily. "Do you know who?"

"We have com evidence of communiqués with a doctor named Gruber, and I spoke to Captains Sirkin, Redolan and Merther myself. It's all logged. And I've got drones following every one of my women." She waved a hand upward to the small drone that still followed her every move, recording all.

"Human tech?" Tigh tried to focus uncooperative eyes on the small hoverdroid over her shoulder. "I didn't know you brought those on board."

Ginny gave him a small smile. "Just a little insurance, in case things went bad. Henny activated them when she realized you'd all been gassed. We converged on the bridge. Thank heaven you'd given me access. Your doctor had himself locked in."

"Emperor," Doctor Heller said as she walked over and

caught Ginny's eye. "I'm glad to see you coming around."

"How are the men?"

"All doing well. The younger crew members are already bouncing back. This agent appears to affect the older men more strongly. I have some concern for Councilor Torm, but his vital signs are good. It may just take him longer to come out of it than the rest of you."

"Please watch him closely, Doctor. He is a dear friend and one of the few men I can trust without question." Tigh looked back at Ginny. "I thought all the men on this ship were trustworthy, but I was wrong. I'm not sure who we can trust with your safety, Gin. You and your crew."

Ginny squeezed his hand. "It's all right, Tigh. We knew going in that this wasn't going to be an easy mission. We're used to looking after ourselves."

"Thank the Goddess you were immune to the gas." Tigh's eyes closed as he struggled with consciousness. "But what about the babies? They are half jit'suku."

Ginny's gaze shot to the doc's. Cat had that little frown between her eyebrows that meant she was thinking. "It's possible they were affected when you breathed in the contaminant, but you've also been breathing the antidote for some time, so they'd have received it the same way. Did you feel anything, Captain? And abdominal pains or cramping?"

"No, nothing." Ginny's pulse leapt with worry.

"While you're here, I'll run some scans, but chances are anything that might have entered their systems has already been negated. The agent knocks out jit'suku fast, but its poisonous properties take hours to be fully realized. We got the antidote circulating within less than an hour of initial exposure."

"Please run your scans now, Doctor. I believe neither Ginny nor I will rest easy until we are certain our babies are all right."

"I understand," Cat said. "If you can sit up, sir, we can use this medbed. All the others are occupied." Tigh moved slowly, but he managed to get out of the way enough for

Ginny to sit on the medbed. The doctor set the scanners and spent a few minutes fussing over the jit'suku designed equipment. She ran two scans, finishing up with a blood sample. "It'll take a few minutes to figure out how to get the blood analysis results. Sorry, ma'am. I'm learning as I go with this equipment. But the scans are clean. The babies are fine, swimming around happily inside from what I can see."

"Thank the Lady," Tigh said with feeling.

Ginny breathed a sigh of relief and gave Tigh a hug. He was sitting up stronger now, getting better by the minute. He wasn't completely steady on his feet yet, but he was improving rapidly. Councilor Torm woke up a few minutes later, though the poison had affected him more severely than anyone else on the ship, due to his age.

A short time later, Ginny and Tigh reclaimed the bridge. Tigh brought in a few members of his bridge crew to relieve some of the ladies, but he and Ginny were both wary now, unable to trust any of the jit'suku crew members completely.

Their fears proved out a few minutes later when Krysta erupted from her seat at the nav console and grabbed her co-worker by the throat. She lifted him off his feet and into the air, using all her martial arts skill and what Tigh now realized had to be a cybernetic arm of some sort. The man flailed, unable to breathe as she held him with superior strength of an implanted arm that looked very realistic otherwise.

"What is it?" Ginny demanded.

"He just tried to reroute com through his panel, ma'am." Krysta spoke fast, fending off the man's attempts to dislodge her mechanical arm. "He's one of the conspirators."

"Stuff him in the brig!" Tigh surged to his feet, as those loyal to him moved in.

It took several men to subdue the navigator fully, taking the burden of the big man from Krysta. Tigh watched with grim approval as they secured his hands and dragged him from the bridge. Tigh then turned to the female navigator as he reclaimed his seat. The sad truth was he was still weak from the poison and needed to sit.

"Are you certain, Ensign?"

"Yes, Your Majesty. When I took over at nav, I noticed we've been on a very strange course. While on this station for the past hour or so, I traced the navigator's logs and realized he was taking us on a circuitous route. I thought at first, it was a security measure, but now, I suspect it was so we could be in ambush position when the doctor gassed everyone."

"Can you plot us a faster course, Krys?" Ginny asked.

The ensign nodded. "Aye, aye, ma'am."

"I think we ought to get to Solaris Prime as soon as possible, don't you?" Ginny asked Tigh as she stood at the side of his command chair.

"I think you're right, my love. The sooner we get home, the better."

Tigh sent word ahead and dispatched a number of ships he thought were loyal to him to escort the three traitorous vessels back to the nearest military base. Tigh both hoped and feared the revelation of the plot against him would make it clear just what side the rest of his men stood on. If there was one thing he couldn't abide, it was a sneak.

When they finally reached the Solaris system, an honor guard made up of both military and Zenai ships awaited them. Tigh was taken aback by the presence of the brotherhood. They rarely involved themselves in matters of politics, but then, word of Ginny's call sign had probably already gotten back to the Zenai. Tigh wondered what sort of reception the human Valkyries would meet from his old teachers.

CHAPTER 10

Krysta waited to disembark down the wide gangplank alone, as usual. The doctor would leave last, with so many patients still to care for, even if she was technically higher in rank. Because of the diplomatic nature of this voyage, the disembarkation would probably be recorded for playback all over the empire. They had to pay at least some attention to protocol, as well as security.

To cover the security angle, Henny and that big brute, Hansa, had gone down the plank first, together. Krysta could tell there was something brewing there. She'd never seen Henny so radiant as when she was with the jit'suku warrior. Lieutenant Darlington, as executive officer, went next, accompanied by the jit XO. Sally seemed to be friendly with the man, but Krysta didn't read any attraction between those two, at least, though there were a few other jit warriors who'd caught the eye of some of the other women. The rest of the female bridge crew would walk side by side with their jit counterparts as a deluge of news bots recorded their every move.

Krysta herself was somewhere in the middle of the pecking order, and since her jit counterpart was a traitor, she would have to face the news bots all alone. It wasn't anything she wasn't used to. Growing up differently from everyone else had set her apart from the moment she'd lost her arm at age eight. She hadn't been fitted with her final cybernetic arm until she was fully grown. Losing a limb was one of the few disfiguring injuries that still couldn't be fully—unnoticeably—repaired until adulthood. As a result, Krysta had grown up as the object of pity. On a world where everyone swam and many lived in habitats built on and in the water that comprised over ninety percent of the planet, having only one arm was a definite drawback.

She'd never had a boyfriend. Never dated. All the usual games young adults played—frolicking in the water—were off-limits to her. Her balance was all off for swimming anywhere fast. She was fine on land, though the basic mechanical arms she'd worn as she grew to adulthood had drawn stares, pity and sometimes horror.

Krysta had begun to dream of other worlds, where swimming wasn't so necessary to everyday life, when she was still a little girl. She'd studied hard and applied herself to navigation calculations until she could do even the most complex of them without difficulty. Her dream had been to work as navigator on a trading vessel—to see the worlds beyond her home and maybe find a place she could finally fit in.

Then, the virus struck. The only good part of that whole horrible time was that her nav skills were needed by the human fighting forces, though she never would have considered joining the military before the plague. Still, when she saw her father and brothers die of the virus, she knew where she needed to be to put a stop to the beings who would harm the only men who had ever looked on her with love in their eyes. Her mother was proud of her, but they weren't in contact often. She'd sent a message home to tell her mother where she was going before they left on this mission, but hadn't received a reply. Her mother was a healer by nature and inclination. She didn't understand the military, though she was always supportive of Krysta, if distant.

"May I act as your escort, Ensign, since Navigator Jeviar is in the brig?"

Krysta snapped back to the matter at hand. She looked up to find a kind smile directed at her from one of the most handsome men she'd ever seen. She remembered him. He'd sparred with Henny that first day they'd practiced in the shipboard gym, and she'd noticed him then. He'd been in the gym watching them practice a number of times since, but then, so had a lot of the men. They couldn't seem to comprehend women practicing a fighting art. But Krysta had noticed this man, time and time again. Unpracticed as she was in the ways of flirtation, she'd had no idea he even knew who she was or what job she did on board, but apparently, he did. That thought sent a warm, scared feeling to the pit of her stomach.

"You're Commander Xeer." Krysta felt like an idiot the moment the words left her mouth. She'd asked around about him, and she'd just betrayed herself.

But his widening smile made her feel tingly inside and less embarrassed. "I am. And you are Ensign Krysta Verity, navigations officer. I'm sorry I didn't introduce myself to you before now, Ensign, but my duty station is on the other side of the ship, and our rotations were opposite. When you were going off-duty, I was going on. I only managed to find a few hours where you were free when I was, but at those times, you were usually in the gym under the tutelage of your armsmaster."

So, he'd been asking around about her too. She was flabbergasted at the idea that he'd made an effort to seek her out. It was simply mind-boggling to a girl who'd never had much male attention thrown her way.

"I—" She didn't know what to say.

"I have made you uncomfortable, and that was not my intent. I apologize." He stepped back, and it looked like he was going to leave. Suddenly, that was the last thing Krysta wanted. She reached out to stop him, grasping his arm. She'd unthinkingly used her cybernetic arm and immediately pulled back on the power, but it was too late. He stopped dead in his tracks.

"I'm sorry." She released his arm and turned away, tears threatening. How could she be such a fool? She didn't know how to talk to men—especially not ones she found attractive—and this one lit her up like no man ever had before.

She felt a soft touch on her shoulder, just at the join between her cyber parts and her human flesh. "Don't apologize, Ensign. I am the one at fault here. I am too direct. Always have been. But I sensed something in you that resonated with my own experience. I, too, have had limbs replaced. It is not something done often among my people, but my family had access to experimental medical facilities while my mother lived. She was a medical researcher. When I was maimed as a teen, she did all she could to put me back together."

Krysta's spine went rigid with shock, and she turned slowly to face him, meeting his gaze. "You know about my arm?"

"I thought I recognized something familiar in the way you moved and the way the other women worked with you during those gym practices, though I'm sure nobody else would suspect. But then, you incapacitated Navigator Jeviar. All the men talked about it. No one has ever seen such a strong female, even among our race." His eyes twinkled as he made light of something that had worried her to no end. His casual treatment of her differences made her feel much more at ease. Then, a thought occurred to her.

"But you sparred with Henny. If you've got cybernetics too, you could've walloped her. Why didn't you?"

"I have not the finesse with my implants. Your armsmaster is simply too good and too fluid to succumb to brute strength, no matter how powerful."

Krysta felt herself warming to this devastatingly honest man. "She is very talented. I'll never be half the fighter she is."

"Half her skill is more than many warriors ever achieve, so

you should feel proud. You are nimble and strong. I've watched your practices. You never rely on the enhancements of your arm. I suspect it is your secret weapon, no?"

Krysta actually laughed, feeling that comfortable with him. "You're right. I keep it in reserve for when it's needed. Otherwise, I like to be like everyone else."

"Ah, yes," Xeer nodded. "I understand completely. Ensign," he seemed almost shy for a moment, "I would very much like to see you again. Perhaps, you would honor me by sharing a meal as soon as our mutual duties allow it?"

Was he asking her on a date? Krysta could hardly believe it.

"I'd like that," she said, trying to sound casual, fighting the butterflies that started winging around in her stomach.

His eyes lit up, and he seemed encouraged by her shy response. "I live in the palace barracks, so I will be nearby. I've heard they will house you all in the palace, and I believe I'll be assigned to arrange security for some of the ladies of your crew when they venture out on the grounds. I'd like you to feel free to call upon me at any time. It would be my pleasure to show you around the palace."

"I'd like that, too." She sounded like a broken recording, but the butterflies were getting more active the longer he looked at her with those piercing dark eyes. Not only was he handsome, but kind and understanding, as well. And cybernetic. Here was a man who not only understood but shared her affliction. "I don't know what they have scheduled for us, but I'd like to talk more with you, Commander Xeer."

"Please call me Noln. It is my first name. Xeer is my family name."

"But you outrank me." Krysta could have bitten her tongue for pointing out such an obvious thing and ruining the mood. But he laughed, putting her at ease again.

"When we are on duty, I will be happy to give you orders, and my first order would be to call me by name. May I use your name, as well?"

His tone softened, and his gaze held hers with... Was that

hope? Krysta felt like she was tumbling headfirst into the breakers, being swept out to sea by the look in his beautiful, mysterious eyes.

"Yes, Noln. I like the way my name sounds with your accent. It makes it seem special."

"As special as you are, Krysta." He took her hand in his and brought it to his lips, kissing her knuckles as she watched in wonder. He turned her hand over and slipped a small length of data tape into her palm. "My private com nodes. I hope you will make use of them if ever you'd like company."

He'd slipped her his number! Never had a man done something so brazen or intimate, no matter how hard she'd dreamed of just such a thing. And she hadn't even stepped foot off the ship, yet. Would all the jit'suku men be as willing to court a woman with her defects? Judging by the trip here, it seemed unlikely. The members of the jit crew had been respectful, and though many had made overtures to the other women, none had bothered Krysta at all. Only this one had caught her eye, and now, he'd made a move toward her. Krysta decided to bask in the attention. Xeer—make that Noln—was a good man from all she'd seen of his character. She would be happy to share a meal with him. What happened from there, only heaven knew.

Commander Xeer escorted Ensign Verity down the gangplank. Newsbots abounded as did officials who'd come to greet the emperor and his new bride-to-be. Often there would be a priest or two in attendance for a homecoming, but even Xeer was taken aback by the Zenai presence. Warrior priests lined the walkway, all fully armed and ready for battle. It was an honor guard that meant business, and all knew where the Zenai stood in regards to Emperor Tigh. He was one of their own.

Xeer steered the lovely navigations officer to the side area where the rest of her crewmates waited. The males stood behind the women they'd escorted, ringed by warrior priests and high officials, awaiting the emperor and his woman. This was an historic moment for the jit'suku people. Xeer felt proud to be even a small part of it.

He felt even more elated to have finally spoken to the woman who had haunted his dreams since the moment he'd first seen her. He'd spent the past weeks of the voyage learning all he could about her and watching her from afar. He'd almost missed his opportunity, but he'd seized on the absence of her navigations counterpart to speak to her and guide her on her first steps on his world. If he had his way—and if the Lady Goddess so blessed him—Krysta Verity would become Krysta Xeer before too much longer.

A kiss would tell him all he needed to know, but he was too shy to accost such a gentle woman. Plus, she had that cybernetic arm. She could fight him off if he scared her. Even though he could probably overpower her with his own implants, that definitely wasn't the way he wanted to start their relationship.

She seemed so oblivious to her appeal, so innocent and untouched. He thought he understood why, but he'd like to hear about her growing years, her thoughts, her dreams. He'd never before desired to hear such things from the females he bedded, but this woman was different. She might very well be the woman meant for him. That kiss would tell, but he wanted their first kiss to be special. If, as he suspected, it would be but the first of the rest of their lives together, he wanted her to remember it with joy, never fear or confusion.

So, he'd court her. He wouldn't act the barbarian as many of his brethren so often did. He'd give her the human ritual courtship as best he could. He'd gentle her first, then he'd kiss her and discover if she was indeed the woman he hoped she'd be.

*

"Are you ready, my love?" Tigh put his arm around Ginny's waist, tugging her close for a quick moment.

The others had gone ahead, including the last female to

leave the ship, the conscientious doctor. All waited below for them to make an appearance. Tigh and Ginny, flanked by Councilor Torm, who was feeling much better, and a contingent of Hansa's most trusted men. Hansa himself had been sent ahead with his female counterpart to be certain all was secure below.

"I'm ready, I guess." Ginny didn't sound too enthusiastic.

"What is it? Don't fear my people. They will love you once they get to know you."

"It's not that, per se. It's more a feeling of dread in the pit of my stomach. Like life as I knew it is now going to be radically different." She shrugged. "I know it can't be helped, but it's daunting, to say the least. I never expected to be anybody's empress. I never even dreamed of being a ship's captain until the virus left me no choice."

Tigh gathered her close, resting his chin on top of her head. "All is the will of the Goddess. I gave up the empire, only to be called back from the brink of priesthood to make an effort at peace for both our peoples. We're the only two who can do it, Ginny. We've been brought together for the purpose of peace. I can't think of anything more important— except perhaps our love. Even the fate of the empire pales beside that." He leaned down to kiss her, glad to see she understood his half-teasing tone.

"I do love you, Tigh. I never thought I would, but I do."

He caressed her hair. "My love knows no bounds for you, my Velkir. You are magic to me, and you will bring that magic to our children and our people. I believe in you." He kissed her once more then pulled back, searching her eyes. She looked better. "Are you ready to greet the future?"

"With you beside me, I can do anything, Tigh." She clutched his hand as they started down the ramp together, flanked by guards and with Councilor Torm at a discreet distance.

Tigh was impressed with the abundance of his Zenai brothers. He'd never seen so many warrior priests gathered together anywhere but on the sacred mountain. That they'd come to greet the Valkyrie and her crew was significant. In fact, Tigh was amazed to see High Priest Jurdan himself waiting for them in the small clearing set aside for the official welcoming ceremony.

Tigh sank to one knee in front of the high priest. As emperor, the high priest was the only being to whom Tigh would bend his knee, though he'd done something similar with the human leader when he'd surrendered. That act had been noble. This one more ceremonial in nature, though the high priest had always been both friend and teacher to Tigh.

Protocol demanded Tigh show respect to the high priest, but Ginny didn't know any better. She stood at Tigh's side, unsure, he could tell, as her hand trembled in his. He squeezed her fingers to let her know it was her decision. But words would help her understand what was going on, so he spoke to the priest.

"High Priest Jurdan, you honor me and my bride-to-be with your presence at our homecoming." Tigh stood, deciding to gloss over the moment with formal introductions. Why hadn't he considered that Jurdan would come off his mountain for this? "Master, this is Captain Gineva Starbridge, my mate." He kissed her hand, drawing her eyes as he waited to see how Jurdan would react.

The high priest surprised him by sinking to one knee before them, as all the Zenai warrior priests all around did the same. The Zenai bowed to no one. The very idea of it was shocking. Tigh glanced around again, taking in Torm's quickly hidden surprise, as well as the shock on all the jit'suku faces nearby. The human women merely looked curious. They didn't fully understand the import of the priests' actions, but they would before long.

"The prophecy comes to pass," Jurdan intoned, raising his hands, even as he remained on one knee before Tigh and Ginny. Energy crackled in the air as Jurdan drew the power he commanded down to him. "The Velkir have come through adversity to save us all. May the light of the Mother

Goddess prove my words so that all shall know the truth."

For the first time, Tigh grew afraid. The high priest commanded strange and mystical powers that could be dangerous. Tigh had seen Jurdan draw the light of the Goddess before to judge priests who had been accused of breaking their vows in the most heinous ways. The light had flowed through the men, marking only the guilty. Tigh had seen it and marveled at it. And he'd seen it kill. He tugged on Ginny's hand, drawing her close to his side, but it was too late.

Jurdan clapped his hands together, and sparks showered down from above, pouring through the women, lighting them from within as they met the sensation with raised eyebrows, some starting in surprise. Ginny, at his side, glowed with the heavenly light, as did her abdomen. For a split second, Tigh thought he saw the tiny outline of two babies there, nestled below her heart, and all was right with his world. The light of the Goddess didn't harm her. It flowed through her, bathing her in its goodness. She was the Velkir!

As were her crew.

Armsmaster Henny Sonata glowed with the light, at peace in the presence of the Goddess, unlike most of the other women. She neither jumped nor questioned the glowing sparks that suffused her being. Hansa had drawn nearer when he realized what High Priest Jurdan was doing, fearing for his mate, but he needn't have feared.

His dearest Henny was not only a skilled warrioress, the likes of which the jit'suku hadn't seen for many generations, but she was blessed of the Goddess. Hansa stood behind her, basking in the glow that sparked from her and through her, touching him with the same blessing.

Henny shocked him, turning to face him. She smiled and reached for him, pulling him down for a kiss that sealed her light to his inner core, joining them in a way that would unite them forever. At length, she drew back and smiled up at him.

"Do you understand what you've just done, my love?" His

whisper touched them both as they continued to bathe in the light of the Goddess.

She nodded, an unearthly light in her eyes. At that moment, Hansa felt the presence of the Goddess stronger than he ever had before. He sank to one knee, staring up at the face of his beloved, who was no longer only his beloved, but also the Goddess made flesh.

"Together, we will teach new generations of warriors to protect our people." The words issued from Henny's mouth, but Hansa knew they came straight from the deity he served. She tugged him to his feet, proclaiming them equals, though his Henny was still possessed of the Goddess' light. The priests all around regarded her with awe as Hansa spared a glance to their surroundings, ever vigilant.

The light was fading, leaving Henny and Hansa last of all.

Ginny didn't understand what had just happened, but she felt warm and loved—by someone or something beyond her understanding. The light faded, and she was sorry to see it go but reassured by the knowledge that a small part of it resided in her, and in her babies. She looked to her crew, concerned for their welfare and caught Henny's words. Her master-at-arms and friend was acting out of character, and Ginny grew concerned.

Regardless of what protocol demanded, her crew came first. Ginny released Tigh's hand and went over to check on Henny.

"Chief Sonata, are you all right?"

Henny turned to face Ginny, her face still aglow and wearing a broad smile. "Aye, Captain. All is finally right with the world. The teachings of my line will not die with me. They'll live on in our children and for generations to come."

Ginny's gaze went from Henny's ecstatic face to where her hand joined with Hansa's. The big jit armsmaster stood too close to Henny for a mere acquaintance, and the happy, defiant look on his face said he didn't care who knew they were lovers. Ginny had to bite back a smile.

"Your father would be pleased to know his teachings will live on, Chief, and from all I've seen, I think he also would have liked your choice of husband. Congratulations to you both."

Henny actually teared up but was too stoic to let the drops fall.

"Warrior priestess," the high priest intoned from over Ginny's shoulder as he addressed Henny. Jurdan had snuck up on her. The man moved more quietly than even Tigh. "Be you welcome on Zenai Mountain."

"Thank you, sir." Henny clearly didn't know how to address a high priest, but Jurdan didn't seem to mind as he turned his shrewd gaze on the man who stood almost protectively over Henny's shoulder.

"Hansa of Clan Poltar, is this warrior of the Velkir your true mate?"

"She is, Master." Hansa's deep voice rang with pride.

Jurdan smiled then, his old face splitting into a grin of true affection. "You were ever one of our best, Chi'gor Hansa. Your duties as a masked protector are now over. You will, with your mate, train successive generations of warriors, as the Goddess has decreed. I expect to celebrate your mating on the sacred mountain very soon, Master Poltar. You and your mate will always have a place there, in the Warrior Goddess' domain. And she is but the first of the new caste of warrior priestesses heralded by the fulfillment of the ancient prophecy. But that is talk for another time." Jurdan backed off a pace. "Our duty is to first welcome our emperor and his bride-to-be, then to talk of the changes the Goddess' appearance here heralds for all jit'suku." The high priest made a show of respect, though as the most senior servant of the Goddess, he bowed to no man under normal circumstances.

But Henny bowed to the old man in the way of her martial arts tradition, from the waist, with one clenched fist resting in an open hand, signifying respect for the high priest, but not in the kneeling tradition of the jit'suku. Oh, yes, times would be a-changing, Ginny thought as she watched the interaction.

It was then that she became aware of the multitude of newsbots flittering here and there, all seeking some different angle to record the action. They hovered at a distance, but they were there all the same, recording each and every word, from all angles, for posterity.

Something of great significance had just happened here, she knew, but she didn't understand the full extent of it. She'd meant to read more on their Velkir prophecy, but then, she'd been busy with Tigh and then the traitors. She knew they considered the Velkir something special, but she didn't understand all of the implications for her or her crew. It would be best to play it cool until she knew more.

She turned to Tigh, seeing the approval and love in his eyes. It gave her strength and an idea of what to do next. She then turned to face Jurdan.

"Sir," she addressed Jurdan, "my crew and I are honored to be welcomed by you and your brotherhood. We are simple soldiers who have had a long journey to an uncertain future. It's reassuring to have your Lady's blessing and your presence here as we come to the jit'suku galaxy for the first time. May our futures hold friendship and understanding."

Jurdan regarded her for a long moment, until she was almost ready to squirm, but her training and backbone held firm. Then, he smiled. "It is the fulfillment of my life's work to have the Velkir walk among us. You are welcome here, Empress-to-be. As will be your children, the heirs to the empire!"

CHAPTER 11

Cheers met his pronouncement, though they weren't the disorganized accolades of human response. These were shouts made with military precision in the deep voices of the priests and the other believers who'd been invited to witness the historic occasion.

Tigh came up behind Ginny and put one hand on her shoulder as he bent to whisper in her ear. "I knew they would love you as much as I," he said, warming her with both his words and his warm breath on her skin. She fought to suppress the shiver of awareness his touch always stirred as she turned her head to look up into his eyes. He was smiling, love reflecting back at her from his gaze.

He'd warned her that he'd be expected to address the crowd and had even prepared a short speech. Sure enough, there was a podium emblazoned with the imperial seal set up a few feet away. Tigh squeezed her shoulder one last time and headed for the spot, facing the multitude of recorders and bots along with the crowd that had gathered to welcome him home.

"Thank you all for this warm welcome home. Thanks especially to my brothers in the priesthood. I truly did not expect such a grand welcome, though I suspect it is more for my lady and her crew. And it is well deserved, for they not only come in peace to save our future, but they have saved my life and my mission of peace by dealing with traitors sent to destroy myself and my crew." Murmurs went through the assembled crowd of officials and civilians, though the priests and other soldiers were too well disciplined to speak as Tigh went on. "I expect advance reports have already reached some of you. The rest will learn of the way a coward incapacitated me and all the men on board my ship, attempting to turn the women over to Goddess only knows what terrible fate. Thankfully, they underestimated my beloved Velkir. She and her crew took command of the ship while the rest of us were unconscious, won a space battle against three traitorous ships—showing mercy by not destroying them—and had her doctor administer an antidote to revive us. At first, I debated over whether to make this matter public knowledge, but I believe the time for truth in this empire is long past. In short order, I will be making recordings of the action that took place onboard available to you through the news streams. I think you should all see the bravery, skill and heart of your empress-to-be. In that way, I believe you will come to respect and love her and her crew, as I have."

This was all news to Ginny. She felt a little conspicuous, knowing that everyone in the empire would be able to see exactly what she'd said and done during those precious hours when Tigh was unconscious. She thought back quickly over that time and hoped she hadn't said anything that would be embarrassing. But Tigh was right. The jit'suku needed truth more than anything. Only in her conversations with Tigh and the other men on board did she find out that most warriors had no idea Elius planned to release a bioweapon until after it was done. At that moment, Elius had lost the respect of most of his army, but he was still emperor, with enough loyalists who were as crazy as he was to support him. Elius had hidden most of his crimes—perpetrated by the select few who had the same bloodlust he did—from the majority of the jit'suku galaxy.

When she'd discussed this with Tigh, he'd told her that he planned to do things differently. He wanted honesty to be his byword, and she agreed. Still, letting the news air every moment of her life was something she wasn't looking forward to, but in this particular case, she understood. The jits probably had no idea what to expect with her and the rest of her crew. They needed to understand her, and this was perhaps the best way to accomplish that quickly. There was no truth like a person's behavior when under fire. Soldiers bonded fast under those conditions, and a large portion of jit society was based on warrior ways, so showing them how she captained in a crisis was a good way for them to take her measure.

She'd still have those who hated humans and distrusted her, she was certain, but any fair-minded man would at least give her a chance after seeing how well she and the crew worked together in such a difficult situation. At least that's what she hoped for. It was the best possible outcome as far as she could see—a lessening of hostility toward her presence and perhaps even the beginnings of acceptance.

Tigh was still speaking, moving on to more personal matters.

"We will celebrate our mating one week hence with a galaxy-wide holiday. We'll dispatch credits from the imperial treasury to each and every citizen of the empire to commemorate our happiness." Again, that deep, organized cheer sounded from the assembled guests. "And I will confirm what the high priest alluded to earlier. My lady is already with child. Most likely, twins, in fact." The cheer was longer, this time, as Ginny blushed and smiled, her eyes only for Tigh as he gazed back at her. She couldn't resist the urge to put one hand over her stomach, where her babies rested content for the moment.

Tigh finished his remarks and headed back to her. They'd discussed whether she'd want to speak before they landed, and she demurred. She'd wanted to get the lay of the land here before she got up in front of everyone and made a fool of herself. Tigh had assured her they'd all love her no matter what she said, but she rather thought that was an overly-optimistic opinion.

Tigh headed for the line of vehicles that waited. He held back a moment to invite Hansa and Henny to ride with them, and Ginny was glad. She wanted to ask Henny about that weird moment back there.

The cars were designed to allow people to see the imperial party as they made their way to the palace. The landing site was inside palace grounds, but far enough away from the palace proper to limit noise and assure security. The cars were transparent on top, but secure.

Tigh let Ginny precede him into the car then sat beside her. Henny and Hansa followed, sitting opposite them.

As soon as the hatch shut, Ginny turned to Tigh. "Can we talk in here? I mean, can anyone hear us?"

"We're secure, my love. Everyone can see us," he gestured to the fleet of newsbots flying alongside and over the car, "but nobody can listen in."

"Good. Then, can anyone tell me exactly what just happened back there? Henny, were you actually... uh... possessed for a minute there?"

Henny's laughter rang out, putting Ginny more at ease with the strange happenings. Regardless of what had happened, this was still Henny, her long-time friend.

"I guess that's as good a word for it as any, but I was definitely feeling something there when the jit Goddess spoke through me. Weird, huh?"

"You can say that again." Ginny sat back in the plush seat. "I can't believe you're so calm about it, Hen. That was some strange stuff."

"It was, but it felt... right somehow, Gin. I don't pretend to understand it, but the Goddess is amazing. She's pure and good, and she welcomed us. You felt that, didn't you?"

"I did," Ginny admitted.

"It was a miracle," Tigh chimed in. "I've seen the Goddess' light used to both bless and burn. It can kill if you

Henny.

BIANCA D'ARC

are not of true heart."

"Really?" Ginny turned to him. "Then, it was a test?"

"Of sorts." Tigh looked uncomfortable. "I had no idea Master Jurdan was going to do that or I wouldn't have allowed it, but I guess in hindsight, he needed to know exactly who and what he was dealing with. He's waited his entire life to see the fulfillment of the ancient prophecy. More generations than I can count have held that responsibility sacred. For you to come now, when we're on the brink of destruction—and for you to truly be the Velkir of legend—will give us renewed hope. Master Jurdan needed to know if he was indeed, in the presence of true Velkir before he could know for certain. But I'll not thank him for having put you and your crew in danger."

Tigh's hand rested over hers, and she saw the fire in his eyes, along with the worry he'd felt when he realized what Jurdan was doing.

"It's all right, Tigh. I expect that won't be the last test we're subjected to. I didn't expect this to be easy, but for the sake of both our peoples, it must be done."

"And for us, Gineva. Don't forget us."

"How could I?" She cupped his cheek, smiling up into his eyes.

A throat clearing across the small space of the car drew her back. Henny was shaking her head with laughter. "You two really have it bad, don't you?"

Ginny liked her friend's teasing. It reminded her of her younger days, when she'd been free to just be a girl and not had the responsibility of a starship captain or empress-to-be.

"As if you and Hansa aren't making goo-goo eyes at each other at every opportunity." She teased Henny right back.

"I object to the term goo-goo eyes," Hansa said in his droll voice. "I don't even know what it means, but it doesn't sound very manly."

The women laughed outright as even Tigh chuckled. "You have good instincts, my friend," Ginny said after a moment. "Now, why didn't I know about this budding romance?

138

Henny, I thought you were my best friend."

"Well, gee, let me think… Maybe it's because your head was so in the clouds over your own imminent marriage that I never quite found the right moment to tell you? Nah. To be honest, I wasn't sure what we had until the big lug fainted dead away at my hatch. I knew then, that I'd be broken forever if he died."

"Oh, Henny." Ginny reached across and took her friend's hand, squeezing once in comfort. "I'm happy for you both." She included Hansa in her wishes as she drew her hand back.

"Thank you, ma'am," Hansa said, drawing Henny's hand into his own. "I have not yet thanked you and your crew for saving our lives and our mission. Blessings upon you, my lady." He nodded to Ginny then took Henny's hand to his lips for a gentle kiss. "And you, my love."

"So, you are chi'gor?" Tigh asked Hansa unexpectedly. Hansa looked pained for a brief moment but quickly recovered.

"I was, but you heard the Master. That's over now," Hansa replied.

"What is chi'gor?" Ginny asked.

"The title literally translates to 'masked protector'. It is a secret order of the priesthood. Only the most skilled are asked to pose as less than they truly are so that they may be placed with those who may someday need their aid," Tigh explained. "It seems my friend, Hansa of Clan Poltar, has been my shadow all these years as part of his duty. Am I not right, old friend?"

"It was always more than duty, my liege. I valued your friendship and still do, if you can ever forgive my deception. When the high priest first approached me with the task, I was both honored and afraid that it would drive a wedge between us if you ever discovered that protecting you was something I'd been asked to do by the brotherhood."

Tigh was silent a long moment, gazing consideringly at his friend. "I have one question."

"Anything, my liege."

"How often did you let me win when we sparred?"

A grin stole across Hansa's angular face. "Not as often as I'd like, I'll admit. We are fairly matched, my liege."

Tigh sighed. "Chi'gor—now Master Poltar—we're alone here. Why are you suddenly using my title to come between us? Don't you wish to still be friends?"

Hansa's face went blank. "I wasn't sure— I didn't want to presume— Dammit, Tigh, after learning I'd lied by omission to you all these years, I wasn't sure you'd still want to talk to me, much less retain our friendship."

"Then, be at ease, my friend. All I want is a chance to see which of us is really the more skilled. You're a Master now, after all. If I can beat you in a fair fight, I can earn my own ranking."

"You're on, Tigh. And I believe you'll earn that rank before long. You've always been one of Jurdan's favorites and not just because of your pretty face. As you know, the high priest values anyone who can come close to kicking his backside across the training hall, and you've come closer than most."

Both men laughed, and the easy camaraderie was restored between them. Ginny was glad of it. If her best friend was going to be married to one of Tigh's men, it would help if they were all on speaking terms.

The palace was a dream. Soaring towers gave way to sharply angled roofs and architecture that was distinctly not human, but welcoming all the same. Ginny liked the look of the place and was impressed by its beauty.

"What do you think, my love?" Tigh bent to speak into her ear as he stood behind her on the landing pad, looking up at the main entrance hall.

"I don't know what I expected, but it wasn't anything like this. It's beautiful."

"I'm glad you think so." She could hear the pride in his voice, as well as the true happiness he felt in finally being home. "For now, I'll have quarters assigned within the royal apartments for your crew. It's the most secure portion of the palace, in addition to being the most beautiful. I thought, for the time being, you'd want your friends and family nearby."

"Thank you, Tigh. That'll be perfect."

The doors opened as they approached, and they were greeted by a double line of servants standing at attention like soldiers on review. Ginny was duly impressed by their starch and order, every servant a strong example of jit'suku genetics in male form. Only one old woman stood in a place of honor off to one side, and Tigh went to her as he greeted his people with handshakes and nods.

He stopped before the lady and took both of her wrinkled hands gently in his. He leaned in and placed a soft kiss on her weathered cheek, sparking a smile.

"Grandmother, I've returned with my mate. Thank you for being here to greet her. May I present Captain Gineva Magdalena Starbridge, my wife-to-be."

The old lady stood with all the grace and style of a former empress and looked Ginny over with measuring eyes. Ginny wanted to squirm under that perusal but resisted. The old woman was a surprise. Tigh hadn't talked about his grandmother at all. Ginny knew that some older jit'suku women had survived the mutated virus, but she'd had no idea any of the royal family had been so lucky.

"Is she your true mate?" The old woman demanded in a leathery voice.

"She is, Grandmother. And she carries our children, even now."

She raised one eyebrow as she turned her gaze back to her grandson. "Children? Humans breed more than one at a time?"

Tigh chuckled. "Twins, grandmother. You know very well that humans breed very much like ourselves. I was a twin. Ginny has twins in her family history. Her mother is a twin. In fact, her mother and aunt are right behind us, as is her cousin. They came with us to attend the marriage ceremony."

"She comes from good family?" his grandmother persisted

with skepticism in her tone.

"Grandmother." Tigh sounded like a boy teasing his parent, and Ginny warmed to the relationship she sensed between the two. More than anything, she felt like she was being put on by the older woman, but she'd wait to see if her instincts were right. "She's a Starbridge. A direct descendant of Diva and John whom our ancestor Tren entertained so many years ago."

Wise old eyes turned back to her. "You're one of those Starbridges. I see the distinctive eyes you share with your ancestress. She very nearly became empress, but she was not a true mate to Tren. Be welcome here, Gineva. I've long desired my grandson to find his true mate. In you, I hope he will have that and more."

The old lady extended one wrinkled hand, and Gineva put out hers to meet it, smiling. "Thank you, ma'am. It's an honor to meet you."

"To be sure, I'll be glad to have female company, once again. You say your mother and aunt accompanied you?"

"Yes, ma'am, and my cousin, Amelia, plus my crew. Ten women, plus myself."

The old woman's gaze went from her to Tigh. "It's a start. You've done well, grandson. Better than I expected, in fact. The Lady Goddess smiled on your path to allow you to find your true mate at such a time."

The former empress looked downward, and Ginny was surprised to find a young boy of about four or five years old tugging on the old lady's skirts. Since Tigh's grandmother was clearly not strong enough to lift the little boy, Ginny bent down to him, smiling as he stuck his thumb in his mouth.

"Hello, little one. My name is Ginny. What's yours?"

"This is Mattie, my newest page." The former empress bent down beside Ginny and reached out to tuck a strand of curly blond hair behind the boy's ear. "He doesn't talk much yet, but we're working on it, aren't we, Mattie?"

The little boy nodded, big blue eyes wide with interest as he looked at Ginny. She was enchanted by the boy and wondered with a pang what had happened to his family. It was likely his mother had been among the victims of the virus. Ginny sent a questioning look to the former empress. The old woman shook her head, and Ginny knew her fears were confirmed.

"It's nice to meet you, Mattie. I'm sure we'll be seeing a lot of each other."

Tigh's grandmother patted the little boy on the back, sending him back to the corner behind her where a small contingent of young boys of various ages stood. Ginny hadn't seen them before, but now, she realized they all wore a sort of uniform bearing the imperial crest. They were probably all 'pages', she realized, motherless boys the former empress had taken charge of. Immediately, Ginny's heart softened toward the old woman.

"As you'll learn, my grandmother increases the number of imperial pages every day," Tigh teased the old woman.

"It's my prerogative to have as much or as little help as I desire, Tigh," the former empress reminded her grandson.

"I believe I can assist you, ma'am," Ginny said, "if you find yourself with extra pages. My family, crew and I have missed having youngsters around."

Tigh's grandmother beamed at her as she took Ginny's arm, leading her away from the main hall toward a side corridor. "I believe we're going to get along very well, indeed, Captain."

Tigh's grandmother accompanied them to the family portion of the palace, making idle small talk as they walked along beautifully decorated corridors, accompanied by an honor guard of men who left them at the entrance to the family's private sector. As soon as they were alone in the dowager's sitting room, she turned shrewd eyes on Tigh.

"Now, tell me the truth, boy. This mating. Is it just a ruse to make this more palatable for the masses, or is it true?"

Tigh pulled Ginny into him, his arm tight around her waist as they faced his grandmother together. "The Goddess truly blessed us, Grandmother, and if you don't believe me, ask your friend, Jurdan. He subjected my true mate to the light of the Goddess before I even knew what he intended. Thankfully, she passed the test, as did her crew. Grandmother, they truly are the Velkir, and Ginny truly is my mate."

Tears gathered in the old woman's eyes. Ginny was touched by the display of emotion. She moved out of Tigh's arms and took his grandmother's hand, hoping to reassure her.

"I love your grandson, ma'am. I wouldn't lie about that."

"Bless you, Gineva. You lighten my heart."

Tigh moved forward and cupped his grandmother's cheek. "Rest easy, Nana. We wouldn't lie about mating, though I was prepared to take any woman who would have me when I arrived in the human galaxy. But then, I saw Ginny, and I knew, from the moment I saw her, she was special. I subjected her to the nij'ta not five minutes later, and that's when I knew she was destined for me, though she made me work for her compliance, courting her in the human way."

"Good for you, Gineva. It's not good for a man to have everything handed to him. Even an emperor should have to work for things, from time to time. Though, of all the emperors I've known, Tigh is the least pretentious. Even my own beloved Theotren always took too much for granted."

Ginny realized then, that this woman wasn't Tigh's grandmother. If she'd been married to Emperor Theotren, she was the Empress Rilanda, Tigh's great-grandmother!

"You've worked it out, have you?" Empress Rilanda smiled at Ginny as she sat down in an overstuffed chair. Tigh moved to a sideboard and poured three glasses of what looked like some kind of wine. He served his grandmother first, then Ginny, and kept the final glass for himself. "I helped raise Tigh and Elius, just as I helped raise their father, Renalt. There's not much for old empresses to do when their husbands die and their sons take over. Tigh still calls me Nana in private, but in public, I prefer 'Grandmother'. I need no reminder that I am 'great'." The old lady chuckled as she sipped from her glass.

"I understand, ma'am. I never knew my great-grandmother, but my own grandmother preferred not to hear that word. She said it made her feel old. So, we called her Nonny," Ginny admitted as Tigh urged her to sit. "This isn't alcoholic, is it?" she asked him, referring to the glass she held.

"Barely," he admitted. "But it's safe for the babies, if that's what you're asking. I would never give you anything that could hurt them. Try it. It's a drink first bottled for women's tastes, but I like it too. Nana served it to Elius and I when we were just teens."

Ginny took a cautious sip and was pleased by the burst of fruity flavor that hit her tongue. "It's delicious."

CHAPTER 12

Tigh grinned at her, as did his grandmother. They spent the next hour getting acquainted. Tigh checked discreetly on the arrivals of the rest of Ginny's crew members, assured by his household staff that they'd all been welcomed and shown to their rooms along with their bags. The ladies were reported to have declined the help of adult male servants, but without fail, each allowed some of the dowager's page boys to help them unpack. He was warmed by the thought. Those little boys had flocked to his Nana—the one rare source of maternal presence in their short, troubled lives. It was a good sign that the Velkir seemed to understand and were already showing compassion for the youngsters.

"Your crew are unpacking in their quarters, Ginny," Tigh said as he returned to the ladies. He could tell his Nana was tired, though the old lady would never admit to any such weakness. "I think we should do the same. I had your belongings moved to my suite. I hope you don't mind. We're not married according to your laws yet, but mated pairs in our society are not kept apart."

"I don't mind, Tigh. I came here to be with you." Ginny rose, following his lead beautifully. She tucked her smaller hand in his. "Will we see you at dinner, ma'am? I hear there's a celebration planned."

"I wouldn't miss it." The dowager smiled broadly.

They took their leave in short order, and Tigh's pulse leapt as he drew nearer the emperor's suite. They'd have an hour or two to themselves, and he knew just how he wanted to spend that time.

He stopped beside a large doorway attended by two liveried soldiers. He bent down and swept Ginny into his arms, picking her up before nodding to the men to activate the portal.

"What?" she asked breathlessly as he hoisted her into the air. She had a smile on her face but was clearly caught by surprise.

"I read up on your customs, my love. I am merely carrying my bride over the threshold of our new home. It's supposed to bring good luck. Personally, I think we can use all of that we can get."

Ginny laughed as he crossed into the emperor's suite. He was glad he could make her smile. He lived for her smiles.

"Oh, Tigh, this is beautiful."

Tigh set her down and looked around the front room of the suite. It was the one place he'd left intact after returning to the palace. It was his one reminder of happier times with his brother and sister-in-law. Tigh remembered those first few months after Elius had taken the throne and how excited Marla had been to redecorate everywhere in the palace, including this room—the drawing room to Tigh's old suite.

Marla had been friend to both brothers as they grew up. She'd probably hoped to marry Tigh at one time, but when he decided to follow the path of the Zenai priest and give up the throne, she'd turned to Elius, instead. Tigh didn't mind her defection. They'd been good friends. Nothing more. He'd kissed her once, and that one time was enough to tell him she was not his destined mate. He didn't hold her desire to be empress against her. She was a good woman at heart, though a little more hungry for power than Tigh.

Then again, it seemed everyone was hungrier for power than Tigh himself. Perhaps that was the distinction that would make him a good emperor. Goddess willing, he'd give it his best shot. Memories came rushing back as he looked at the room Marla had been so proud of.

"I had a lot of the rooms cleared out when I came back to the palace. All except for basic furnishings in most of the suites have been removed to storage. You can rummage around in the storage areas for any pieces you might like, or commission new things from artisans. Whatever you like." He picked up a trinket Marla had put in the room to make it look more lived in than the rest of his suite. He distinctly remembered her teasing him about how stark his tastes were. He'd appreciated her efforts, though the room had never felt comfortable to him with all the artificial decorative items left lying around that he had no use for. "I left this one room as it was to remind me, but it's not necessary now." Tigh tugged Ginny back into his arms and nuzzled her neck from behind. "I want you to redecorate the whole palace, Gin. I want you to put your mark on this place and make it a home for us. This room included. I don't need any more reminders of the past. We have a future to nurture now." He let her go and walked toward a set of doors that led to another part of the large suite.

"I'll be happy to redecorate, if that's what you really want."

"As you can see from the rest of this suite, my idea of decoration is sorely lacking. If you don't take this place in hand, it'll look more like a monk's cell than an emperor's home." He laughed as she joined him at the door. The bedroom was indeed, sparsely decorated, with only Tigh's ceremonial swords draped above the large bed that dominated the center of one wall. The bed linens and hangings around the room were red and black—the colors of the Zenai priesthood. "My sister-in-law, Marla, went in for all kinds of frills and ruffles. While I wasn't fond of that, even I can see this is too stark for a lady."

Ginny snorted. "I'm not exactly the frill-and-ruffle type myself, in case you haven't noticed."

"Oh, I noticed." Tigh looked her up and down as she stood at his side. He licked his lips. She looked good enough to eat.

The nervous fire that flared in her eyes was enough to set his hunting instincts on full alert. She backed away, and he moved after her, quietly stalking her as she moved closer to the bed, leading him just where he wanted her.

"Those are beautiful swords. Ornamental?" She turned a questioning, challenging gaze to him.

Tigh's lips spread in a predatory grin. "Functional, as well. They have passed down the centuries through my line from emperor to emperor. They've been used in battle more than a few times and have seen their share of blood. I keep them nearby to guard my sleep. It's something quite a few of my ancestors have done, though my brother thought it a silly tradition. Too bad, for they might've saved him when his wife killed him in his sleep."

"That wasn't here?" Ginny looked appalled, and he was glad he'd upset the floorplan of the palace when he reclaimed it.

"No, love. There are no ghosts in these rooms. They were my quarters even before I left for the Zenai mountain. They were kept empty while I was gone, and since I returned, the only things I added to this suite were those swords. They'd been hanging in the audience hall when Elius was emperor, but I wanted them nearby, as my father had kept them close. They bring back good memories of my parents and my childhood. They're what inspired me to train with the Zenai in the first place. I used to sneak into my parents' room during the day while they were both busy and just stare at them, wondering what tales they could tell."

"That's a nice memory, Tigh." Ginny moved back to him. "I'm sorry for all you've lost. I know how it feels, if that's any consolation."

He tugged her close, burying his face in her hair, inhaling her luscious scent. "It is, my love. Though I could wish that neither of us had been through such sorrow, I'm glad for it in a way, because it brought us together. I wouldn't want to have lived this lifetime without you."

"You say the sweetest things, my liege." She blinked up at him, teasing him with her saucy glances.

Tigh pinched her bottom, liking the way she squeaked and tried to move back, but he didn't let her get far. He herded her toward the bed, sweeping her legs out from under her when she was close enough so she fell backward onto the plush mattress.

"Strip, slave girl. Then attend me."

"My liege?" She blinked up at him, playing along.

"You heard me, girl. Undress yourself, then me. I'm impatient tonight. Don't make me wait or you'll feel the consequences."

Ginny knelt up on the bed, sliding her nimble fingers to the closures of her clothing, undoing each catch slowly while she teased him with her eyes. "What sort of consequences, my liege?"

"You're tempting fate, my dear. Tease me much longer, and you'll find out firsthand."

"Do you promise?" When she licked her lips, he knew she was playing the same game and loving every minute of it.

This was something new for them—a foray into fantasy where he could dominate his powerful mate. It was something he needed. Most jit'suku males were dominant by nature, though human females weren't always suited to the kind of submission most jit males wanted from them. Tigh had been willing to take whatever Ginny would give him, and he had no complaints, but she'd yet to give him that final, total, complete trust that would state more clearly than anything else her love and utter trust in him. It was something he discovered he needed, much to his surprise, before he tied his life to hers in front of their people. This moment out of time was an epiphany for him—for them—though she didn't realize it yet.

With a growl, he joined her on the bed, rough, yet mindful of her delicate condition, as she jokingly called it. He'd never hurt her or the babies, but he would discover the limits of her trust—her love—for him. It was suddenly something more important than anything else.

Tigh would have stopped to wonder why now, but the light of the Goddess pulsed its demand. It hadn't quite fled either of them, though neither would realize that until much later. They came together with sparks showering from where they touched. Tigh grabbed her wrists, locking their lips together in an act of domination and love that merged his breath with hers until he didn't know where he left off and she began.

And it was only the beginning.

He pushed her down on the soft mattress, pinning her wrists on either side of her head, kissing her with all the pent-up passion in him. When he let her go, it wasn't far. He still held her wrists but levered up a short distance to look down into her smoldering eyes.

"You don't obey very well for a slave girl."

"Good thing, since I only answer to a man who can master me. So far, no one has." She lay down the gauntlet, playing the game as he'd hoped she would. His vixen of a mate was up for anything, it seemed.

"That's all over, now. I'm the only man who will claim you," he placed a quick love bite on her jaw, "and master you," another bite near her collarbone, "and have you." He zeroed in on her breast, this time, making her yelp, though not with pain. She was surprised more than anything, if he judged her tone correctly. A quick glance into her eyes reassured him that he hadn't given her anything she didn't want or couldn't handle. "For the rest of your life."

She moaned as he returned his attention to her other breast, sucking and laving the taut peak with a slightly rougher touch than he'd ever given her before. She spasmed in his arms with need, and he knew she liked it.

But the game wasn't over, yet. Not even nearly.

With only a small bit of reluctance, he rolled off her to sit on the side of the high bed.

"Stand here, girl. Between my legs." She complied readily, standing there, watching him with curious, excited eyes. "You are disobedient and willful." He tugged at the closures on her clothing as he spoke, stripping her with rough movements that had her naked in short order. She stood before him in a puddle of her clothes, her lush body making his mouth water, her luscious scent filling his nostrils with yearning. "Turn," he instructed, twirling a finger in the air as he looked his fill at her voluptuous form. She complied, but slowly, so he swatted her fleshy ass, satisfied when she jumped and turned a bit faster.

He stopped her when she faced completely away from him, cupping her ass in both hands and squeezing. She had a bitable ass that was just begging for his hands, his mouth, his teeth. He leaned forward and nipped her, pleased when she jerked and her breathing came faster.

"Bend over, slave girl. Show me your charms."

She hesitated long enough to earn another soft whack on her quivering cheeks, but eventually, she bent from the waist, revealing a thin strip of pink between her creamy thighs.

"Spread your legs, girl, and lean all the way forward. Touch your toes and show me your pussy." He nudged her bare feet with his booted toe, forcing her feet wider apart as her creamy center was slowly revealed. "That's nice, slave girl," he said approvingly as he feasted his eyes on the look of her and felt the satisfaction of her compliance. Would she be as up for what he planned next? Tigh would take it in slow stages, both to savor her surrender and to secure her participation. They both liked it when things progressed from spark to flame in the fullness of time.

Tigh reached out and stroked through the wetness already gathered between her thighs with one finger as she shuddered. He brought his other hand forward and used his fingers to spread her inner lips, revealing the tight hole that wept in anticipation of his claiming. Spearing inside slowly with one finger, he felt her whole body tremble in awareness of that most intimate touch. He felt an answering tremble in his own body as she stood there and took what he'd give her, a willing slave to his passion and her own.

Rubbing lightly, he began to stroke inside her core with deliberate movements while his other hand gathered the moisture that spilled from her needy core and moved upwards toward the little opening that teased him so. She shied away when he pushed inside, but he pulled the finger from her pussy and slapped her inner thigh. Just once. Until she stilled.

"You're my slave girl, remember. I can do with you as I will." Tigh renewed his efforts, pushing one finger into the small pucker of her ass while she stood there, taking it. "Repeat my words, slave girl. I can do with you as I will." His other hand hadn't returned to her pussy, and he used it to slap her once more as he pushed that lone finger a little deeper into her anus. "Say it, girl," he demanded.

Another whack brought forth the words he so wanted to hear.

"You can use me as you will." Her breath came in pants as he slid his finger all the way inside her, rocking only slightly as she got used to the feel of him.

"You're a good little slave girl," he praised her as he leaned forward to nip her ass. It was just too tempting to resist. "For that, I will give you a reward."

Tigh pulled away, taking only a moment to drop his pants low enough to release his cock and balls. A second later, he was impaled in the tight depths of her cunt, gripping her hips with tense hands as he began moving in a hard rhythm that brought her to an explosive climax in mere moments.

But he wasn't done with her yet.

As she went limp, he caught her in his arms and lifted her onto the bed, positioning her on her back with her arms and legs spread wide. Tigh looked around, improvising by using the ties that held back the bed curtains to tie her to the four corners of the bed, spread eagled for his pleasure.

She didn't object, letting him do what he liked without any protest. In fact, he saw only the glimmer of interest and returning passion in her beloved eyes as he finished securing the last knot.

He rid himself of his own clothes then lay at her side, running one hand over her curves, as if memorizing each and every dimple and rise. He lingered on her sensitive breasts for a long time before settling between her legs. He'd left plenty of give in the ties around her ankles so he could bend her knees and position her the way he wanted.

"I will have the imperial craftsmen make me a plug for this pretty ass of yours, slave girl. What do you think of that?"

She sucked in a breath before answering. "Whatever you desire, my liege."

"Ah." He smiled up at her as he fingered her slit. "That was the right answer. You have earned another reward."

He leaned closer still, inhaling the sweet perfume of her excitement. He had to taste her! Using his tongue, he traced a path around her nubbin and down to her opening, sweeping inside for a few pulsating licks before pulling out and sweeping up to her clit once more. He repeated the process several times before she came with a keening cry that he felt in his very bones.

He wanted to claim her like nothing else in the world, but he also wanted this moment—this breakthrough in their relationship to last as long as he could possibly make it last. His time was drawing near though. He couldn't hold out much longer without exploding.

"Now, slave girl. What was that you were saying about never having been mastered? I believe you have revised your opinion, haven't you?"

She didn't answer fast enough, which gave him an excuse to slap her tender pussy. She squirmed at the sting, but her cunt wept fresh juice for him, betraying how much she liked it.

"Who is your master, girl? I won't ask again." While he spoke, he poked two fingers into her, stroking in and out as she began to thrash in excitement on the wide bed.

"You are." Her words were a mere whisper.

"What was that? I must have it louder, girl."

"You are." The breathy sound was better, but still not loud enough to suit him. He removed his fingers and slapped her eager pussy.

"You are!" She screamed as he levered himself over her and pushed deep inside, sliding home within her as her excitement level went higher still.

"And who am I?" He panted as he pounded into her, his balls slapping her ass on every stroke.

"My master," she sobbed as she neared her peak. He moved higher and faster as he felt her inner muscles clench. She came on a screaming sob. "Tigh!"

He answered her passion with his own, bathing her core with his seed as they came together in bliss. He'd never felt so close to another human being—not even to Ginny. Something had been riding them both, pushing them toward this culmination, and he couldn't say he regretted any of it. He'd needed her submission, though he hadn't quite recognized that need fully in himself. He'd thought the Zenain training would help him be more tolerant of her human independence than most other jit'suku men would have been, but when it came right down to it, he was just as primitive as his brethren jit'suku. Thank the Goddess, his woman was understanding and adventurous.

Tigh rose up on his elbows, gazing down at the woman he loved beyond all others still beneath him. "Are you all right?"

"Mmm," she answered with a broad smile. "Never better." She wiggled her hips, drawing aftershocks where they were still joined. "Master." Her gaze teased him, her words played with him, but her heart was his alone. He knew that beyond any doubt whatsoever. His strong mate would submit only to him.

Tigh kissed her, thanking her without words for her understanding. "I love you, Gineva Magdalena Starbridge."

*

Dinner that night was a grand celebration, and if the emperor and empress-to-be were a little late to the start of the feast, that was to be expected. The jit'suku males of all castes of their society waited patiently for their new emperor, though they shared more than a few knowing looks and ribald jokes between them as they waited.

The human women were given places of honor. Tonight, they would be formally introduced to the emperor's advisors and the rest of the imperial court. There was a large contingent of Zenai warrior priests present, as well—more than had been seen at an imperial feast than at any time in recent memory. The high priest himself sat at the head table, overseeing all in his wise, silent way.

CHAPTER 13

When Ginny and Tigh arrived—late, as was becoming usual—to the state dinner, it was to find everyone already there, waiting for them. Ginny intercepted a few knowing, teasing looks from her crew while some of the men looked downright envious as she noticed their gazes locked on Tigh.

They made their way to the dais through the throng standing in respect. When they sat, so did everyone else. Ginny was used to a certain amount of military precision and the accolades due as captain of her own ship, but this was several steps above that, though Tigh was a lot less formal once they all sat down. He encouraged everyone to eat, drink and be merry, but Ginny still got the feeling a lot of the men were watching her and her crew with a weird mixture of fear, respect and, in a few cases, repressed hostility. But to a man, the warrior priests spread strategically around the huge room gave off a totally different vibe. They seemed invigorated, vigilant, and eager in a way she couldn't quite explain, but it felt protective to her, which was reassuring.

Ginny tried to keep an eye out for her crew, but most seemed to be well entertained by the men sitting around them. The high priest was sitting next to Henny and Hansa, sharing conversation from time to time, mostly about Henny's family history and fighting tradition. No big surprise there. But seated next to them, farther down the table, truly was a surprise. Krysta had the full attention of Xeer, one of the men Ginny had gotten to know a little aboard Tigh's ship, though she'd had no idea there was any interest in that direction. In fact, Krysta was one of the few women who never spoke about men or seemed the least bit interested, but that looked to have changed, now. She laughed with Xeer more freely than Ginny had ever seen Krysta behave, and Xeer seemed to be well and truly smitten.

Tiggy was chatting with a trio of older jit'suku men, and Sally had taken the seat next to the dowager empress. The two women talked quietly, and Ginny knew Sally's natural reserve led her to sit back and watch while the former empress' age probably held her back from more boisterous participation in the feast. They were good company for each other, for the moment. Ginny shot Sally an inquiring look and received the 'all clear' hand signal in return. As she thought, Sally was enjoying her talk with the elderly woman, which gave her the added chance of watching the proceedings without really needing to participate in a more vocal way.

Cat was sitting with Councilor Torm, probably still keeping an eye on the old man who'd taken the poisoning a lot worse than the younger crewmen. But Torm had included a few younger men in their small group, and they were talking medicine when Ginny managed to overhear a few snippets of their conversation. Justina and Penny both had a contingent of younger jit'suku men vying for their attention near the end of the huge banquet table, and were enjoying the attention from what Ginny could see. That left her mother, aunt and young cousin, who sat together, garnering a great deal of attention, though few men dared to speak with them.

"Why are they staring at my mother and aunt like that?" Ginny asked Tigh in a whisper when she had a chance to speak to him privately.

Tigh looked up, glancing around unobtrusively. "I think it's probably a combination of factors. First, they are twins. Jit'suku females can have twin males, but never twin females.

It is a rare, once-in-a-century happening among my people. To see two identical women isn't something they're used to. Also, one of them is your mother. They're probably afraid of offending either one of them, and thereby offending you. It wouldn't be good to start off on the wrong foot with the new empress—or her mother—now would it?"

She chuckled as he teased her, but she knew there was some element of truth in his words. "I didn't know that about female twins being so rare here. Do you think it's wise to parade them around together? Doesn't that sort of remind everyone that we're human?"

"My love," Tigh brought her hand to his lips for a brief kiss, "there's no hiding the fact that you're human. They're just going to have to get used to it. The sooner the better, is my belief."

"I guess you're right, but I can't help but worry that I've made my family targets by bringing them here."

"Perhaps, but they would be targets in your galaxy, as well as here, now that you've been identified as my mate. Better that they're here, under our watchful eyes. I don't think my brethren among the Zenai will let any harm come to any female associated with the Velkir, and you are their leader."

Ginny chuckled. "I think Henny is in charge of the whole Velkir thing now, don't you?"

Tigh looked down the long table to where Henny sat talking to the high priest. "Not necessarily. She is almost certainly the teacher foretold in our prophecies, but she does not lead the Velkir. That is your duty, and one you have performed for years already. Your crew look to you for direction, Ginny. You will still fulfill that role, even though you no longer operate within the confines of a starship. Your ladies love you as both leader and friend. I would hazard to say, you are part of their family, as they are part of yours."

"You're right." Ginny regarded him with tears in her eyes that she refused to let fall. "You're more perceptive than I gave you credit for, Tigh. Forgive me. Most human males would never have realized how close we are or put it just that way."

"Don't give me too much credit." Tigh chuckled. "Most jit'suku men wouldn't understand it either, but most warriors would have some idea. And the warrior priests, most certainly. Our training is deeper, more emotional than the others. We are trained to take all factors into consideration, including the relationship that often develops between a beloved leader and his men. Or, in this case, a remarkable captain and her crew." He tipped his head to her in respect, and she did likewise.

"Speaking of remarkable, I can't believe you were once one of these grim-faced priests, though I see the same spark of intelligence and observation in their eyes. Henny told me what she knew about your Zenai friends, but seeing them in the flesh is, I'll admit, intimidating."

"Never fear any Zenai, my love. You are Velkir. Each and every one of them would die to protect you and your ladies. For example…"

Tigh looked around the room, searching for something. His eyes lit when he spied one particular priest, and he stood, stalking down the table to everyone's surprise. Ginny watched him head for the priest, who stood when Tigh reached him, a broad smile lighting his swarthy face. Tigh pulled the man into a huge hug and pounded him on the back, and the priest did the same.

Tigh brought him back to the high table, motioning Ginny to the back of the dais that was only a foot or so off the polished stone floor. The meal progressed in the hall as Tigh commanded his people to continue eating, but he dragged the poor priest away from his food and toward Ginny. She hopped down from the low dais to make it easier on the man, though like Tigh, he stood head and shoulders above her. She probably still would have had to look up, even if she'd stayed on the dais, she thought with a shake of her head.

"Ginny, my love, this is my good friend Tolo, warrior priest of the Zenai. He was promoted while I was away and is now a third-level novitiate, the highest level before taking vows. We trained together for many years on the mountain."

Tigh kept one hand on the man's shoulder, and it was apparent they were close. It was just as apparent that Tolo was uncertain how to greet her. She decided to take matters into her own hands, so to speak, by taking his hand for a good old human handshake. He looked at her with bemusement in his dancing green eyes but smiled broadly and returned the gesture.

"It's nice to meet you."

"My lady, it is an honor and a privilege to meet you."

He looked like he wanted to bow, but Tigh still had him by the shoulder. He shot such a worried look at Tigh that Ginny had to laugh.

"Please, I've never been called 'my lady' before. I'm more used to answering to 'captain'. Considering you're such an old friend of Tigh's, would it be terrible if I asked you to call me Ginny?" She sent a questioning look to Tigh, hoping she'd done the right thing, but his wide grin said all she needed to know.

Tolo looked scandalized, but at least the bowing was forgotten in his shock. "It wouldn't be proper."

"Seems to me, we were never very proper, my friend," Tigh chided. "After this circus is over, I want you to accompany us back to our rooms for a nightcap. We have much to discuss, and you are one of the few I can trust implicitly." Tigh's expression grew more serious, and Tolo forgot his discomfort. Ginny liked the glint in his eye as he stood facing Tigh. These men were clearly cut from the same noble cloth and knew each other well enough to not need a huge explanation when one needed help from the other.

"Jurdan will no doubt organize protection for you. I aim to be part of that group," Tolo assured Tigh with a grimly determined look on his chiseled face.

"Meet us here when the meal is over, and we'll discuss it more in private. I'm sorry I dragged you away from your dinner." Tigh laughed, but his friend took his easy words as dismissal.

"Yes, my liege." Tolo backed away, making a short bow as he left, and Tigh sighed.

Ginny took Tigh's hand and squeezed. "This bowing and scraping stuff is going to get old really fast." Her tone was matter-of-fact but elicited the desired response when Tigh laughed out loud. He turned, sweeping her into a brief hug, a smile lighting his eyes.

"You're good for me, Ginny." He kissed her cheek and set her away. "But you're right. We're going to have to work through this in the early days until our friends find their footing with our new status. It'll be up to us to put them at ease enough to work with us, but still maintain the respect of the rest of our people. It's a fine line my parents were able to walk successfully, though from what I hear, Elius swept away all their informality and instituted a lot of the bowing and scraping we're seeing now. It'll be up to us to change it back. I think we're already off to a good start."

Tigh helped her back up onto the dais with a solicitous hand. "If you say so."

After the meal was mostly over, it was time for the speeches. Tigh had warned her that she'd be called upon to formally introduce her crew and family to the entire assembly. She didn't mind. As a ship's captain, she'd gotten used to speaking in public on the spur of the moment. She even took pride in the fact that she barely ever got tongue-tied anymore, though she'd no doubt said some really stupid things during her early days of command.

Tigh had introduced his circle of advisors and some of the palace officials first. The steward was an austere man who'd retired from soldiering to run the palace with military precision. There were others in the hierarchy of the palace that had been put in place when Tigh took over, such as Xeer, who'd been on the ship and now headed up the palace guard. A few others had performed different duties aboard ship and were now resuming their regular posts.

When it came Ginny's turn, she stood to address the assembled men with only a little trepidation. She knew many of them from the voyage here, and if she was any judge of expressions, most of the rest were reasonably receptive to her and her crew. Regardless, she decided to keep the introductions short, sweet and to the point. She gave name, rank, and a brief background for each of her women that touched on their military careers but avoided anything truly sensitive about their personal lives. Ginny figured those things would come out—or not—at each woman's discretion.

The crowd seemed already in awe of Henny, so Ginny felt free to tell them a little bit about her father's dojo and accomplishments in addition to the regular fare. Henny was proud of her family's history but reticent to speak of their accomplishments. Ginny had known the family almost her whole life and felt no such compunction. She missed the men of Henny's family as much as she missed her own father and brothers, and she respected the knowledge they'd passed down to Henny and to her that had saved their lives more than once during the war.

Ginny saved the introduction of her mother, aunt and cousin for last. Her young cousin was only eighteen and visibly dazzled by all the masculine beauty in that hall. For a girl who'd grown up without male attention, this had to be a very odd situation, to say the least. Yet, she was handling it well.

"Amelia," Ginny introduced the young woman first, "is my cousin. She was studying physical sciences at university before agreeing to come here. She's eighteen years old, which in human terms usually means she'd have about six more years of schooling before she started working in her chosen profession. I'm hoping she can continue her studies here and find an occupation that is both rewarding personally and helpful to jit'suku society."

Murmurs of approval sounded from the older councilors, and Ginny was glad she'd decided to tack on that bit of personal information. She only had her aunt and mother's introductions to finish now, though in some ways, knowing that just their identical appearance made them extra noticeable among jit'suku, those introductions would be the most difficult of all.

"My aunt, Jane Kerlew-Johnson is Amelia's mother, and as you can see, my own mother's identical twin. The emperor informs me that twin females are incredibly rare among jit'suku, which we did not realize. Twin births of both males and females are not exactly common among humans, but apparently, more than it is here. In my case, not only is my mother a twin, but there is a history of twins on my father's side of the family, as well, going all the way back to Diva and John Starbridge's twin sons." Ginny looked around the room to see how her words were being received. The eyes she met indicated a mix of surprise, interest and a strange kind of awe at the mention of her most famous ancestors.

"My Aunt Jane had a very successful psychotherapy practice back on our homeworld and has council certifications in both medicine and psychiatry." Ginny waited for her aunt's high level of education to sink in, glad when she saw indications that some of the men, at least, were duly impressed. "My mother, Janet Kerlew-Starbridge, is a medical nurse with training in botany and apothecary science." Ginny took a deep breath. "I'd like to take this opportunity to thank each and every one of my family members and crew—who are my extended family—for pulling up stakes and moving to this new galaxy with me. They are brave and loyal, one and all, and they have my respect, thanks and love."

Ginny sat, indicating she was through speaking. A polite round of applause sounded, and Ginny was glad she'd gotten through the formal part of the evening's festivities.

Entertainment had been arranged, including a demonstration of agility by some acrobats and a hand-to-hand fighting exhibition put on by two of the Zenai novices who moved like lightning. Some musicians played background music, but there was no dancing, as there would have been in years past.

"I'm sorry our entertainments are skewed toward what warriors find interesting," Tigh said at one point.

"I find it all interesting," Ginny told him. "Don't worry. Everything here is new and intriguing to us." She sat back and watched the evening unfold, learning more and more about her new home and its people.

When the entertainments wound down and only the musicians were left playing soft music in the background, people started to take their leave. There didn't seem to be any formal order to the end of the evening. Folks just got up and left when they felt like it, and Ginny was relieved to see that nothing further would be required of herself and Tigh in the way of formal declarations, speeches or gestures. The whole arrangement was very practical, and little by little, the tables emptied out.

Tigh turned to her and smiled. "Are you ready to leave?" he asked solicitously.

She nodded, noting that her mother and aunt had already left, as had some of her crew, though others were engaged in discussions that might go on for a while. She caught Henny's eye, and a series of expressions along with a discreet hand signal told her that Hen would look after the stragglers and make sure everybody was safe for the night. Relieved to have Henny looking out for the few who remained, Ginny was ready to leave.

"It was a lovely evening," she said as she stood from her seat.

"It was," Tigh agreed, gallantly sliding her heavy chair back so she could step away from the table.

A small group of guards were waiting to see them safely to their destination. Ginny noticed that Tolo was among the honor guard that escorted Ginny and Tigh back to his private suite. Tigh left the rest of the men at the door but asked Xeer, Hansa and Tolo to come inside for a nightcap.

After the men settled that while Xeer was in charge of the palace guard, Hansa would resume his leadership of the imperial guard. It was the imperial guard that would work with Tolo, who was heading up a special group put together by Jurdan, in order to provide close bodyguard coverage for the imperial couple. Hansa seemed glad of the help and not at all put out that the Zenai priesthood was going to be more active in this imperial household than they had been in the past.

The division of labor was easy to sort out. Xeer would secure the buildings and grounds with his forces. Hansa's group would be providing the visible deterrent while Tolo and those priests assigned to the special group would be guarding Tigh and Ginny from the shadows. It was during this discussion that Xeer revealed that Elius had run the palace guard down to a skeleton crew both by his policies and his actions.

"I didn't mention it before," Xeer admitted, "because we're recruiting as fast as we can, but our current numbers aren't anywhere near what they should be. And, with new recruits, it will take time to be certain of their abilities and assign them where they're best suited."

"Good. Keep doing that," Tigh told him approvingly. "You must see to the rebuilding of the palace guard as quickly and securely as possible. With Ginny and her ladies living here, protecting the palace is vital. Hansa and Tolo can worry about babysitting me and my bride, but perhaps they can lend you some personnel until everything is as it should be." Tigh clapped Xeer on the shoulder. "I hope the three of you can work together on this. I didn't expect the Zenai would step forward with such an offer, but I am happy to accept it. It sounds like, right now, we can use all the help we can get. Protecting the women is imperative to the future of our race."

A significant glance passed between the men that Ginny let pass. They probably were still thinking of her and her ladies as helpless, but if push came to shove, they'd all be fighting, not sitting back, waiting to be rescued. Still, she wasn't about to disabuse them of the notion that she might need a little extra looking after. She could handle herself in most situations, but she knew the men wouldn't see it that way.

Plus, she was pregnant. She'd promised Tigh not to do anything too risky in her condition. If having Zenai priests as bodyguards made him happy, she'd do it. At least while she was pregnant. After that, they'd renegotiate.

Tigh, Hansa, and Tolo got into detailed discussion about how they would work the bodyguard schedule and duties, so Ginny took the opportunity to speak somewhat privately with Xeer. She'd noticed the way he'd been looking at Krysta throughout the dinner, and while Ginny wasn't usually much of a meddler, Krysta was special. Most of the crew thought of her as a shy little sister, and Ginny wanted to make sure Xeer understood that Krysta was somewhat...not exactly fragile, but her feelings could be delicate.

"I noticed you were talking with my friend, Krysta," she said to Xeer, watching his reaction closely.

"She is a very intelligent and interesting woman," he replied, without missing a beat. Ginny liked that response.

"I'm glad you think so. The thing is, she's usually very shy, but she didn't seem to have any problems chatting with you. I'm curious. Do you have any interest in her? Because I think she has one in you, and I'd hate to see her disappointed if you're not serious." Ginny decided to just lay it on the line since these warriors seemed to respond well to plain speaking.

"My lady." Xeer looked insulted. "I would never hurt her in any way. I believe she is my mate. I only wait for her to get more comfortable with me before I prove that belief to her. I didn't want to scare her off, for I sensed she was not used to dealing with men and particularly not a male who was interested in her as a woman."

Ginny was surprised by his astute evaluation. "You're very observant. I'm glad to know you've figured her out and won't rush her. Krysta is..." Ginny struggled with a way to say what she wanted without insulting her friend. "Well, she's a little different, Xeer. She didn't have the typical experiences most young women of our generation had growing up."

"Rest easy, my lady," Xeer said. "We've spoken of her differences. It is something we share, to a certain extent."

"Really?" Ginny was surprised and a little alarmed. If he had cybernetics, it was because he'd been irreparably injured at some point in his life. She didn't like thinking about the massive trauma that might cause someone to have to replace a limb with a cybernetic one.

Xeer nodded. "I have several implants, though I received them later in life than your friend, Krysta. Still, I do understand what she went through physically, and I have a good idea of the psychological issues that come with the affliction we both share."

Ginny touched his arm, moved by his candor. "I didn't really mean to pry, Xeer. Krysta is...special. I'm glad you can understand just how much."

"If the Mother Goddess so decides, I will share my life, my hearth and my strength with Krysta. I'll do my best to protect her and court her in the human way, since I don't believe she would respond well to the normal jit'suku methods." A devilish smile lit his face, and Ginny was glad this understanding man might just be the one for Krysta. She needed a special guy, and Xeer showed every sign of being just the right one.

CHAPTER 14

A few days later, the women took a field trip to the Zenai monastery at Jurdan's invitation. Tigh was busy with affairs of state. Apparently, one of the many duties of the emperor was to hold court and settle disputes among his subjects. Quite a few cases that needed to be heard had piled up in his absence, so he was holding court for a few hours every day until he got through the backlog.

Today, he'd be doing a marathon session while the women were safe in the heart of the Zenai monastery. He'd told Ginny before she'd left that there was no place safer for her in the universe than there, and so, he would be able to work without worry for her safety. His plan was to clear his desk, if at all possible, of the old matters so that anything new could be dealt with more quickly.

Jurdan had been especially eager to learn more about Henny's fighting style, so he'd extended the invitation to the entire crew. Ginny participated in some of the kata exercise as part of the all-women group, but when they started actual fighting practice, she sat back to watch.

Jurdan and a number of highly-ranked priests surrounded the outdoor square they were using for their practice, and when time came for individual sparring bouts, a few of the priests squared off for some friendly contests with the ladies.

This was a much higher level of training and teaching than what had occurred on the ship with Tigh's crew. These priests were truly interested in learning how Henny accomplished take-downs that they clearly didn't expect.

They were especially interested in how the smallest of the women could face off against huge warriors and manage to not only hold their own, but occasionally prevail. Each time one of the smaller ladies landed a blow on a stunned male, they slowed and asked for details on how the move had been accomplished. Henny would step into her role of teacher, at that point, and the men listened with intense concentration.

Over the course of the afternoon, Henny went a long way toward cementing her role as teacher and expert fighter. She also did a bit of exhibition kata and even sparred with some of the top-level priests. Jurdan clearly gave her respect for her skills, and the other priests followed suit. All in all, it was a good day, Ginny thought, for improving their position and gaining friends and admirers among the warrior priests.

Ginny, Krysta and Sally were on the way back to the palace. Henny and the others had decided to stay a bit longer at the monastery and would return later that night, but Ginny was feeling a bit queasy and wanted to go home and lie down.

She was in the air car they'd been using when something rocked the sturdy vehicle, and it began an unscheduled descent. They weren't anywhere near the city yet, so the farmland below was a mostly flat patchwork of crops. Tolo had been piloting the vehicle, with Sally sitting in the co-pilot seat and learning how to operate the vehicle. Krysta had been sitting in back, relaxing and chatting quietly with Ginny, but when the car started to go down, everyone snapped to alert.

Tolo tried to get a message out on the comm, but it was pretty clear he wasn't getting through. Sally took over the comm task, telling him to concentrate on flying while Ginny looked on helplessly. This wasn't like being in battle in her ship. This was far too small a craft with few weapons, and although it was very maneuverable, if the engine went out for whatever reason, its only option was to glide to the ground and await rescue.

They were gliding now, heading for a country road with no traffic on it. That would do for a landing strip, Ginny thought, as she looked out the window. She caught sight of pursuit behind and alongside them. This wasn't a simple malfunction. This was a deliberate attack.

She tried her personal comm, but it, too, was jammed. Grabbing a pen and paper out of her bag, she wrote a quick note the old-fashioned way and jammed it under a corner of the carpet. Unless the attackers burned the vehicle—which she didn't think they would, since a fire like that would attract too much attention too soon—Tigh's people would find her note. She hoped.

She also snapped a few images on her personal comm of the pursuit vehicles, trying to document as much as she could, and ordered Krysta to do the same. The attackers might find and destroy their comm devices, but at least they would have tried.

And Ginny had one last thing she could do. She activated the small robotic recording device that Tigh insisted she carry with her at all times. It was the same small camera that had been part of her gear aboard his ship, which had come in so handy when all the men had been incapacitated. The memory of those units had been downloaded and reproduced for analysis, and the units returned to the women with Tigh's blessing. He encouraged them all to carry them, and Ginny had acceded to his wishes.

Ginny activated the little unit. It detached from her belt and began to hover, recording everything.

"Oh! I've got mine, too," Krysta said, seeing Ginny's device appear over her shoulder.

"Don't activate it yet," Ginny said quickly. "Keep it in reserve. My unit will probably get captured if we end up in their trap." She glanced out the window and frowned. "And it certainly looks like we're going to get caught. What we need to do now, is leave clues for those who will come after us. To help them find us quicker."

Ginny positioned the floating camera near the window to record what it could of the pursuing vehicles. Then, she took the camera and reattached it to her belt, this time, facing outward on the buckle, as if it was some kind of ornament. With any luck, the bad guys wouldn't realize what it was, and she'd get a chance to discard it somewhere Tigh's people would find it. In the meantime, it would continue to record everything.

"Do you think they're going to kill us?" Krysta asked, her expression grim.

"If they'd wanted to kill us, they would have blasted us out of the sky already. I'm betting on capture, so stay alert. If you can get away, do it."

"But—" Krysta objected, but Ginny was having none of it.

"That's an order. They'll keep me alive, but I'm not sure about the rest of you. I'd rather have you free to come get me than dead." Harsh words, but it was how she felt. She saw Krysta nod and was glad she understood.

Tolo had his hands full guiding the car down to the ground safely, and Sally was still working on coms, to no avail. The com system was supposed to be triple coded and unassailable on this royal vehicle, yet somehow, someone found a way to jam them. They'd also punched through the shield that should have been protecting the engine like it wasn't even there. It was simple. Someone had to have given the enemy their codes.

"None of this is supposed to be possible with all the precautions," Krysta said, sounding grim as they kept coasting, ever downward.

"Inside job," Ginny muttered, but everyone in the small cabin heard her.

"I fear you are correct, Highness," Tolo said, fighting with the stick to keep them in line with the roadway as they drew ever nearer to the ground.

"Orders?" Sally asked, as if they were back on their ship again. What Ginny wouldn't give for a fully armed warship, right about now.

"You three do your best to escape. They want me. Probably not you guys." She hoped.

"I cannot comply, Highness. I am sworn to protect you to my last breath," Tolo said, sounding grim. She wasn't going to argue with him. There just wasn't time.

"Do what your conscience demands, then," she said, focusing her energies on the women because she didn't think she'd have any luck dissuading a Zenai warrior priest from whatever it was he thought he was supposed to do. "Don't get yourselves killed," she said to Sally and Krysta, meeting each of their gazes for a heartbeat. "Do your best to break free. If you can't, do your best to stay alive, whatever that entails. They will be looking for us. Do what you can to help the searchers. Drop clues, if possible."

"Aye, aye, Captain," Sally replied, her tone subdued but resolute.

"We've been in tough spots before," Ginny reminded them. "We'll get through this. Just keep your wits about you."

"Roger, that." Krysta braced as the air car made contact with the road.

It was a bumpy landing, but they made it down in one piece. Krysta popped the hatch but was thrown back into the cabin by some sort of grenade that hit her in the shoulder with great force before popping and releasing a cloud of gas. Ginny tried to hold her breath, but it was useless. She felt the effects of whatever was in the gas putting her to sleep—hopefully, that was all it was doing.

She felt herself being lifted. Someone had her ankles, and someone else had their hands under her shoulders. They weren't all that gentle, but at least they were taking her someplace rather than killing her on the spot. She was able to open her eyes just enough to see a squad of jit'suku men, some of whom were wearing what passed for medical clothing in their society, along with a few soldiers.

As they loaded her into a waiting vehicle, Ginny bided her time before taking the opportunity to detach the miniature floating camera from her belt. She pressed the tiny button that would order it to remain hidden and to stay on station before releasing it to land on the ground. The little chip inside the floater was smart enough to conceal itself using whatever cover it could find for the next hour.

By that time, she'd probably be long gone, but at least she was leaving behind a recording of exactly what had happened to her. She only hoped it would help Tigh find her. She wished she had some way to tell him just one more time how deeply she felt about him, but at that point, the effects of the gas took her completely under, and she didn't wake for a very long time.

Tigh was hearing one of the last cases of the day when the court chamber doors burst open, and Xeer came running in. He was followed by an equally hasty troop of palace guards who stationed themselves around the room and the participants in the current trial.

"My apologies," Tigh said to the parties who were seated at separate tables in front of him. "We will have to resume this later. Please follow the guards' instructions." Tigh rose and removed his robes of state, discarding them on his chair as Xeer joined him.

"Sire, there was an attack on the Velkir's air car. The car went down, and all three women—your lady, Sally and Krysta—were abducted from the scene. Tolo is in critical condition and may not live through the night." Xeer's voice was low and urgent as they walked through the private door at the back of the court chamber. More palace guard were present all over the rooms and corridors they walked through.

"When?" Tigh asked, already considering his options. One thing was certain. He wasn't going to sit around in the palace while his soul mate was out there, somewhere, in danger. He was walking rapidly toward the hangar where his personal vehicles were stored.

"No more than half a standard ago," Xeer answered promptly. "When the air car did not show up on the next radar station as expected, the alarm was raised. The attendants at the previous radar station were found dead. The enemy planned this operation to the minutest detail."

"I'm sensing there's a qualification to your words," Tigh said tightly, even as he worried. "What is it?"

"Your lady, sire. She was brilliant! She left one of those little floating recording devices at the scene in stealth mode. We have retrieved it and downloaded the footage. Sire." Xeer stopped walking to face Tigh. "It was Gruber."

Tigh saw red for a moment before he managed to calm himself enough to speak. "Gruber? You are certain?"

The bastard responsible for the virus that had killed so many in both galaxies. Gruber was the one war criminal Tigh had searched for and been unable to find. He was a thorn in Tigh's side, having been behind the attempt to subvert his ship on its way home from peace talks with the humans. If not for Ginny and her crew, Gruber would have derailed that, as well. If evil had a name, in Tigh's opinion, Gruber was it.

"I saw his face on the camera. He was definitely commanding the force that took the women. You can even hear him speak, and we have voice-matched the recording with our files. It was definitely him." Xeer began walking again, following in Tigh's tracks as he paced toward the hangar with renewed determination. "Sire!" he called. "Tigh!"

Xeer's use of his name turned Tigh around. It had to be pretty important to get Xeer to forget the new protocols that Tigh insisted he didn't like and didn't need but that everyone around him seemed unable to relinquish. Xeer had his attention now, and he came closer, lowering his voice to keep their discussion as private as possible.

"Tigh, there had to be an accomplice—or many—on the inside. Gruber had the codes to the air car and was able to jam coms and fire through shields that should have held off anything up to, and including, a nuclear warhead." Tigh's blood boiled as Xeer's words penetrated. "Whatever you're planning to do, choose your wingmen and crew wisely. Only those you trust implicitly. There are, without doubt, rotten apples among us."

"I'm trusting you to figure out who they are," Tigh said, between gritted teeth. "I'm giving you authority to investigate anyone and anything within this palace and its grounds. Run it to earth, Xeer. Find out who has betrayed me and arrest them. Do this for me while I find my mate." Tigh reached out to put one hand on Xeer's forearm, impressing on the warrior how important a task Tigh was giving him.

"I will not let you down," Xeer pledged. "I knew you would want to go out and find them, which is why I directed everyone to meet you in the hangar." Xeer smiled just a bit, and Tigh had to shake his head.

"You know me too well, my friend." Tigh resumed walking. "Who is everyone?"

"The Velkir's crew, and the remainder of the men who traveled with us to human space, for a start. Jurdan sent some warrior priests along with the ladies. I believe they're readying the Phenix, even as we speak."

The Phenix was the emperor's personal warship. Small but fast. Light but sturdy. It was designed to allow the emperor to either escape the palace, should all other defenses fail, or to join in the fight as highly specialized strike battleship with minimal crew. His men could handle it. As could the ladies, he now believed, if given half a chance. Tigh decided to let them sort out who would control what station aboard the ship. They probably already had.

"Bring them back, Sire," Xeer said in a low voice.

Tigh noticed the emphasis in his friend's voice and remembered that Xeer had seemed particularly impressed by Krysta. Tigh knew it wasn't just his own future at stake here, but Xeer's as well.

Tigh paused to meet his friend's gaze. "I will bring them all back. This, I vow."

Xeer nodded. There was a great deal of emotion in that simple gesture, but there was no more time to waste. Tigh kept moving. He had to find them and bring them back, not just for himself, but for Xeer and for all jit'suku.

Xeer stayed behind with his guardsmen as Tigh mounted the ramp that led into the Phenix. He climbed up to the bridge and came upon a well-ordered group of people— males and females—working together to prepare for launch.

Tigh spotted Jimnai Burk sitting in the nav position. He'd been the first officer during the trip to human space, and Tigh trusted him implicitly. Hansa was standing next to Henny, over by the weapons consoles. It looked like he was showing her what they had and how to use it. They all looked up when Tigh entered the bridge.

"Thank you all," he said, overcome by the determination he saw on all of their faces. "I understand there is a recording of the abduction?"

Just like that, they got back to business. The petite ensign everyone called Tiggy motioned Tigh over to her station. She was Ginny's coms officer, he recalled, and she was sitting at the primary coms board on the Phenix, with his own coms officer backing her up. They had the display screens up and running to show Tigh what Ginny had recorded.

He watched the take down with his jaw clenched. He heard Ginny declare what Xeer had told him—that this was an inside job. Someone—likely more than one person—on the inside had betrayed them. He vowed they would find those responsible and bring them to justice, but first, he had to rescue his mate.

Ginny had been so brave. He was impressed, all over again, at how cool his mate was under fire. She had left the device behind, ordering her people to do all they could to get away or leave clues. At least one more of those human recording devices was out there, with Krysta. He'd heard them discuss it, and Ginny had told her friend to save it for later. But what about the other woman?

"Sally was co-piloting." Tigh stated. That had been easily seen on the early part of the recording. "Does she also have one of the recording devices?"

Tiggy looked up at him. "We all do," she answered a bit sheepishly. "Captain told us to keep them with us at all times, just in case, but I can't guarantee Sally had hers with her today. She should have, but there's no mention of it on the recording we have."

"Understood." Tigh watched the rest of it, his gut twisting in knots to see Ginny tossed into an air car like a sack of grain. "Is there any way to track these devices?"

"Yes," Tiggy said at once, giving Tigh hope. "Captain said to keep that to ourselves, but I think she meant it for just this sort of situation. If the floater is recording, I can track it, but if it's in standby, or shielded, there's no signal for me."

"This hangar is shielded, so we'd better launch," Tigh said, already moving toward his command chair. "Start scanning as soon as we're airborne."

"Aye, Captain," Tiggy replied, giving Tigh a little start of surprise. He supposed he was the captain of this ship, but he hadn't expected the title. Just one more of a dozen new titles he'd never expected to wear.

He talked to the other stations, finding everything in readiness. On his command, they flew through the open hangar doors, using their atmospheric drive. Although this ship was fully capable of traveling in space, it was also small and maneuverable enough to do well near the surface of a planet.

He had wanted to take the ship out for a shakedown cruise—more for him than for the ship, itself. He hadn't gotten the chance to do so before now, but he would certainly put this little marvel of cutting edge jit'suku technology through its paces today.

"I've got a signal!" Tiggy didn't look up from what she was doing, but her expression was relieved. "Make that two signals. The XO and the navigator's floaters are both operational and broadcasting."

"Can we see the feed or is it strictly a homing beacon?" Tigh asked the woman.

"At this range, we can only use it to get closer. Once we're near enough, I should be able to get enough of the transmission to give us something." Again, Tiggy focused on her board, but the news was good.

Tigh felt a grim satisfaction go through him. They would at least be able to track the women to their current location. That was a damned good start.

Ginny woke by slow degrees. It was like coming out of a fog, and she realized she must have been drugged into unconsciousness by whatever was in that gas grenade. She only hoped it hadn't harmed the babies, but she couldn't really worry about that at the moment. Her first priority had to be getting out of this mess, so she could get to her own doctor and be assured that the babies were okay. She tried to take heart in the fact that she felt all right and her abdomen didn't give any indication of problems. She hoped it would remain that way.

Ginny knew Tigh was probably already on his way to find her. She just had to help things along, if she possibly could. Escaping would be nice, but if she couldn't manage that, she'd be happy with just figuring out where they were and what the situation was.

Opening her eyes just a fraction, she looked around, trying not to draw any attention to the fact that she was waking up. She was laying on a slab of some kind in a windowless room. A quick look around told her that Sally and Krysta were in the same room, on matching slabs sticking out from the opposite wall. Krysta was sitting up, rubbing her head, but Sally was still unconscious.

Seeing Krysta up, Ginny sat up, too. "Any clue what's going on here?" Ginny asked, rolling her neck to loosen the crick in it from laying at an odd angle.

"I've only been awake for a few minutes. Haven't seen anyone or anything besides these four walls, Captain." Krysta made some casual hand gestures, alerting Ginny to far more than her words revealed.

For one thing, Krysta was able to communicate that she'd activated both floaters, which were firmly attached to Sally and Krysta's belts. Ginny felt good about that. If their luck was holding, the signal would get out and be received by those looking for them. Tiggy knew how to track the low-tech signal. She'd tell Tigh, and they'd follow the beacons, if at all possible.

"How are you feeling?" Ginny asked, just to keep the spoken conversation going while Krysta continued to fill her in with gestures only her team understood.

Krysta's hand signals alerted Ginny to surveillance cameras Krysta had already spotted around the room. They were definitely under observation, so the cautious approach was best.

"I'm okay. I suspect they gave us some kind of counter-agent to wake us up," she went on. Krysta had specialized sensors as part of some of her hardware. If she said they'd been deliberately awakened, Ginny could take that as fact.

"How about Sally?" Ginny gestured to the other woman who gave every appearance of being out cold.

"I think she got more of the gas than we did, even though she was sitting up front. You held your breath, right? Like I did?" Again, Krysta's words said one thing while her hand gesture talked of something completely different. In this case, she was indicating that, if someone came in through the door visible just to her left, she was going to take them out with her cybernetic arm.

"Yeah, as soon as I saw that grenade hit you, I did my best not to breathe, but eventually, I had to," she admitted.

"Yeah, me too," Krysta replied. "But Sal didn't see the gas come in the door. I don't think she knew to hold her breath, so she got more of a dose than we did. Plus, they took us out of the cabin first. She was in the gas longer. As was the pilot."

Ginny felt a pang for Tolo. She had no doubt Tigh would mourn if the man had died. She felt pretty bad about it herself. She hated to think of that skilled, big-hearted man dead because someone wanted to get to her.

"Makes sense, I guess," Ginny replied while giving the hand sign that she understood Krysta's plan and wouldn't get in the way.

CHAPTER 15

As it turned out, they didn't get a chance to use that plan because nobody came into the room. Sally woke up much more slowly than the other two. Krysta had her implants to help her rid her body of the toxins, and Ginny had managed to not inhale too much of the drug, but Sal had gotten the full whammy.

They couldn't do much of anything until Sally woke up because there was no way in hell that either Krysta or Ginny would leave her behind. Krysta could have carried her, but that would have been difficult. She'd have had to put Sally down each time she needed to use her cybernetic strength to do anything else. So, Ginny decided to wait until Sally could at least walk on her own.

In the meantime, they kept up the simple conversation about how they felt physically, and speculation about where they were. All the while, they were plotting their next move using subtle hand signals and code words that only they understood.

The plan evolved as time went on, and eventually, they arrived at the idea that as soon as Sally was mobile, Krysta would use her cybernetic strength to wrest the door from its hinges. Depending on what they found outside, they would do their best to escape. Ginny was certain Tigh was mobilizing heaven and earth to find her, but she would be damned if she just sat around waiting for rescue like some princess in a tower. She would do all she could to aid in her own rescue. As a soldier, she could do no less.

"Oh, my word, there she is," Tiggy whispered as the signal started to clear. Tigh was instantly alert and on his feet, leaning over the coms station to see what was going on.

"What do you have?" he asked, feeling a sense of urgency. They'd followed the signal to this mountainous region, and now, they were just trying to home in on exactly where the women were being held.

"It's fading in and out, but for a moment there, I saw the captain." Tiggy looked up at Tigh. "Beg your pardon, I saw Captain Starbridge, sir. She was sitting opposite our navigator, Ensign Verity. Krysta must have activated the device but kept it camouflaged on her belt. It was showing the view right in front of her, which included Captain Starbridge."

The screen in front of her wavered again, going from broken black and white fuzz to the image she described. Tigh's heart clenched with relief. Ginny was alive!

"There she is again. We're getting closer. The image is clearer this time," Tiggy reported as she fiddled with her controls. "No audio. Visual only," she reported, still fine-tuning the image, which was getting clearer all the time. "Hot damn. Sir, they're planning something."

"How can you tell?" Tigh asked the coms specialist.

"We have our own set of signals. Hand signals. Gestures. Stuff we've worked out over the years," she admitted to him. "I can see the captain's orders from her gestures. She's saying to wait for Lieutenant Darlington, then they go. The lieutenant is either incapacitated or not with them at present," she surmised. "Once they have her, they're going to make a break for it."

"How? Does she say how?" Tigh wanted to know.

"Well, Krysta has...uh...cybernetic implants. If she

doesn't want to stay someplace, it's pretty hard to keep her there. I would guess they're going to break out and make a run for it."

Tigh felt a rush of both pride in his mate and concern for her safety. "We'll just have to be there when they go," he said, firming his resolve. "Jimnai, can you get us a precise location?" he asked the man who had acted as executive officer on their mission to the human galaxy. His trusted friend, Jimnai Burk, was running the nav board, searching for the exact location of where Ginny and the other two women were being held.

"We're over the signal right now, Captain," Jimnai replied immediately. "They must be underground, for there are no structures on the surface here."

"Search for anything that looks like an entrance. Then, bring us down nearby. I want a clear shot at the area from the main weapons array, should it become necessary." Tigh had to plan for all contingencies, though he would never fire on the location unless he was certain Ginny was safe. "And Henny, I want you running the weapons board," he told the human master-at-arms. He trusted Hansa implicitly, but he knew Henny's loyalty to Ginny was beyond question. It was also an act of faith on his part, trusting the Velkir to do their best for everyone.

"Aye, sir," Henny replied, one eyebrow raised in a sort of pleased surprise.

"I've found a small structure, sir," Jimnai called out urgently. "Scans show it's an entry point to what has to be an underground complex. Scans can only penetrate the first layer of rock and soil, and there's a definitely a lift, as well as a staircase, heading downward quite some distance."

"Any reference data on this site?" Tigh asked.

"Nothing in the database," Hansa replied. "But I remember hearing rumors of an underground facility here during your brother's time."

Now, that sounded ominous. "What kind of facility?"

"Medical. Experimental. I heard it directly, just once, from a fellow who claimed to have been stationed at a top-secret laboratory in the eastern mountains, but most of the other soldiers thought he was speaking out of turn. I heard later that he'd died in a training accident."

"That doesn't sound suspicious at all," Tigh mused sarcastically. "And it fits with Doctor Gruber's field of expertise. What did this fellow say about the base?"

"It was small. Deep in the earth. One main laboratory and a few offices. It only had one way in or out," Hansa replied at once. "The idea was that it would be easily contained, and if they needed to bury the whole place, they could do it easily, and no one would be the wiser."

"Why would they need to bury a place like that?" Tiggy asked, her eyes wide.

"It was probably a failsafe in case one of their experiments got out of control," Tigh said. "It sounds to me like they were experimenting with bioweapons. That's one of the few uses I can think of for such a place."

"Then, this might be where the virus was created?" Tiggy's voice was tinged with anger.

"It's possible," Tigh concluded. "Especially since the fugitive, Doctor Gruber, was the one who created the virus."

"When we find him," Henny said, her voice solemn and strong, "he's a dead man."

"You'll get no argument from me, Chief," Tigh assured her. "He's already been sentenced to death for his actions. The fact that he's been eluding justice for so long is a thorn in my side, and a disgrace. The sad fact is he still has many allies—the faction that wants war at all costs."

"And kidnapping Captain Starbridge?" Tiggy asked. "How does that help?"

"Straight out assassination would've been easier and more disruptive," Henny put in, her tone contemplative, even as Jimnai maneuvered the ship in for a landing. "Unless he's counting on you to come after her, and you're the real target, Your Highness."

Tigh thought about it. "Possible, but unlikely, unless he

knows we can track them and doesn't mind burning the location of this hidden facility."

"He's a desperate man," Henny reminded him.

"Yes, but he's also a scientist to the core. He wouldn't want to give up his lab. At least, that's what I'm betting on."

"Then, how much do you want to bet there are sensors that have already told him we're here?" Henny posed the question, that arch in her eyebrow.

"I'm counting on it," Tigh answered back. "This ship has a lot of special capabilities." Tigh deliberately brought his hand down on a new console that rose out of the armrest of his chair. He grimaced as something sharp pricked his hand, then the console lights blinked into the green position. "Hansa, deploy the bots."

A few clunks sounded from below the flight deck and a moment later, a series of self-propelled bots shot out from under the ship, heading for the ground, unfolding into battle bots as they went. Each landed lightly on their feet, weapons at the ready, while several specialized bots with large wheels rolled over every inch of the proposed landing site, making certain it was safe. When they were done, the bots formed a ring, facing outward while the ship came in to land smack dab in the center of the well-armed circle of bots.

"Don't you worry about mechanicals being corrupted?" Henny asked quietly.

"Not in this case," Tigh answered just as quietly as he watched the scene unfold. "These bots, and this entire ship, for that matter, are DNA-keyed to the emperor. My brother commissioned this ship, but we were identical twins, so the special features respond to me, as well, but no one else."

Ginny was impatient to leave the cell in which she'd awakened. When Sally finally started to stir, Ginny went over to her and helped Sally sit up.

"How do you feel, Sal? You got a bigger dose of the knockout gas than we did," Ginny explained gently.

"I feel like a herd of elephants is running through my

brain wearing spiked heels," she admitted, rubbing her forehead, "but I'm good. Where are we?"

"Your guess is as good as mine," Ginny replied. "Do you think you can walk?"

Sally rested both of her palms on her thighs and patted them just once. "Let's find out."

With Ginny's help, Sally got to her feet and took a few tentative steps. The more she moved, the easier it became, and the less she leaned on Ginny's supporting arm. Once Ginny was sure Sally would be able to walk on her own, she maneuvered them both to the area by the only door. With a nod to Krysta to indicate they were through waiting, Ginny set their escape in motion.

Krysta walked over and, using her cybernetic arm, ripped the door off its hinges. Ginny didn't get to see Krysta use her mechanical strength often, and it was always impressive. Krysta peeped out the open doorway first while Sally and Ginny stayed behind cover next to the now-open doorframe. When Krysta gave them the signal, they rushed out of the cell and into a long hallway, leapfrogging each other's positions as they went, doing it by the book, like the troopers they were, even if they were mostly unarmed.

Only Krysta had a weapon, and it was her actual arm, so nobody could really confiscate it. Not easily, at least.

Ginny was surprised by what they found as they moved along. The place seemed almost empty. Oh, there were signs that people had been living here. Refuse bags were lined up in one of the cubbies they'd passed, full of garbage and sealed behind an odor-blocking field. But they didn't encounter any people until they happened upon a doorway that was made of a clear substance. Thick, Ginny could tell, from the optical distortion, but clear enough that she could see the laboratory beyond.

There was one man in the lab, and he saw her as she peered through the transparent door. His eyes grew round, and he immediately hit a control to his right. Ginny assumed it was an alarm, but instead of locking down, the transparent door opened.

The man came around his lab bench and walked right up to Ginny. He wasn't armed. He looked upset, but he didn't seem threatening. Curious, she waited to see what would happen. She didn't have a weapon, but Krysta was as good as. She stood beside Ginny as the man approached.

"How can this be?" the man asked, clearly dismayed at something. Their escape? Somehow, she didn't think so. "You are human! But you are not. Not entirely. You are," he said, pointing at Krysta then dismissing her as he turned back to Ginny. "But you are not."

"You took DNA samples while we were unconscious?" Ginny asked. Things were starting to make sense to her. Maybe this jackass needed to see it with his own eyes that what they'd claimed was true.

"I never believed what they said," the man admitted. "It was preposterous to think that the pure jit'suku race would have merged with humans at some point in our history."

"What about the empress whose marriage to your Emperor Tren brought about the long period of peace. Did you think that was a hoax? Did you not realize she was just like me? A human hybrid with jit'suku DNA?" Ginny felt outrage fill her, even as something else began to burn in her veins. A righteous anger that felt familiar. And somewhat...divine.

"It had to have been a hoax. There were no formal records kept of that time. No way to prove those claims," the man countered, his voice rising.

"But you have proof now," Sally said, her voice low and deadly. "You saw the evidence for yourself. The Valkyrie is one of those hybrids."

The man turned red with anger then white as a sheet as emotion rode him hard. "She is an abomination! And you're even worse. Human, jit'suku, and something I've never encountered before. You have codes from some other race, entirely."

Ginny felt more than saw Sally detach her floater from her

belt to let it capture the moment from a better angle. Sally had their backs, should someone else come down the corridor, but so far, this strange man was the only one they'd encountered. Ginny wasn't altogether certain he was even sane. Especially after what he'd just said about Sally.

"Emperor." Tiggy's voice came over Tigh's earpiece as he left the ship with Hansa and Jimnai at his side. Henny remained in the ship, at the weapons station, in case of trouble, and Tiggy was still monitoring coms. "Valkyrie has left the cell. The trio is heading down a long hallway. I'm getting a live feed from Krysta's belt-cam."

This was good news. They were all together and mobile. He just hoped they didn't run into any trouble before he got to them. Summoning his bots, he left a smaller circle of protection around the ship and took a well-armed platoon with him. Between himself, his two friends, and the platoon of incorruptible bots, they would meet any resistance with deadly force, if necessary.

As the bots opened the access to the underground facility like they were peeling a metal can, Tigh and his friends stood back. The bots were designed with multiple sensors that could detect hidden traps and unsafe atmospheric conditions. When the report came back that there was no threat of gas surface agents in use, Tigh and his friends advanced into the stairwell. The bots were already at the bottom, scouting ahead and giving Tigh a running account of their findings.

Tigh opted for the stairs, rather than the lift. He left a bot at the lift opening to deal with anyone that might come up that way, but he wasn't too worried about it. If anyone managed to escape out to the surface, the women aboard the Phenix would take care of them, he was sure.

When he reached the bottom of the staircase, he found himself in a chamber containing a multitude of hooks with various kinds of coats hanging on them, as well as a row of footwear along one wall. This was a vestibule, of sorts, where inhabitants would gear up for going outside or relieve themselves of outerwear before going deeper into the facility.

"Tiggy, status?" Tigh asked, taking a moment to observe the chamber and plan his next move.

"They're moving down a long hallway. They came across one cubby that was loaded with bags of trash, but that's it, so far," she reported.

"Roger that," he told her. "Alert me the moment something changes."

"Aye, sir," Tiggy replied.

Hansa and Jimnai also had earpieces and had heard Tiggy's report. Tigh looked at them now. He had given access to the bots, reporting feed to both men, and all of them were seeing data on one side of their combat displays showing what the bots had discovered so far.

"Looks like a straight shot down to a lower level," Jimnai observed a moment before one of the bots encountered a room where five men were sleeping.

"A barracks?" Hansa asked rhetorically as Tigh ordered a thorough scan of the room. "Only one exit," Hansa observed as the report came back from the bot. "Seal them in for now. We can deal with them later," he suggested.

Tigh ordered the bot to do exactly that and stand guard at the lone entrance with orders to stop anyone from leaving, should they somehow be able to bypass his lockout codes that sealed the door. As emperor, he had backdoor and override codes to every piece of tech made by jit'suku—including every programmable door lock in this place.

"I could lock everything down," Tigh mused as they began walking again.

"You could, but the ladies are on the move. Better, perhaps, to let them move freely and keep the bots doing recon and dealing with problems as we find them. With any luck we'll meet in the middle," Hansa offered.

Tigh nodded. He wasn't sure which was the better option, but he knew Ginny wouldn't like being locked in anywhere, even if it was for the best of intentions. As they began to move again, another bot reported activity in a compartment it was about to search. Since Tigh had ordered all the bots to approach with caution and stealth, it waited to receive orders.

He paused for a moment, shifting the feed from that bot's sensors to his display. There were four life signs in the room, and they were talking and moving around. Tigh instructed the bot to climb to the top of the open doorway and deploy a miniature sensor stalk at one corner, where it probably wouldn't be noticed, to do a sweep of the room.

The data came in, confirming this room, like the other barracks chamber, had only the one entrance. Tigh ordered the bot to return its sensor, and he quickly issued the order to the door's electronic system to close it and lock it down tight. He stationed the bot at the door, in case the men inside found a way through, then resumed moving. He and his friends were in the next long stretch of hallway that spiraled gently down into the rock of the mountain when Tiggy's voice came to them.

"They're at a doorway to what looks like a laboratory. There's one man inside. The door is closed, but transparent," she reported.

"Can you send us an image grab of the man?" Jimnai asked before Tigh could get the words out.

"Done." Tiggy's confirmation preceded the image of a man in a lab coat by a fraction of a second.

"That's Gruber!" Tigh cursed under his breath as Jimnai exclaimed.

"He's seen them. He's coming over to the door," Tiggy told them breathlessly.

If only they could communicate with Ginny and tell her to get as far away from that madman as possible. But the cameras weren't receivers. Just transmitters. Tigh started running, his two friends bringing up the rear. The time for subtlety was over.

"He's shouting at them about DNA samples and how he didn't believe that Ginny had jit genes. He's ranting," Tiggy said as Tigh and his friends moved ever downward in the underground facility.

Tigh commanded doors to lock as he encountered them, but there were not many, and the base was mostly empty except for those few the bots had already discovered and locked in. The pathway was clear, at least. Any rooms they passed were just rooms, not side passageways. They kept going down, meeting up with the bots and sending them out ahead at a fast clip. If anybody started shooting, hopefully, they'd engage the bots first, but Tigh wasn't waiting. The whole group was moving at the warriors' top speed.

"I've got two feeds now," Tiggy said excitedly. "Sally detached the floater from her belt and activated it. It's giving me a better view. The lab guy looks like he's about to pop a vein, he's so upset, but the captain is... Oh, man...she's starting to glow. I think we're about to have another divine visitation. You guys had better get your asses down there, pronto."

"Yes, ma'am," Hansa said, almost laughing at the comm tech's candor. "I believe we're almost there."

CHAPTER 16

Ginny felt calm take her body and recognized the touch of the jit'suku Goddess. She'd felt it as an observer before, but this time, it was coming through her. She didn't question it. Somehow, the Light that filled her left no room for questions, only peace and acceptance.

"I made my virus to destroy you. Aliens that have the temerity to look like us, but are far inferior." The man was raving now, but she suddenly understood he was the designer of the virus that had killed off so many people throughout two galaxies.

"We were not the enemy, Doctor Gruber," Ginny said. The words were hers but also came from the Goddess. Somehow. "Humanity was found according to My plan and would have created the next evolution of two races, blending together to become stronger and better able to cope with what will come in the future. Your interference—your misuse of your free will—has brought two mighty races low, but you will not win. I am Light to your darkness. I bring wisdom to your ignorant fear. I prevail where you fail."

Ginny raised her arms. Or maybe it was more accurate to say that something raised Ginny's arms, and light began to form and glow all around her hands. Light that was so bright and so pure, it could burn, but Ginny had no fear of it. Even as Gruber recoiled, Ginny saw the Light flow into him. It simply blew him away. Disintegrating the being that had caused so much heartache, pain and death across two galaxies.

"That was almost too good for the likes of him," Krysta said as she watched the Light begin to fade.

"It is not My way to make beings suffer," Ginny said, knowing it was the Goddess who spoke through her, even as the presence of the divine began to fade.

"No, it's not. We bring that on ourselves, for the most part," Sally agreed. "Now, Captain, if you're back with us, I think we need to make tracks and get out of this hole."

"Roger that, Ensign. Let's go." Ginny was back to normal as the Goddess's presence faded. "The men can investigate this place later. Right now, I want to get outside and figure out where we are."

Tigh arrived at the end of the long corridor in time to see the Light of the Goddess flowing through his mate and out into an open doorway in front of her. Tiggy was giving them the run-down on everything she could see through the lens of the floater cam, and he wasn't surprised when she reported that the man in the lab had dissolved in the Light.

He also heard Ginny's last statement as he drew closer. He ordered the bots to guard their backs while he went forward to meet up with Ginny and her friends. She turned from the doorway and stopped, catching sight of him as he drew nearer. The smile that lit her face warmed his heart as he closed the distance between them.

Wrapping his arms around her for a quick, reassuring hug, he allowed those around them to take on the responsibility of keeping a lookout for the short moment it took to reassure himself that his mate was alive and well. She hugged him just as tightly, and he felt the slight tremble of her shoulders as he moved back to meet her gaze.

"Are you all right?" he asked, his voice low and urgent.

"I am now. I knew you would come for me." Her eyes

shone with love that he felt in his own heart.

"Always," he replied at once.

"Uh, Captain…" That was Krysta's voice interrupting their moment. "Sally doesn't look too good."

Ginny stepped back and turned to check out her executive officer, and sure enough, her face had gone gray. Jimnai was there to catch Sally as she fell unconscious.

"That's it. Let's get out of here. We need to get her some help," Ginny said, her decisive nature coming to the fore.

"As you wish, my empress," Tigh said, issuing orders for the bots.

He divided them into two groups. The larger group would sweep the area ahead of them as they retraced their steps out of the underground facility. The smaller group would act as rear guard.

The men and women would walk between the two groups of bots, Hansa and Krysta in front, Jimnai carrying Sally in the middle, with Tigh and Ginny bringing up the rear. Tigh gave Ginny one of his personal weapons and was pleased to see how naturally she handled the blaster.

"Let's move out," he issued the order, and within moments, they were on their way back up to the surface.

"Where are we?" Ginny asked as they moved briskly along. "Underground?"

"Yes," Tigh answered, keeping his attention on the bots and his display, but happy to have his lover at his side once more. "This was some kind of secret medical or weapons lab. So secret there is no record of it in the imperial databases. Not even the ones I have access to as emperor."

"That man. Gruber. He said he'd designed the virus," Ginny said slowly, even as they walked along at a fast clip.

"That's what the courts found, after I took over. I'm glad, though, to have evidence of him saying so, himself." Tight glanced up at the floating camera, keeping pace with them and still recording. "Those little floaters are handy gadgets."

Ginny shook her head just once, to the side, a smile lifting the corner of her mouth. "Human tech is good for some things."

"In this case, it was invaluable. It led me to you, my love, and for that, I will be forever thankful."

He touched her arm, wishing they could stop and embrace but knowing that would be foolhardy. They had to get out of the facility as soon as possible and back to the safety of the Phenix.

"Is it just me, or is this place kind of empty?" Ginny asked as they trod along.

"I don't think there were many people living or stationed here, even at the height of its operation. We only found one room that looked like a barracks and one rec room. I've sealed both off," Tigh told her. "Less than ten warriors, from what the bots saw."

"Yeah, speaking of those bots..." Ginny glanced significantly behind them. "I've never known jit'suku to use bots in battle. I didn't even know you had that kind of technology."

"Sending machines against an enemy is thought to be cowardly among warriors," Tigh answered immediately. "We've had this sort of technology for centuries and use it mostly in peacekeeping applications to supplement local police forces, and the like. These bots are DNA coded to me, so I know they cannot be corrupted by even the most sophisticated enemy."

"You had a bunch of bots made just for you?" She seemed incredulous, and he had to explain.

"They were first made for Elius, but since we're identical twins..."

"Oh, I see." She nodded at the bots leading the way, and those behind, once more. "Handy."

"Very," Tigh agreed.

As they passed the two locations where Tigh had sealed warriors inside the chambers, they slowed to make sure all was still as he had left it. The rec room door had some dents in it, but it was holding against the warriors trapped within.

"I will send others to deal with these warriors," he

decided, ordering the bot to guard until he gave it the signal to return to the Phenix. He would give that signal only when he had the women safely aboard. "Sally needs help sooner rather than later. The warriors will keep for a while longer."

The barracks chamber was quiet as they passed. It was likely the men within hadn't woken up yet, which Tigh figured was just as well. They made good time back to the vestibule chamber, pausing only to let the bots scout ahead, including outside the upper door. When the scans came back clear after only a minute or two, they continued their trek upward.

"Those bots are really handy," Ginny observed.

"They are not something I would have asked to be made, had it been up to me, but Elius did have some good ideas, on occasion," Tigh allowed. "And your floaters are something just as useful, if not better."

"Well, they've come in very handy lately," Ginny admitted with a rueful shake of her head.

"Emperor Tigh?" Tiggy's voice came to Tigh over his earpiece.

"Go ahead, Ensign," he signaled back.

"I've been able to tap into the facility's coms, sir. With your permission, I'd like to play the recording of what just happened to the men in those two chambers."

Tigh was surprised. Not that the human woman would show initiative, but her suggestion to play the recording of Ginny's confrontation with Gruber was startling.

"Why is that, Ensign?" he asked her.

Tiggy's response took a moment, as if she was thinking how best to phrase her answer before replying.

"Sir, if you'd ask Captain Starbridge, she might explain that…uh…I'm prone to a bit of foresight on occasion. Right now, it's telling me these men need to see what just happened. I can't explain it any better than that," Tiggy said, her words tinged with a bit of hesitancy, though he heard a conviction in her beliefs, as well.

"Just a moment, Ensign," Tigh replied, calmly, turning to

Ginny to do as the younger woman had suggested. "Tiggy says she thinks she should play the recording you just made to the men we have isolated below."

"She did?" Ginny's eyes widened. "Did she say why?"

"Something about foresight?" Tigh replied. He would have scratched his head, if he wasn't in the middle of an evacuation.

But Ginny's eyes cleared, and she started nodding. "Do it, then. I've learned to follow Tiggy's flashes of insight. Her family is a bit famous—or, perhaps, that should be infamous—for the gift of clairvoyance. If she says we should do it, we probably should, and really, there's no downside to this particular action." Ginny shrugged. "If you're asking my opinion, I'd do as she says."

"I will always value your opinion, my love," he took the time to tell her, earning a sparkling smile for his efforts.

He gave Tiggy the go ahead as they reached the door that led outside. The bots formed a defensive perimeter around their small group as they made a dash for the ship. Tigh didn't breathe easily until they were inside. He recalled all the bots and sealed the ship so that they'd be ready to go at a moment's notice.

Tigh had Jimnai put Sally in a stasis pod. She wouldn't get any worse before they could get help for her, and she'd be safe if they needed to make evasive maneuvers. That done, they all went to the bridge.

Ginny went straight over to Tiggy's comm station as soon as she hit the bridge.

"Status?" Ginny asked her coms officer quietly.

"All clear, Captain. I'm playing the recording now. Do you want to see their reaction?" Tiggy replied, smirking a bit at her own brilliance.

"There's a two-way comm you've tapped into?" Ginny surmised.

Tiggy nodded, enlarging the feed on her screen so Ginny could watch over her shoulder. She felt Tigh join her a moment later, his warm presence at her back as he watched over Ginny's shoulder.

The men in the barracks were sitting up in their cots, awakened by the bright light of the comm screen that took up one wall of the small room. On the other side of Tiggy's screen, the warriors in the rec room took a moment from their ongoing bids to escape to watch the communal comm that was also playing Ginny's confrontation with Gruber.

She shuddered as he shouted at her. He'd been a vile sort of man. Knowing that he'd been the architect of so much death across two galaxies made it hard for her to look at him, but she'd never shirked from her duty, so she watched, her lips held in a grim line. Then, she noticed that the recording of her got really bright as she started to glow.

She knew what would come next, but it was still startling to watch. The view was intensified from the floating camera that zoomed around the action to capture the best angles. Ginny hadn't paid the floater much attention at the time, but the static view from Krysta's belt was somewhat one-dimensional compared to the angled views of Sally's fully-independent floating cam. Ginny silently applauded Tiggy's choice for using the floating cam's footage interspersed with the steady cam's recording.

Tiggy had skillfully cut together the two views to create a running narrative that required little explanation. When Gruber disintegrated in the Goddess's Light, Ginny sighed. Tigh's hand rested on her shoulder, and she reached up to place hers over his, accepting the comforting touch and returning it, in kind.

"You know, I was there. I saw it happening, but that's not something I'll ever really understand," she said softly.

"The Goddess works in mysterious ways," Tigh replied. "That She chooses to work through you and your crew is something all our people are going to have to come to terms with. It won't be easy, but perhaps that is why She is doing so in such an open way, for so many to witness."

"You may have something there, Emperor," Tiggy said,

her voice a bit smug. "Take a look at the men in those two rooms." She focused her screen on one face after another, the shock and horror in their eyes was easily read.

In both chambers, discussion soon erupted, and one warrior even started sobbing and praying to the Goddess to forgive him. Ginny listened to some of the talk for a bit and was astounded to hear pretty much every one of those men— who had helped Gruber abduct her and her friends—admit to being terribly wrong.

"I think, rather than warriors, you should probably send in some warrior priests of the Zenai to deal with those men," Ginny suggested to Tigh as she finally turned away from the screen.

He looked at her with respect in his gaze. "I suspect you're correct." He walked with her the short distance to the captain's chair. They both stood behind it, together. "I also think perhaps that we should allow that recording to be seen widely. There are hold-outs all over the empire. If some of them react as strongly to seeing you wield the Goddess's Light as those men, then our work may be done for us in convincing them to repent of their ways."

"Now, you're talking like a priest," she teased him, smiling and receiving an answering smile that held promises of delight along with utter relief.

"I almost was a priest," he reminded her. "I never thought I would be truly happy on any other life path, but you've shown me the error of my thinking, Ginny." Tigh's hand cupped her cheek gently. "Thank you for turning my life around and making it so much better than I ever expected."

"I could say the same to you, Tigh," she replied, softly. There was no bridge. No crew. In this moment out of time, it was just the two of them, staring deep into each other's eyes.

Someone was giggling, and it sure sounded like Tiggy O'Roarke. The moment broken by her crewmember's irreverent sense of humor, Ginny stepped back from Tigh, rolled her eyes at Tiggy, then looked around for a likely place to sit on the small bridge.

"I would give you the captain's chair, but this ship is DNA coded to me," Tigh said, somewhat apologetically.

"Don't mind me, I'll just make do," Ginny insisted.

There were already two on weapons—Hansa and Henny—and Tiggy had a backup at coms. Jimnai was in the navigator's chair, and there wasn't room for much more on the small bridge, but there was one open chair where the engineer would have sat. Ginny didn't know much about engineering, but the chair would put her close to Tigh and securely positioned should they encounter trouble.

"Looks like I'll monitor the engines," she said brightly, sitting down at the board. "You know," she said to Tigh conversationally, "this makes me miss my own ship."

She sighed heavily, lamenting the fact that she'd never know what the human military had been going to assign her out of the shipyards. That ship would go to another captain. It probably already had, by now.

"My brother commissioned this ship," Tigh replied, his voice contemplative. "But I don't see any reason why the jit'suku empress should not have her own warship. Especially when she has proven herself in battle the way you have. And you have your own crew, already. I think we could arrange to build something suitable for you, if you like. Of course, I hope our reign to bring in a new era of peace. With the grace of the Goddess, you won't be called on to fight anywhere."

"That suits me just fine," Ginny replied quickly. "Just having a ship to take out, now and again, would be amazing." Then, she thought of all those orphans and the fractured society she was going to live in and backpedaled. "Of course, I don't want to use resources that would be better spent elsewhere."

"I think the shipyards could use the work," Tigh responded. "But it is good of you to think of our people's welfare first. Rebuilding our society will take time and lots of initiatives. Getting the shipyards building again, is actually a good way to start. They can build you your warship with the supplies already on hand. Then, perhaps, we can start them on cargo and passenger ships. I hope to encourage emigration from the human galaxy to ours, if at all possible. We'll need transports for those people."

"You think big," Ginny complimented him.

"I like to plan ahead," he replied. "For example, here comes the backup I requested." He flicked a control that brought the outside view onto the main screen so everybody could see what he had. Four large air cars were approaching their position. "One transport from the Zenai monastery and a trio of peacekeepers."

Tigh spoke with the captains of the transports and related the situation below ground. He gave specific orders for the warrior priests to deal with the prisoners before he issued the commands that would send the Phenix airborne, on its way back to the palace.

The adventure, for now, was over, and Ginny was just glad they'd all lived through the experience. Sally's condition still worried her, but they'd get her the best possible medical help as soon as they landed. For now, she was in stasis and wouldn't get any worse.

"I wonder what Gruber was grumbling about Sally having alien DNA?" she thought aloud, then looked at Tigh. "The jit'suku have been around the universe a few times. Have you ever run into other humanoid races?"

"None that I know of," Tigh answered quickly. "Of course, there might be something in the archives. We can take a look when we get back to the palace. There are restricted sections of the imperial archives that require my personal authorization to access and cannot be seen outside special rooms set aside for such research."

"Secretive," Ginny said, feeling a new adventure in the works. "I like it."

Her heart was giddy with relief at being out of Gruber's hands. She also thought, perhaps, the Light of the Goddess had done something to lighten her mood. Or, maybe, it was just being around Tigh. Believing that he would come for her—and knowing he had—was making her feel all bubbly inside. Not a sensation she was used to feeling. Not by a long shot.

They arrived back at the palace a while later, without incident. The path back to the palace had been a much straighter line than the trail they'd followed from it. Sally was sent immediately to medical. The doctor who had come with Ginny, from human space, was there to meet the ship when it landed. She had help from the court physician and medical staff, and they rolled Sally out of the ship, stasis pod and all, and took her away, already taking measurements. Tigh stood beside Ginny as she watched them go.

"Do you think she'll be all right?" she asked him.

"I hope so, but her fate, like all of ours, is in the Goddess's hands," he replied truthfully, earning a measuring glance from his mate.

"Sometimes, you sound just a little too much like a Zenai priest," she quipped, her smile taking the sting out of her criticism.

"I shall attempt to tone it down in future," he told her with mock seriousness.

"Oh, don't bother in my account," she replied, taking his arm as they began to walk away from the ship. "I think it's kind of sexy."

"Truly?" He was surprised.

"Well, it's a heady thought to realize that I tempted a priest away from his vocation," she mused, a smile dancing around her lips. "I, personally, never saw myself as the femme fatale type before."

"You give yourself too little credit," he told her as they walked out of the hangar and into the more decorative parts of the palace.

Xeer was waiting for them, as was a group of Zenai priests who all regarded Ginny with increased reverence. Tiggy must have already released the recording. It was clear from the way his Zenai brothers looked at Ginny that they'd seen what she'd done when the Goddess worked through her. Seen it and understood it for the miracle it truly was.

"Sire, there's an urgent meeting in the Council chambers. They've asked if I would invite you and your lady to join them," Xeer said promptly. "I'm glad to see you back in one piece, milady," he added, smiling at Ginny.

"Glad to be back," Ginny replied casually, smiling back at Xeer. Krysta joined their group, and Xeer fell in to walk beside her.

"I reinstituted the Grand Council when I came back to the palace," Tigh explained to Ginny as they walked. "It's made up of men of power and wealth from all across our space. Those who cannot be here in person participate over dedicated and highly secure comm channels. They've been in charge of rebuilding our society since the disaster, and they've done a good job, so far. The thing is, there are some hardheads on the Council. I've left them alone because smothering dissent is something Elius did that I do not want to repeat, but I'm afraid you are not universally liked by the men on the Council. I just wanted to warn you, and I'll understand if, after your ordeal today, you'd rather skip this meeting."

Ginny took a deep breath and squared her shoulders. "I've never run from a fight," she told him. "Let's just get this over with."

"That's my beloved Velkir," he murmured for her ears alone. As a result, she was smiling as they entered the Council chambers, as was Tigh.

What he didn't expect, and couldn't have predicted, was the utter silence as the men within the chamber noted their arrival. One by one, as Ginny passed, every man in the room dropped to one knee. On the comm screens set up all around the chamber, cams zoomed out to show the men at the other end of the comm channels doing the same. Even those who Tigh had noted as being especially hostile to the idea of taking a human woman to be empress.

Their tunes had changed. Radically. Had the recording of today's events done that? Tigh had to think it probably had.

Amazing.

Lord Alfar, who had been particularly brutal in his words against Tigh's mission to the human galaxy, came forward and dropped to one knee right in front of Ginny. Tigh stayed alert, wondering how this would unfold. Whatever happened, he'd be ready.

"My lady," Lord Alfar began, his words loud but trembling a bit, a far cry from his usual bombastic style. "We have seen what transpired today, and we acknowledge the second miracle of your arrival. Those of us who doubted the wisdom of doing as our emperor has done are in doubt no more. We offer welcome to you, and apologies to the emperor, and seek both of your forgiveness."

Tigh stood back to see what Ginny would say or do. This was a test for her, and he could not help. If he tried to step in, that would set a bad precedent. She had to sink or swim on her own for the moment, though Tigh would always be there to try to save her, should she do the former.

"I accept your welcome, my lord," she replied graciously. "But forgiveness must be given by the Goddess. I am not Her, though she has seen fit to use me as Her weapon." Ginny's ironic tone was apparent to Tigh, though he didn't think the others would hear it. "I guess you've all seen the recording?"

Nods all around from the men still on the ground confirmed Tigh's suspicions. It was time for him to say something. Ginny had hit just the right tone. Now, it was time to show them all that they would rule together, as a pair.

"Please rise, my friends," Tigh said, gesturing for them all to get up off the floor. "I am pleased beyond words to find you willing to accept my lady," he told them as they hesitantly rose, a few at a time. "I know we have not always seen eye to eye in this chamber, nor do I expect us to do so always, but on this, the path is clear. I'm glad you see that now."

"And I'm glad to say that Doctor Gruber is no more. He has paid for his crimes with his life," Ginny put in, like the bloodthirsty war commander she was. Anyone who saw her now, saw not the mild-mannered empress, but the Velkir, in all her glory. "Anyone who aided him in my abduction is welcome to repent their ways. The Zenai priests are willing to listen to their confessions," she said for all to hear. "I'm prepared to let bygones be bygones, if—" she paused significantly, "—we can all agree that bioweapons will never be used again. I know the human government is prepared to sign a treaty to that effect, and I would hope you will, too. There has been enough suffering."

A cheer went up throughout the Council chamber and on comm feeds the galaxy over. It certainly sounded to Tigh as if his lady had won over some of her most argumentative detractors. How long it would last, he wasn't sure, but it was definitely a good start.

CHAPTER 17

Over the next days, as the recording of Gruber's end circulated to the farthest reaches of the empire, it seemed to strike a chord with even the worst of skeptics. To have the father of the virus show his confusion over being wrong about jit'suku DNA mixing so well with human was really something. It seemed a lot of the people who had refused to accept that Ginny truly was the prophesied Velkir had objected on the basis that a human couldn't fill that role.

The fact that Gruber had ranted about Ginny's jit'suku DNA somehow made it easier for those skeptics to believe. It was one thing to be told the facts by people who supported the new regime. It was another, apparently, to have the father of the virus confirm it.

Faced with prophecy and the undeniable presence of the Goddess, not once, but twice, working through the women, the skeptics and supporters of the old regime had no choice. They either slunk away, taking a backseat and letting the new galactic order take hold, or they allied themselves with Tigh and Ginny.

The warrior priests of the Zenai were kept very busy with hearing confessions and redirecting those who had gone astray. The concept of confession wasn't really part of the Zenai way, but Jurdan had agreed with Ginny's desire to have the priests evaluate each of the former enemies, to judge whether or not the repentance was real. Acting as judges of character and reform were well within the purview of the warrior priesthood, so in the end, it all worked out.

Having the Zenai work with the former transgressors also kept a buffer between those bad actors and the emperor. Tigh feared that, if he'd had to sit in judgment on any of the warriors who had helped abduct Ginny, he wouldn't be able to be lenient. Yet, leniency was what Ginny desired, as long as the men truly repented.

Much better to have actual priests take care of making that judgment. Tigh could not be objective where the safety of his beloved was concerned.

As the days progressed, another topic became foremost in his mind. He'd proposed to Ginny, and she'd accepted, but they had yet to have the formal ceremony. The wedding of an emperor to his empress wasn't something that could be undertaken quickly, and the dowager empress was heavily involved in the planning.

She roped Ginny's family, and the ladies of Ginny's crew, into helping with the preparations. Tigh feared the party was going to be something that the jit'suku empire had never before experienced. It seemed there were many human traditions they wanted to include, and the dowager empress was inclined to indulge them—as long as they included all the necessary jit'suku traditions, as well.

The wedding, from all accounts, was going to be a true mix of their two cultures.

Ginny kept tabs on her crew over the next days. She also visited Sally daily, to check on her progress. She was still too ill to move to her own room but was being kept entertained by Tolo, who was, likewise, still taking up a bed in the infirmary. Both of them had been laid low by the drug Gruber's men had used to knock them all out.

Ginny sensed a little spark between Sally and Tolo. They weren't admitting to anything, just yet, but Ginny had high hopes for a budding romance between the two. It felt like, now that she'd found a man to share her life with, she wanted all her friends to be as happy as she was.

The dowager empress had befriended Ginny's mother and aunt, and she was taking them around to the orphanages and medical centers. Once Ginny got wind of it, she realized her family was going to settle in well. Her mother and aunt were already working with the dowager to develop ways to help with all the boys left motherless by the virus. Already, the number of young pages in the palace had tripled, each woman having taken a group of little boys under their wings.

It was good to see the children laughing and playing around the halls of the big building. There was more than enough room for them, and the ladies were educating them, as well as mothering them. Ginny wanted to encourage that sort of thing throughout the empire, and she was taking careful notes on what worked…and what didn't.

After the wedding was over, Ginny had plans to put out a special call to any women in the human galaxy who had an enhanced ancestor—and therefore jit'suku DNA in their profiles—to come help restore the balance here. If the human government was interested in allowing some jit'suku men to move there, Ginny was already thinking about ways to screen and select suitable candidates.

The first few groups of men to go back home were going to have to be especially patient fellows. They were likely to get a cold reception in many places. They'd have to earn the women's trust, and that could take some time. She wanted to set up classes to prepare them for the traditions, beliefs and customs they might encounter. Her crew would be the teachers, but they weren't even close to that stage yet. The wedding had to come first, and then, all her plans could be set into motion, though she was already discussing some of it with Tigh.

He was supportive and offered very good suggestions, which was a great help. Between the two of them, she'd already prepared some notes on how to go about the various steps in the plan. All it needed now, was the right timing.

When the wedding day arrived, the pomp and circumstance was even greater than Ginny had expected. News cams floated everywhere along the route she took from the suite where she had slept the night before. There was a tradition among the jit'suku that all the women of the family would gather together in one place the night before a wedding to tell stories, laugh and keep the bride-to-be company. It was something like a hen party, only it included all ages of women and didn't focus so much on the party aspect as it did on the camaraderie and family ties.

Ginny liked it. She hadn't had a lot of time lately to just hang out with her crew and family. Her crew had become part of her family, and it was good to renew those ties and gossip about the men they had met so far. It was clear to them all that Krysta and Xeer were getting very close, as were Hansa and Henny. There was also something between Sally— who had been released from the infirmary just the day before—and Tolo. Good-natured teasing was passed around evenly until Ginny's mother and aunt started talking about how their marriages had been before the virus.

The mood grew a bit somber when they remembered the way things used to be and the good men that had been lost forever. They drank a toast to Ginny's father and uncle, the crew members' fathers and brothers and cousins. All those men, just wiped away by something so tiny…and deadly.

But there was hope, too. Hope for a rebirth of both races that had suffered so badly. Now that the man who had crafted the virus was gone, they all felt that they could truly start over and make both races stronger. United. At peace.

There hadn't been peace between the jit'suku and humanity for centuries. There had been brief periods of ceasefire and one long stretch of quiet during Emperor Tren's time, but it hadn't stuck. This time, though, Ginny was certain the peace would endure. For, after the next generation or two, there would be no more jit'suku and human. There would be one race of people with shared DNA.

That would stop the jit'suku warriors in their tracks. It was one of the tenants of their warrior's code that they did not make war on their own people. Humanity was going to become jit'suku, and jit'suku would, likewise, merge with humanity. It was an elegant solution for an untenable situation, but she'd take it.

They discussed many topics that night from the peace treaty that would be formed by her marriage, to scandalous teasing about the jit'suku men. The women dined together and spent the rest of the evening talking and laughing and remembering. Ginny enjoyed it immensely and thought it was a great tradition that humans would do well to adopt from the jit'suku.

They all slept in the big room that had been set aside for this event, on colorful couches designed for lounging. It was like a pajama party or a camp out, where the women talked until the wee hours of the morning and remembered why they were friends…and family.

In the morning, a late breakfast was served buffet style in the room next door. Everybody cleaned up and put on fluffy robes that had been prepared for them, for the next part of the day involved dressing for the ceremony. Since this particular marriage involved the head of the entire empire, it had to be more elaborate than a simple provincial wedding. There were heavy ceremonial robes to be worn for the actual ceremony, with underclothes that were much more comfortable, that would be revealed once the party began, later that evening.

In between, there would be a few hours of sitting in state on the throne, receiving emissaries and lords from far-flung regions of space within the empire. It seemed like everyone who could possibly do so had sent a high-ranking representative or come themselves to pledge fealty to the emperor and see the new empress for themselves.

Ginny knew she would be under close scrutiny. She just hoped the Goddess who'd been taking such an active interest in this situation would stick by her now. She would need a deity's stamina to sit through all the rigmarole expected this afternoon after the wedding ceremony.

Maybe that's why they made the formal robes so stiff and cumbersome, she thought. Sitting for hours was hard enough, but with the support of the robes, she wouldn't slouch. She couldn't. The bead-encrusted fabric wouldn't allow it.

When Tigh saw his bride walking down the aisle toward him, his heart skipped a beat in pure pleasure. She was radiant. The formal wear made her move slowly, but she had a grace that was all Ginny and owed little to the restrictive clothing.

She met his gaze and smiled at him as the news bots hovered in front and behind. They were less obtrusive than he'd thought they'd be, but both he and Ginny understood the need for everyone in the empire to see this event. Those who couldn't be here in person would be able to view it live on their newsfeeds. It was an historic day that deserved to be marked.

Therefore, they'd agreed to the newsbots. Ginny's crew also had their own floating cams arrayed around the room. Tiggy had rigged a monitoring station where specially trained and screened security agents were watching the direct live feeds from the floaters, watching the crowd for potential trouble.

Tiggy would also be recording this to send back to human space so they could see the result of the Valkyrie's adventure. The wedding would cement the deal and make everything official. Which was why it was so important that it go off without a hitch.

The palace guard was on high alert, and the new palace contingent of Zenai priests hadn't let either Ginny or Tigh out of their sight. During the ladies' party, they'd posted themselves at every entrance to the large chamber where the dinner and slumber party had been held, and examined everything in minute detail before letting it into Ginny's presence.

The tight security was a bit tiresome, but Tigh knew Ginny understood it was necessary. For that matter, he wasn't comfortable with it either, but he endured. It helped that he knew these men and had studied with them. He'd started setting up a wing of the palace specifically for the Zenai. If they were going to guard him and his empress, he wanted them to be in familiar and comfortable surroundings.

To that end, Tigh had begun remodeling some of the unused rooms into something resembling the rooms and facilities he'd become accustomed to on the Zenai mountain. He'd given the men leave to create a shrine to the Goddess, an exercise area both indoors and outside in a disused courtyard, and whatever else they wanted. Tigh only asked that they allow him to train with them on occasion, to keep his skills sharp.

But the warrior priests had gone even farther. They'd welcomed Henny and the ladies who wanted to continue learning the fighting arts to their outdoor courtyard. The mixed group of martial artists had drawn quite a few onlookers from the palace staff when they'd started training together, and almost all of the little page boys wanted to emulate what they saw, which led to a few accidental black eyes and bruises.

Seeing that, one of the warrior priests had suggested adding a class for the youngsters into their training schedule, and when it was mentioned to Ginny, she'd supported the idea wholeheartedly. She'd even been known to observe the class with some of the other ladies, like proud mamas watching the little boys learn how to respect themselves, their fellow beings, and the Goddess, through the discipline of martial arts.

Before too many days had passed, almost all the little boys had started training in the ways of the Zenai. It would do them no harm to learn to defend themselves and get a bit of exercise, Tigh thought. And, if it turned out that one or more of them felt a true calling to the priesthood, they could pursue that path when they were ready.

Such training also helped focus young warriors who chose that path later in life. Tigh had often thought that, if more of the warrior class had been trained under Zenai principles, they never would have let Elius get away with half the things he had done.

For his part, Tigh hoped the presence of the Zenai in the palace would become a permanent addition. It was good to have them around. Their mere presence stood as a symbol of righteousness, and Tigh knew enough about the order to know that they would have something to say if Tigh somehow strayed from the path of the Lady's Light as he grew into his new role as emperor. He was counting on it.

Ginny finished her long walk down the aisle and joined him in front of High Priest Jurdan in the area in front of their thrones. Tigh took her hand in his, and for a moment, as he looked into her shining eyes, time stood still. His heart filled once more with the deep and abiding love he felt for her, and he didn't care who saw the look on his face. Let them look. Let them see the reality of their mating and know, once and for all, that this is what had been ordained by the Goddess, Herself.

Together, they turned to face Jurdan and listened to what he had to say. A lot of the ritual was formulaic, but there was a point during which the High Priest would impart a teaching of wisdom he wanted to share with the particular couple standing before him. But Jurdan surprised them. The message he shared was not for them, alone, but for all jit'suku and all humans who would see this recording. It was a message of hope and peace, forgiveness and love, prosperity and Light.

At the end of the ritual, they kissed, and it felt like that very first nij'ta, when Tigh had first discovered the truth about this amazing woman, who was now, legally, his wife. He didn't realize it during the kiss, but he would discover later that there had been an ethereal glow around them when they kissed. All the priests knelt when it appeared, believing it to be a manifestation of the Goddess's blessing.

All the news bots floating around caught it and recorded it from many angles, which would be looked at later, in great detail, lending validity to the fact that the Light was real and not some manufactured effect. When the kiss ended, so did the glow, going back to wherever it had come from just as mysteriously as it had arrived. Tigh noticed the priests on their bended knees all around them, but he didn't know, at that point, why they'd taken that position.

The stunned faces of the assembled crowd registered next as Tigh turned with Ginny on his arm, to face the audience in the chamber. The moment of stunned silence continued until someone started cheering in the back of the room, and the sound started a chorus of cheers that shook the rafters of the vaulted ceiling far above.

The stunned faces turned to happy faces, some with tears streaming down their cheeks. Emotion was running high, and for once, it was all positive emotion. Tigh had taken over a troubled empire, and it had been a struggle to give people any reason to be hopeful, much less happy. Today, it certainly seemed as if the tide had turned.

The audience, filled with men, was cheering as if they'd just seen their own salvation. Perhaps they had. Tigh wanted to think he'd finally brought hope back to this people. Ginny was the embodiment of that hope—for his empire and for himself.

"I didn't expect quite this reception," Ginny said to Tigh as he leaned down to speak with her over the din.

"I didn't either, but I'm grateful for it," he replied, kissing her cheek to renewed cheers. "They will love you as much as I do, my heart," he said, feeling the truth of every word. "You will heal an empire, just by your presence."

A group of page boys came over to lift the train on Ginny's dress, signaling it was time to walk to the thrones— two equally majestic chairs placed side-by-side on the dais, behind where the High Priest had performed their marriage ceremony. Ginny allowed the little boys to escort her—and her massively heavy dress—over to the chair, but she didn't let them go without giving each one a touch of affection.

She'd learned from the older women how starved for the simple gestures such as a pat on the back or a touch on the cheek these little ones were. Following her mother's example, Ginny never passed up an opportunity to bestow a gentle touch when she saw one of the orphans in the halls. Each boy beamed at her, the littlest lifting his arms for a hug that Ginny could not resist. She reached down and kissed the boy, who could not be older than about six or seven, on the cheek before letting him go.

Ginny had thought her movements would be well camouflaged by Tigh's arrival at the chair next to her. The protocol called for settling the woman first, then the male taking his own seat. What she hadn't realized was that everyone had been watching her minutest motion—especially the news bots. Ginny wanted to roll her eyes when she finally noticed the bots hovering just a few feet away. No doubt her every movement would be critiqued and commented on before the day was through.

Shrugging it off, she resolved to be more circumspect. The stiffness of her bodice kept her upright with nearly ramrod perfection of posture. Tigh settled beside her, and then, the next part of the ceremony unfolded as each nobleman came forward to re-pledge his loyalty to the emperor…and the new empress.

Ginny had feared there might be a few hold-outs. She knew she was not universally welcomed. She'd thought many still had doubts about her presence, but she was proved wrong. As the day wore on and man after man came forth to welcome her, she couldn't detect any sort of resistance.

Maybe she wasn't as good a judge of jit'suku body language as she'd thought, but it certainly seemed as if they were welcoming her with real gladness. A few times, she looked over at Tigh to catch a bemused smile on his face. She wanted to ask him if what she was seeing was real, but she didn't dare speak out of turn with all the news bots covering every angle.

When the parade of nobles was finally over, Ginny and Tigh were able to escape public scrutiny for a few moments by retiring to the antechamber behind the dais. Once again, the page boys helped Ginny with the heavily embroidered and beaded robe. They also helped her remove it to reveal the much more comfortable ensemble beneath, as Tigh did the same.

"Good to be able to move again," Tigh commented as he rubbed his arms and stretched a bit.

"Will we have to wear those again?" she asked, dreading his answer.

"No. They're works of art now. They'll be put on display in the main hall here then moved to a museum where everybody can go look at them, if they wish. There is a collection of such things stretching back to the first emperor. Sadly, the styles haven't changed much in all those centuries." He grimaced then smiled as she did the same.

The page boys left, burdened with the heavy robes, but not before Ginny thanked each one of them. This little crew was really starting to blossom and work together as a group. Tigh had told her they'd all competed for the honor of serving at the wedding ceremony by achieving high marks from the priests who trained them, as well as their teachers in academic subjects. The small group that had finally been chosen had earned their spots in this honor guard.

When they were alone, Ginny rubbed the back of her neck and looked up at Tigh. "I think that went well. Or am I just delusional?"

"No, you're right. It went better than I, or anyone, expected, really." He looked bemused. "I can't be sure, but I think something might've happened. Wait..." Tigh went to the door and stepped out for a moment, holding the door ajar. He stepped back, and Xeer was with him. "Tell Ginny what you just told me," Tigh prompted his friend.

"The Light shone all around you two when you kissed at the end of the ceremony. It was a clear manifestation of the

Goddess's approval of your union," Xeer said, wonder in his voice.

"Is that why all the priests were kneeling?" Ginny asked, wondering aloud as Xeer nodded. "They dropped as one, and the crowd of onlookers went utterly speechless."

"I'd wondered…" Tigh said, shaking his head slightly. "Overall, I'd have to say I'm pleased with the result. I thought it would be much more difficult to get through this day without bloodshed. Or, at least, harsh words and a few feuds declared among the nobles."

"Now, we just have to get through the feast, and we're home free," Ginny thought aloud. "I know I shouldn't have said that, because now, something will happen." She rolled her eyes at her own nonsense, and Xeer laughed.

"We will do our best to make certain nothing bad happens," he assured her.

"I'll hold you to that," she joked with him as she stood and straightened her outfit. The robes of state had been heavy and restrictive, but they hadn't crushed the silky fabric of the dress beneath. A few brushes from her hands, and she was good to go.

They went in to the dinner together, and a smaller crowd of nobles filled the room. Tables had been set up around the walls of the great hall with Tigh and Ginny at the center on one side, in chairs a bit grander than the others, up on a small dais, just a foot or two off the floor. It was so they could be seen, she surmised, as everyone stood to mark their entrance. The crowd cheered when the herald announced them as the emperor and empress. Ginny started a bit. Being called Empress Gineva was going to take some getting used to.

The dinner went well and lasted long into the night. There were many courses, with entertainments between each. One surprise was a boys' choir that performed, made up of boys she recognized from around the palace. Apparently, her cousin had taken a few of the page boys who had an ear for music and the ability to catch a tune, and had taught them some classical music from human antiquity. Ginny knew her cousin had musical talent and training, but she hadn't realized the extent of it.

The jit'suku seemed astounded and enthralled by the sounds the boys made as a choir. Ginny looked carefully at the rapt faces of those listening and realized that, although it was clearly different and surprising, the people who heard the boys' efforts were not appalled by it. Far from it. They seemed genuinely to enjoy it and be intrigued.

"We do not have this kind of music," Tigh said as the performance drew to an end. "It is very different but also very beautiful," he said approvingly.

"I'm glad you liked it. That music, I believe, was from well before humanity reached the stars. It is very old, and the text is religious, I think, but you'd have to check with my cousin for more precise details." Ginny marveled that her shy cousin had done so much in such a short time with the boys.

"I should think that, after tonight, musical scholars will want to know more about these haunting melodies," Tigh predicted.

The rest of the evening passed in a bit of a blur. Tigh was attentive and charming, and his people were welcoming. There were a few speeches and toasts, but Ginny didn't have to speak, except to thank everyone for coming to the feast. When it was finally time to leave the feast, Tigh took Ginny's arm and led her from the great hall.

The party went on without them, but their part in the public festivities was over for now. It was just as well. Ginny was tired. Just in the past few days, she'd been starting to feel her pregnancy a lot more than she had before. Fatigue was her near-constant companion, and certain smells made her want to vomit.

While last night, spent at the slumber party, away from Tigh had been nice, Ginny was glad she would be able to sleep with him again tonight. Pregnancy apparently increased her sex drive, and she was starting to really crave a little private party, just for the two of them.

CHAPTER 18

Tigh and Ginny came together in a long, cool, leisurely lovemaking that spoke without words of the love between them. She went to him as soon as they were alone in their suite, and he gave her everything she wanted...and more.

After the long day they'd had of ceremony and scrutiny, it was good to just relax and be free to be themselves. Together. Ginny asked for passion, and Tigh delivered, treating her like the empress she had just become.

Oh, she wasn't going to let a fancy title and some formal rigmarole change her from who she'd always been, but Ginny had to admit, being in charge felt good. Natural, to her, after the years spent as captain of her own ship. Ruler of her own destiny. Head honcho in charge of figuring out what to do.

She tried not to think of the billions of jit'suku lives she now had influence over. She preferred to think of them the way she thought of her crew—as extended family that she wanted to look out for to the utmost of her ability. True, the number of people she was now responsible for had increased by several orders of magnitude, but she couldn't think of that. She had to focus on the small ways she could improve the lives of those around her and, by extension, the rest of the empire.

In the aftermath of lovemaking, she lay awake in Tigh's

arms, thinking. Ginny had expected to sleep well after the rigors of the day. Though relaxed, she found her mind wandering down those paths, filled with jit'suku. All looking toward her for some sort of salvation. It was a serious responsibility.

"Still awake?" Tigh's voice rumbled above her head. She was snuggled into his side, his arm around her from above as they lay side by side on the enormous bed.

"Yes. Thinking," she revealed. "I want to be a good empress for your people," she told him earnestly.

"Our people, love," he reminded her, squeezing her shoulder for a quick moment. "Just keep on as you have been. The people will come to love you as I do. Already, they're talking about the way you so obviously care for your pages."

"I didn't realize the news bots would be so close. I thought they'd be in front, focused on you," she admitted.

"From what I understand, that's evident on the recording. Popular opinion says that the gestures you made toward the children were not staged, but true gestures of affection. It's a good start. As time goes on, we will build on this day and create a lasting peace for our galaxies."

She could almost hear trumpets when he spoke like that, but she knew he was just saying what he truly believed. There was no need for pretense between them. Not ever.

"You're a good man, Tigh." She snuggled into him, placing a kiss on his chest, over his heart.

He rolled, unexpectedly, coming over her and joining their bodies as he looked into her eyes. She hadn't realized he was ready again, or that such a little gesture would generate such a big response, but she liked it. Somehow, her body was always ready for this man. Her beloved. Her mate.

He set a pace, and her temperature rose almost instantly, along with her desire. Tigh knew just how to touch, how to arouse with just a glance. When he focused on her so totally, she was powerless to resist.

But there was no way she wanted to resist this. Not when

it was so intensely pleasurable. So life-affirming. So real. Nothing had ever been as perfect in her life as when Tigh was making love to her.

And that's what it was, she knew. For the jit'suku—according to the secret research she'd been performing, here and there, in her few moments alone—once a jit'suku male discovered the woman meant for him through the first kiss, the nij'ta, that was it. He was smitten. His whole being was engaged. His mind, his heart, his soul. That's what all the reference sources said, and that's what she felt from Tigh, every time he looked at her or took her in his arms and kissed her.

"I love you, Tigh," she told him, unable to keep from speaking as her body rose in ecstasy. She started to babble, repeating herself as climax hit, but Tigh held her throughout, even as he shouted his own release.

As they came down from the heights of passion together, he held her tight, kissing her face, her hair, her lips. "I love you, now and always, empress of my heart," he whispered, and suddenly, the empire didn't matter. The war didn't matter. Nothing else mattered to her in this moment other than knowing she had Tigh's love.

*

A few months later, when the babies finally appeared, the birth of a male heir was met with joy that spread throughout the jit'suku empire. The fact that the second twin was a girl brought a special kind of hope to every planet of the empire and the human galaxy, as well.

While it was true that twins ran in both families, twins of mixed genders was a truly special event. It was the first such birth since Gruber's virus had been unleashed on the universe. Since then, human females had been able to have mostly male offspring with the Sons of Amber. Jit'suku males had been out of luck with almost all their females gone, but the scientists had claimed female children would be the result of breeding with human women.

The fact that Tigh and Ginny had one of each had given hope to both races and proven that the two races could, in time, become one, ending the war forever. It would take a few generations and lots of work and understanding on both sides, but it could be done.

As Tigh and Ginny presented their twin miracles to the court on Solaris Prime, and the news bots that would stream the images of their tiny little faces all over the universe, their love was clear to all who saw the happy family. There was real affection between emperor and empress. Ginny had endeared herself to the jit'suku people and the many young orphans that had the run of the palace.

Ginny was grateful to the Goddess who had shown such an interest in her and acted so directly, and unexpectedly, in her life. Some of her friends had already found the same happiness she had, and for that, she was also thankful. It was good to see her crew and family doing so well in this new environment. Even her mother and aunt had suitors, which made Ginny want to giggle as much as her young cousin did.

She was grateful for it all. For peace. For a promising future. For the growing acceptance of her presence, and for the two small miracles cooing in her arms. But most of all, she was thankful to have captured Tigh's heart...and, no matter what, she knew, she would never give it back. The stars would fade, and the universe go dark before she would stop loving this man who had given her a life she never expected but was coming to love more with each passing day.

Ginny had been truly blessed. As the people looked for the first time at their new prince and princess, Ginny sent a little prayer up to the Goddess in thanks for all that had happened. They'd been through tough times. They'd lost so many dear friends and family members. They'd been through hell and had come out on the other side.

She didn't deserve to be this happy, but she was thankful to have had this second chance. This chance to heal the rift between two warring peoples. This chance to love and be loved.

And as Tigh revealed the names they had chosen for their newborn babies, a cheer went up in the great hall. They had decided to name their babies for two of their ancestors. Their boy would be called Tren, after the jit'suku emperor who had brought about the longest period of peace between their people to date. This Tren, they hoped, would oversee the peace that would last forever. Their daughter, they decided to name Magdelana, after Ginny's ancestor, the galactic superstar and spy called simply, Diva, who had been such a daring and famous woman in her own time. Both babies were given Starbridge as a middle name, so as never to forget their human heritage.

As the High Priest pronounced a public blessing over the babies, their parents stood over them. Tigh had his arm around her shoulders, and he leaned down to place a kiss on her cheek, much to the approval of those watching. What they didn't hear were the words he spoke near her ear that would live in her heart for all time.

"I love you more than I can say."

She looked up at him, her heart in her eyes as their people looked on. It was clear to all who saw the way they looked at each other that love was possible between human and jit'suku. Love and marriage and children were not to be denied those who would take the chance for happiness embodied by these two.

In the years to come, many would remember this day and that look. The look of love that gave hope to the universe.

# # #

ABOUT THE AUTHOR

Bianca D'Arc has run a laboratory, climbed the corporate ladder in the shark-infested streets of lower Manhattan, studied and taught martial arts, and earned the right to put a whole bunch of letters after her name, but she's always enjoyed writing more than any of her other pursuits. She grew up and still lives on Long Island, where she keeps busy with an extensive garden, several aquariums full of very demanding fish, and writing her favorite genres of paranormal, fantasy and sci-fi romance.

Bianca loves to hear from readers and can be reached through Twitter (@BiancaDArc), Facebook (BiancaDArcAuthor) or through the various links on her website.

WELCOME TO THE D'ARC SIDE…
WWW.BIANCADARC.COM

OTHER BOOKS BY BIANCA D'ARC

* RT Book Reviews Awards Nominee
** EPPIE Award Winner
*** CAPA Award Winner
****Bookie Award Winner

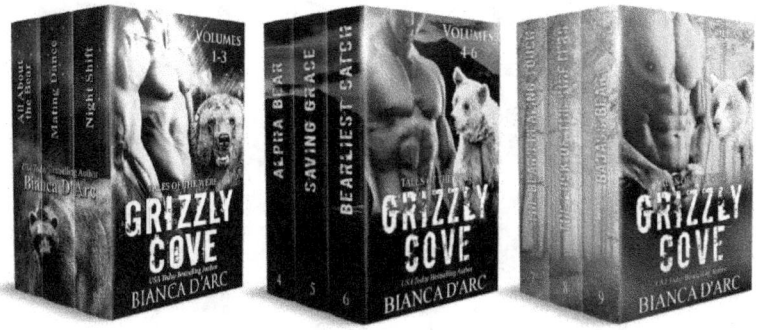

Welcome to Grizzly Cove, where bear shifters can be who they are - if the creatures of the deep will just leave them be. Wild magic, unexpected allies, a conflagration of sorcery and shifter magic the likes of which has not been seen in centuries... That's what awaits the peaceful town of Grizzly Cove. That, and love. Lots and lots of love.

This series begins with…

All About the Bear
Welcome to Grizzly Cove, where the sheriff has more than the peace to protect. The proprietor of the new bakery in town is clueless about the dual nature of her nearest neighbors, but not for long. It'll be up to Sheriff Brody to clue her in and convince her to stay calm—and in his bed—for the next fifty years or so.

Mating Dance
Tom, Grizzly Cove's only lawyer, is also a badass grizzly bear, but he's met his match in Ashley, the woman he just can't get out of his mind. She's got a dark secret, that only he knows. When ugliness from her past tracks her to her new home, can Tom protect the woman he is fast coming to believe is his mate?

Night Shift
Sheriff's Deputy Zak is one of the few black bear shifters in a colony of grizzlies. When his job takes him into closer proximity to the lovely Tina, though, he finds he can't resist her. Could it be he's finally found his mate? And when adversity strikes, will she turn to him, or run into the night? Zak will do all he can to make sure she chooses him.

Phoenix Rising

Lance is inexplicably drawn to the sun and doesn't understand why. Tina is a witch who remembers him from their high school days. She'd had a crush on the quiet boy who had an air of magic about him. Reunited by Fate, she wonders if she could be the one to ground him and make him want to stay even after the fire within him claims his soul...if only their love can be strong enough.

Phoenix and the Wolf

Diana is drawn to the sun and dreams of flying, but her elderly grandmother needs her feet firmly on the ground. When Diana's old clunker breaks down in front of a high-end car lot, she seeks help and finds herself ensnared by the sexy werewolf mechanic who runs the repair shop. Stone makes her want to forget all her responsibilities and take a walk on the wild side...with him.

Phoenix and the Dragon

He's a dragon shapeshifter in search of others like himself. She's a newly transformed phoenix shifter with a lot to learn and bad guys on her trail. Together, they will go on a dazzling adventure into the unknown, and fight against evil folk intent on subduing her immense power and using it for their own ends. They will face untold danger and find love that will last a lifetime.

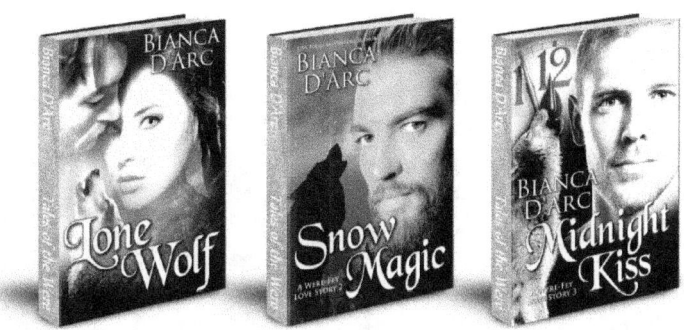

Lone Wolf

Josh is a werewolf who suddenly has extra, unexpected and totally untrained powers. He's not happy about it - or about the evil jackasses who keep attacking him, trying to steal his magic. Forced to seek help, Josh is sent to an unexpected ally for training.

Deena is a priestess with more than her share of magical power and a unique ability that has made her a target. She welcomes Josh, seeing a kindred soul in the lone werewolf. She knows she can help him... if they can survive their enemies long enough.

Snow Magic

Evie has been a lone wolf since the disappearance of her mate, Sir Rayburne, a fey knight from another realm. Left all alone with a young son to raise, Evie has become stronger than she ever was. But now her son is grown and suddenly Ray is back.

Ray never meant to leave Evie all those years ago but he's been caught in a magical trap, slowly being drained of magic all this time. Freed at last, he whisks Evie to the only place he knows in the mortal realm where they were happy and safe—the rustic cabin in the midst of a North Dakota winter where they had been newlyweds. He's used the last of his magic to get there and until he recovers a bit, they're stuck in the middle of nowhere with a blizzard coming and bad guys on their trail.

Can they pick up where they left off and rekindle the magic between them, or has it been extinguished forever?

Midnight Kiss

Margo is a werewolf on a mission...with a disruptively handsome mage named Gabe. She can't figure out where Gabe fits in the pecking order, but it doesn't seem to matter to the attraction driving her wild. Gabe knows he's going to have to prove himself in order to win Margo's heart. He wants her for his mate, but can she give her heart to a mage? And will their dangerous quest get in the way?

The Jaguar Tycoon

Mark may be the larger-than-life billionaire Alpha of the secretive Jaguar Clan, but he's a pussycat when it comes to the one women destined to be his mate. Shelly is an up-and-coming architect trying to drum up business at an elite dinner party at which Mark is the guest of honor. When shots ring out, the hunt for the gunman brings Mark into Shelly's path and their lives will never be the same.

The Jaguar Bodyguard

Sworn to protect his Clan, Nick heads to Hollywood to keep an eye on a rising star who has seen a little too much for her own good. Unexpectedly fame has made a circus of Sal's life, but when decapitated squirrels show up on her doorstep, she knows she needs professional help. Nick embeds himself in her security squad to keep an eye on her as sparks fly and passions rise between them. Can he keep her safe and prevent her from revealing what she knows?

The Jaguar's Secret Baby

Hank has never forgotten the wild woman with whom he spent one memorable night. He's dreamed of her for years now, but has never been back to the small airport in Texas owned and run by her werewolf Pack. Tracy was left with a delicious memory of her night in Hank's arms, and a beautiful baby girl who is the light of her life. She chose not to tell Hank about his daughter, but when he finally returns and he discovers the daughter he's never known, he'll do all he can to set things right.

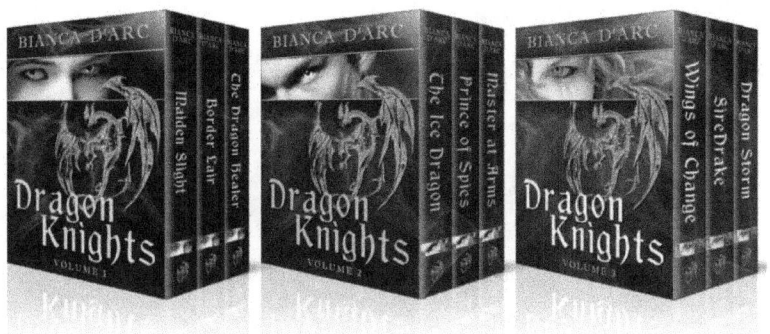

Dragon Knights

Two dragons, two knights, and one woman to complete their circle. That's the recipe for happiness in the land of fighting dragons. But there are a few special dragons that are more. They are the ruling family and they are half-dragon and half-human, able to change at will from one form to another.

Books in this series have won the EPPIE Award for Best Erotic Romance in the Fantasy/Paranormal category, and have been nominated for *RT Book Reviews Magazine* Reviewers Choice Awards among other honors.

WWW.BIANCADARC.COM